D1223482

A WYATT
BOOK for
W
ST.
MARTIN'S
PRESS

Rabbi, Rabbi

ANDREW KANE

A Wyatt Book *for*
St. Martin's Press New York

This is a work of fiction. Any names, characters, and incidents are products of the author's imagination. Although some of the places described exist, they are used fictitiously, and any resemblance to actual events, or persons—living or dead—is entirely coincidental.

 For information, address A Wyatt Book for St. Martin's Press, 175 Fifth Avenue, New York, N.Y. 10010.

Design by Ellen R. Sasahara

Library of Congress Cataloging-in-Publication Data

Kane, Andrew W.
Rabbi, Rabbi / Andrew Kane.
p. cm.
"A Wyatt book."
ISBN 0-312-11879-1
1. Man-woman relationships—United States—Fiction.
2. Jewish families—United States—Fiction.
3. Rabbis—United States—Fiction. 4. Jews—United States—Fiction. I. Title.
PS3561.A465R33 1995
813'.54—dc20 94-45336
CIP

First Edition: April 1995

10 9 8 7 6 5 4 3 2 1

Dedicated, with love,
to the memory of my father,
Mark M. Kane

ACKNOWLEDGMENTS

I am indebted to many. First, my mother, Sally Kane, one of the world's great undiscovered literary critics. Second, the Lenchner and Markowitz clans; especially Denise and Nat for their editorial input, Florence for the public relations, and Michael for the late nights.

I am deeply grateful to Bob Wyatt, my editor, for showing me the way; Pam Bernstein, my agent, for doing what she does best; and Sally Arteseros for loving and improving the manuscript.

Others who were helpful include: Iris Bass, Steve Cooper, Donna Dever, Gershon Kekst, Victoria Skurnick, Daniel Troy, and Alan Winter.

Lastly, always last, are Debbie and Max. It is far more difficult to live with a writer than to be one. Thanks for the patience, forgiveness, and—above all—the devotion.

Our age is not willing to stop with faith,
with its miracle of turning water into wine;
it goes further,
it turns wine into water.

—KIERKEGAARD

PART I

CHAPTER 1

SOME WOMEN capture your eye. Rebecca captured my being. The first time I saw her I was standing in the lobby of The Pineview Hotel in the Catskill Mountains. I felt a nudge in my side. It was my cousin Chaim's elbow.

"Hey, Yankel, take a look at that," he exclaimed, conspicuously pointing somewhere in front of himself.

I followed the line from his finger. It landed on a slender brunette with green eyes that could command from distances far greater than the one already dividing us.

The room was crowded. It was the first day of the summer season and lines of guests were waiting to check in at the registration desk. All the couches and chairs were occupied, and many people just stood around in whatever available space remained. A small welcoming band in the far corner churned out Jewish melodies. There was a lead singer backed up by an electric guitar, a keyboard, drums, and a trumpet. On the floor in front of him was a sign reading, "The Moshe Kleinman Orchestra."

Some young folks were gathered beside the band, singing along. That was where she stood.

The next thing I realized, I was alone. I looked around for Chaim and soon found him slipping in next to her. She seemed not to notice, gazing instead at the lead singer, until Chaim tapped her on the shoulder.

She turned around in curiosity and then smiled as the two of them began talking. Where did he get the nerve to go up to her like that? What were they saying? All I could hear was the music and the tumult of the mob.

In our world, we didn't meet women on our own. Chaim was of marriageable age and, according to the rules, a *shiddoch,* a match, would be arranged at an appropriate time. But Chaim didn't play by the rules.

And I didn't judge him; in fact, a part of me was sympathetic. With his reputation, I knew that he would have a hard time finding a *shiddoch* in the community. I was also jealous.

Their conversation continued for about two minutes, before Chaim waved for me to join them. My stomach grew tense. Despite that, and the lump in my throat, I summoned enough nerve to begin making my way through the crowd.

As I approached and saw how absolutely beautiful she was, my knees weakened. I stopped and stood at Chaim's side. He put his arm around my shoulder and said, "Yankel, I want you to meet someone. This is Rebecca."

She said hello and the corners of her mouth spread into a tender smile. Her voice was soft, as was the unblemished skin on her face and neck. Her light green eyes looked directly into mine.

Her hair, long and wavy, was parted on the side and fell to just above her breasts. Although she was well covered by a long skirt and baggy blouse, one could discern a shapely figure beneath it all.

I said hello and feigned a smile to hide my nervousness. I looked away to escape her intensity, but my eyes were drawn back to her. I could look at nothing else.

Chaim broke the spell saying, "I was just telling Rebecca that we were up here for the summer as waiters."

"Well, Chaim's a waiter, I'm only a busboy," I clarified. Inaccuracy was one of his shortcomings.

"Oh, that's right," he responded.

"Chaim tells me you're from Brooklyn, from Borough Park," she remarked.

"Yes, Fifty-first Street," Chaim blurted out before I could

answer. Then he continued, "Yankel and I live next door to each other."

"Where are you from?" I asked her.

"Woodmere, Long Island," she responded.

"Oh," I reacted, waiting for more words to come. I knew that Woodmere was one of the famous Five Towns on the south shore of Long Island where many Jews were migrating in order to get out of Brooklyn. I also knew that the Orthodox community in Woodmere was less religious than the one in Borough Park. A Jew who was comfortable living in Woodmere wouldn't be so in Borough Park, and vice versa.

Sometime during this conversation the music stopped. At that moment, the band leader walked up behind Rebecca and stood next to her. "Well, Rivki, how'd it sound?" he asked.

"Oh, excuse me," she said as Chaim and I looked at each other, "Chaim and Yankel, this is my brother, Moshe, he's the leader of the band."

We all shook hands. Moshe turned to her, almost ignoring us, and asked again, "So how did it sound?"

She put her hand on his chest to give him a slight shove and affectionately answered, "You know you're always terrific."

Suddenly a voice was calling out, "Rivki, Moshe, we need your help with the bags!"

I turned around and saw a woman who was a somewhat older version of Rebecca beckoning with her hand. "Your father is over by the registration desk getting the keys right now," she continued excitedly.

"We have to go," Rebecca offered. Moshe smiled when he heard the tone of disappointment in his sister's voice.

"Yeah, we should get going," Moshe added. "Got to schlep the bags up and get back down for the next set, which better be soon or the owner will fire me before the season even starts. Anyway, nice meeting you guys," he concluded as he grabbed Rebecca by the arm.

"I'm sure we'll see each other later," she blurted out while being pulled away.

"Definitely!" roared Chaim.

I knew her eyes were on *me,* and I knew why. I'd long been accustomed to women looking at me like that, testing me, tempting me. Being a devoted yeshiva student, I had learned over the years how to deal with this by looking down or in another direction, pretending not to notice. But this time, I stood frozen, my eyes locked with hers. I raised my arm, offering a slight wave and a faint smile as she disappeared into the crowd.

When they were out of sight, Chaim turned to me and said, "Wow! She's something, no, Yankel?"

"She sure is," I confirmed, regaining my composure. "I wonder why she calls herself Rebecca while everyone else calls her Rivki."

"It's a good sign, Yankel. It means she's probably her own person," he observed.

How insightful of him, I thought to myself. She gives herself an anglicized name, different from what she has always been called, and this somehow makes her an individual. When did Chaim become so perceptive? Then again, Chaim did know about breaking away from molds that others impose, so maybe he was able to spot a kindred spirit in her.

Another person who wasn't playing exactly by the rules.

As luck would have it, we were assigned to her family's table in the dining room. Her parents were both educators—her father a principal, her mother a teacher. They had summers off, so for the past ten seasons the family had spent them at The Pineview.

This made her father a *macher,* a big shot, among the guests. It also gave him an attitude problem with some of the help, particularly his waiter. If, God forbid, a steak was too rare, or potatoes slightly singed, Benny Kleinman would send it right back to the kitchen. That was enough to drive Chaim into a spin. After a while Chaim began to make faces at Benny's complaints. They even had a blow-up once, arguing about the temperature of some scrambled eggs.

This most assuredly put a damper on any intentions Chaim may have had for Rebecca. It seemed his disrespect for her father caused her to dislike him. Several times, when Chaim wasn't around, I heard her and Moshe making fun of his manner. They thought I wasn't listening.

I, on the other hand, found myself in an excellent position. Rebecca's mother, Devorah, was always gracious to me, and Benny and Moshe seemed to like me. Above all, there were those frequent glances and smiles from Rebecca.

Chaim became oblivious to all this. His attention turned elsewhere, to another girl, Chani Berkowitz, a counselor in the day camp who was more receptive to his advances. But I still behaved somewhat distantly toward Rebecca; not for fear of Chaim's reaction, but of my own.

CHAPTER 2

THE PINEVIEW HOTEL catered to an Orthodox clientele. Situated in the heart of the Catskills, just outside the town of Fallsburg, it was an unadorned resort with about three hundred and fifty rooms divided among several white buildings set back on a small hill off the far end of a quiet country road. The main building was the largest and newest. It was an architecturally bland edifice, four stories high, with a dining room, a lobby, and a tearoom. The dining room of the hotel was big enough to accommodate more than eight hundred people. The kitchen was enormous, and immaculately clean—a feature my mother would have appreciated. It had two entrances, one from the dining room and the other from the tearoom, where evening snacks and late breakfasts were served. I could tell from the layout that serving and cleaning up were never-ending tasks in this place. Something about Jews and food—perhaps fear of starvation from centuries of persecution—that makes them inseparable. And there always has to be someone to serve and clean up.

Connected to the main building on the north side was a second building which, while also four stories high, was markedly different in structure and design. Its vintage was apparent by the dilapidated window frames and obtrusive fire escape in the middle of the facade. This building also had a lobby, though much smaller, and a "nightclub," which looked more like a school auditorium. The lobby dubbed as a recreation room with a pool table, a Ping-Pong table, a pinball machine, and a snack bar that was open during the afternoon and late at night. On the top floor were the staff quarters where the hotel administration and day camp counselors lived. The other floors had moderately priced guest rooms.

The third building had only one floor. It was strictly for guest rooms, long and rectangular, and stood on the incline of the hill extending from just off the road up to about thirty feet before the entrance to the main building. A path from the road to the main building ran along its length. It was the most quaint of the buildings, bordered by shrubs and trees on all sides.

At the bottom of the hill were three clay tennis courts. Beyond the tennis courts was an outdoor swimming pool, and above that, connected to the north building, was a small indoor swimming pool housed in a makeshift aluminum structure.

There was one more building, a shabby old barracks located behind the main building, where the kitchen and dining room staff lived. It had three floors with five bedrooms, and one bathroom for each floor. Some of the rooms had as many as four beds. Since Chaim and I were lucky enough to be among the first to arrive, we managed to claim a room for two.

When I initially saw this building, I was stunned. The front door was missing, the paint had corroded and chipped, many windows had been replaced by wooden boards, and several screens were torn and holed. The hallways inside were dull with worn plywood floors and matching walls. There was a strong stench of mold in the air.

Our room was on the second floor. The bathroom was at the end of the hall. It had one seatless toilet meant to be shared by about sixteen people, and a tin shower stall with rusty knobs and a slimy floor.

Across the road from the hotel, hidden behind the woods, a river flowed. About a quarter of a mile upstream was a small waterfall beneath a high bridge for Route 52, a two-lane thoroughfare running from Ellenville to Liberty. Children generally played at the waterfall, but the spot I discovered one day while walking through the woods was quiet and deserted.

The stream was bordered by tall trees and in its center sat a large rock, rising well above the waterline. The surface of the rock was almost perfectly flat and at least ten feet in diameter. This was an ideal place for laying out a towel and basking in the sun's rays, especially for a yeshiva student who would only be able to do such a thing in total seclusion.

And so, this was the place to which I would disappear each afternoon, weather permitting, during my break. I would remove my clothes down to my bathing suit, leave them on the bank, and walk through the waist-high water holding up my towel till I got to the rock. I would climb up, spread out the towel, and lay down flat on my back. And, usually after a short while, the rock would begin to feel as soft as a mattress of feathers, comfortable enough for sleep.

Then, one afternoon, about two weeks into the season, my secret was discovered. I was lying there, somewhere between wakefulness and slumber, as I heard my name being called. I rose up on my elbows, turned my head toward the trees, and saw Rebecca standing at the edge of the water.

My first instinct was to grab the towel from underneath me and bring it around my shoulders to cover myself. I did. She smiled, observing my embarrassment.

"Rebecca." Hesitation. "Hi," Awkwardness. "What are you doing here?" Anxiety.

"I followed you." No pretense.

I just stared at her, waiting to hear more.

"I mean," she continued a bit defensively, "I've seen you walk this way many times before, and today I guess I had the urge to follow and see where you went." Still smiling. Quite dangerous.

"You followed me," I repeated, almost casually.

"I guess so." Her turn for embarrassment.

"How long have you been standing there?"

"A little while." Noncommittal.

A moment of silence. We looked at each other across the water.

"Would you like me to go?" she asked.

"No!" I blurted out, surprised at my own enthusiasm. "Wait a minute," I continued. I lifted the towel off my shoulders, held it in my hand, and eased myself from the rock into the water. I made my way to the bank where she stood, holding the towel high so as not to get it wet.

I came out of the water and stood before the pile of clothes I had left by the trees. She wore an inviting smile as she watched my every move, perusing my almost naked body intently with her eyes. I wondered if she was aware of what she was doing, of the power she had. Her seeming pleasure in what she saw aroused my own sensuality, which augmented my discomfort. Nervously, I asked her to look away as I fastened the towel around my waist to remove my bathing suit and replace my pants. I quickly put on my undershirt, then my *tzitzis,* the garment of fringes that Orthodox men wear to remind them of the Torah's commandments. I threw my shirt on over the *tzitzis,* buttoned it, and tucked it in before telling her it was okay to face me. When she turned, she was laughing and trying to disguise it by holding her hand over her mouth.

"What's so funny?"

"Nothing." She continued chuckling as she spoke. "I'm sorry, I don't mean to laugh at you. It's just funny."

"What . . . ?"

"This." She held her hands out in front of her, indicating the situation.

I saw that she, too, was uncomfortable, and I smiled back. I wanted to ask why she followed me, but thought it best not to put her on the spot.

"So this is where you go every day?" she inquired as we started walking toward the road.

"When it's sunny out."

"It's a nice place."

"It's very peaceful, gives me a chance to think about things."

"What kinds of things?"

"Oh, lots of stuff. Life, God, politics. You know, light stuff."

Her smile widened, ear to ear. Her face lit up. I had struck a chord.

"Why do you call yourself Rebecca?"

"I like it. Why do you call yourself Yankel?"

"I don't like it."

"That's good, neither do I." Direct.

"Well, that's my name. I guess I'm stuck with it."

"That's not true. Your Hebrew name is Yakov, and I guess your English name would be Jacob. So, you see, you have choices."

"I never thought of calling myself anything but Yankel."

"Even though you don't like it."

I must have looked dumbfounded.

"Well," she continued, "from now on I will call you Yakov. It's much nicer. I've always liked Hebrew names better than Yiddish ones."

I felt she had nerve, but I sort of appreciated it. "Yakov" did sound nicer, especially when *she* said it. If she wanted to rename me, she could.

Suddenly I looked at my watch and realized that I had to be getting back to the dining room to set up for dinner. We began walking a bit more briskly, crossed the road, and came to the front gate of the hotel. I was concerned about being seen on the grounds with her. It wouldn't look right. And I also wasn't quite sure how Chaim would react if he were to get wind of it. But I didn't say anything and just kept walking with her. I didn't have to worry about such things; I was now Yakov.

"I hope we get to talk about those 'light' matters you think about when you're down at the river," she said as we walked up toward the main building.

"What do you mean?"

"You know, life, God, and politics. I think that was what you said."

"It was, but I lied."

"What do you mean?"

"I hardly ever think about politics. I know nothing about it." We both smiled.

"I see you have a sense of humor," she responded with surprise.

"One needs to, especially when one thinks about life and God all the time."

"Yes, one does."

Suddenly our repartee was interrupted by a familiar voice from behind me.

"Rivki," her father called as he approached us. "I was wondering where you'd gone." He looked at me, smiled, and added, "But I can see you've been in safe hands." He then took her around and kissed her on the forehead.

He was dressed in white shorts, a white polo shirt, white socks, and sneakers, and held a tennis racket in his right hand. His clean-shaven face was wet with sweat, as was his balding head, which was covered by a small, colorful, hand-knit yarmulke. He was as tall as I, about six feet. Our eyes met on an equal plane.

"How are you, Mr. Kleinman?" I asked nervously.

"I'm fine, I guess. Just a bit tired from the run-around I got on the court from Moshe. By the way, Yankel, you can call me Benny. 'Mr. Kleinman's' too formal for my liking."

"Okay," I responded, though my tone was tentative. In my world, we addressed elders with proper titles. It wasn't formal, it was just the way things were done.

"By the way, Yankel, are you by any chance related to the famous Rabbi David Eisen?"

I faltered a moment before responding. It was unreasonable for me to expect my anonymity to last; Mr. Kleinman probably already knew, anyway. "Yes, he's my father," I answered reluctantly.

"I thought so," he replied. "The resemblance is remarkable," he added under his breath.

It immediately occurred to me that he must have known my father in his youth, when he might have looked somewhat like I did now. I had heard this before from relatives, and had even noticed some similarities in old pictures. It was odd, however, hearing it from a stranger, especially this stranger.

"Do you know my father?" I asked hesitantly. I was hoping that he had merely known *of* him and had perhaps seen pictures in one or another of the Jewish periodicals that frequently featured news involving my father. No such luck.

"I used to know him." The equivocation was obvious, as was his vacillating tone. He seemed uncomfortable discussing this, and sorry he had asked about it in the first place. This man had a history with my father and had suspected that I was who I was. Now that it was confirmed, he looked quite rattled.

"Oh, did you attend the Mirrer Yeshiva with him?" I asked, referring to the ultra-Orthodox Talmudic Academy in which my father had studied during his youth. I figured there was no way this modern man from Woodmere, Long Island, with the colorful yarmulke had actually attended the Mirrer Yeshiva considering that graduates of Mirrer typically wore large black felt yarmulkes and black fedoras. But it was the only question I could think of to break the tension.

"In fact I did," he responded, probably aware of my amazement at hearing this. "For a while," he qualified. "But I never finished. I went on instead to Yeshiva University."

Now that was more like it, I thought. Yeshiva University was just what its name denoted: a yeshiva combined with a university. It was a modern-Orthodox institution dedicated to the synthesis of secular and religious studies, a place where science, philosophy, literature, and history were regarded as important affiliates to Talmud.

In the ultra-Orthodox world in which I lived, such a notion was blasphemous. The secular was sinful, and one was permitted to study only the essentials that were required to earn a living. After high school, the men would spend their entire days studying Talmud, and if one had to attend college—usually because there was no family business to go into—he would do so at night. For such individuals, the most common course of study was accounting. Only a handful among the ultra-Orthodox studied law, and even fewer studied medicine. But the highest achievement of all was to be able to continue studying Talmud without having to worry about something so mundane as money. This honor was bestowed only upon those who married rich or were rich themselves.

My father was a prince among the ultra-Orthodox and, like others of his ilk, he harbored severe animosity toward anything secular. He often scoffed at the mere mention of Yeshiva University, particularly deriding the university's rabbinical school for producing supposed heretics. It was widely believed among ultra-Orthodox circles that most of the graduates of Yeshiva University's rabbinical school actually ended up serving in Reform and Conservative pulpits despite their Orthodox ordination. Years later, I would learn that this was indeed not the case, but just another among the many misconceptions of a misguided youth.

"Were you friends?" I asked Rebecca's father, taken with curiosity and well aware that I was overstepping my bounds.

"You might say that," he responded with a tenor of mystery. "Anyway, it's a long story, and if I'm not mistaken, you're probably late for work." His face was tense; the message was clear—he was bringing this conversation to a close.

I didn't push. If there was something to know, I'd eventually find out. I looked at my watch. "Oh my, you're right. I better get going."

"Yes, you'd better, if we're ever going to have dinner," he added.

As I was about to skirt away, Rebecca looked at me and said, "Let's have that talk soon."

"Yes, let's," I responded as Benny stood there watching. I ran through the doors, wondering what that "long story" was all about.

CHAPTER 3

I WAS SEVEN YEARS OLD when my father, the *famous* Rabbi David Eisen, suffered a massive heart attack. I wasn't even told exactly what happened to him. My mother called it "indigestion." And yet, despite her assurances, I can recall my despair seeing the bystanders crowding around as two men in uniforms placed the stretcher into an ambulance. I didn't know what indigestion was any more than I knew what a heart attack was. What I did know was that my father was sick and being taken away by strange men while I was forced to remain in a neighbor's house peering out a window, watching the faces of those consoling my mother. I had a strong sense this indigestion was a dreadful matter.

He was forty years old at the time and, until that moment, had seemed invincible. He was a powerful figure, a descendant of a long line of distinguished rabbis, a pillar in the Orthodox community, a renowned and esteemed scholar. Whether in the yeshiva where he spent his days teaching young rabbinical students, or from his synagogue pulpit where he preached week after week to one of the largest congregations in Brooklyn, Rabbi David Eisen's devotion to his calling was unwavering.

The phone never stopped ringing in our house: students, with intricate questions regarding performance of rituals; congregants, about deaths and births; colleagues, seeking counsel; politicians, chasing endorsements. He took the weight of the Orthodox Jewish world on his shoulders as if he himself were the sole preserver and savior of the tradition, a modern-day Moses. And to me, at seven years of age, he seemed even greater than Moses—perhaps my first irreverent thought.

The one thing my father never had time for was me, his only child. Expectations, however, were plentiful. I was to excel in my studies, be diligent in performance of *mitzvahs,* obedient and helpful to my mother, and invisible when my father came home for dinner.

After dinner, he often disappeared to his study upstairs. I would help my mother clean up, and then go to my room to finish my homework before getting into bed. On my way to my room each night, I would pass by the door to his study. It was perpetually closed, a sign he was not to be disturbed. Often I would stop for a few moments and stare at the door. It was certainly the most majestic door I'd ever seen—deeply stained mahogany with an engraved geometric pattern of small squares surrounding even smaller circles, brass hinges, and a brass handle. It seemed so large, so imposing, certainly fitting for such a man. I would stand close enough to hear what was going on inside. Sometimes I heard talking, my father involved in conversation on the phone or with someone who had stopped by to see him. Mostly, there was a faint humming as he reflected over passages of the Talmud, and if I listened closely enough, I could even hear him turn those pages.

This was his greatest joy in life, the time that he was able to spend uninterrupted in the pure pleasure of learning Torah. And this was the single most important thing for *me* to be doing as well. It was the gateway to my destiny, he would always stress, for I was preordained to take my position, one day, among the ranks of the eminent rabbis who preceded me. He never offered to help me with my studies, or asked if I was having any difficulties. He expected me to be self-reliant, as he was in the eyes of his father—a fact of which he would occasionally remind me. My grandfather had died before I was born, but I knew from all the stories I'd been told over the years that his spirit was very much replicated in *his* son.

Once in a while, when there were guests at the *Shabbos* table, my father would relish the opportunity to show me off as his young budding scholar. Somewhere between the *challah* and the *gefilte* fish, he would typically say, "Yankel, why don't you share with us some thoughts about this week's Torah portion, or perhaps something you learned recently in yeshiva." Yankel is Yiddish for Jacob, or Yakov. I was named Yankel after my paternal grandfather. It was how I was called by all except my mother. She called me *Yankeleh,* my Yankel.

I would say my piece, and everyone around the table would smile, including my father. That was about all I ever got, fleeting smiles when I played my role—my grandfather's legacy.

So I grew up an obsequious, bookish kid with no inclination toward sports, making trouble, or any of the other normal childhood pastimes. Like most of my fellow yeshiva students, I was bespectacled, but that was where the physical similarity ended. I was tall, the tallest kid in my class, with a head of black wavy hair and bright blue eyes.

My mother took great pleasure in my appearance. The earliest memories I have are of her saying things like, "What a gorgeous boy, Yankeleh! What heavenly eyes and beautiful features God has blessed you with! And so tall!" She spoke of this often, indulging herself with friends and relatives, all of whom readily agreed. "The boy will be quite a catch when he grows up. No trouble finding a *shiddoch* for this one," were comments I'd grown used to.

"Why do you fill his head with such nonsense?" my father would react to her. "The boy needs to be concerned with spiritual—*not* physical—matters. He is to be a scholar, not a movie star."

"So he will be a handsome scholar. What's bad about that?" she typically responded.

"If you keep telling him he is so good-looking, he will think that he does not need anything else! He will neglect his studies!"

"Oh, David, come now, the boy is just like you. He is not easily influenced by what I, or anybody, says, and you know it."

At the time, I didn't understand what either of them was getting at. To me, as a young child, how I looked was neither a blessing nor a source of temptation. It was simply another thing that made me different from other kids in the yeshiva, another impediment to fitting in. I had a complex about being tall, and thought my dark hair and light eyes made an uncanny combination.

When I entered my teens and became more tuned in to the way others looked at me—especially the girls in the synagogue—things changed. I began to enjoy the attention, to relish it secretly. My father had been correct—focusing on appearance could easily interfere with my becoming a scholar. The lure of my own carnality was a danger, an impulse that needed to be tamed.

Perhaps my father knew this because he was also tall and good-looking, though less muscular than I. His hair was thinner, too, and he had a neatly trimmed goatee that he habitually fondled. While our eyes were the same color, his were more intense and piercing. Our faces matched, but his skin was rough and mildly scarred from a bad case of adolescent acne, a trait I didn't inherit. And though he had two very pronounced dimples, one in each cheek, I only had one.

We lived in a redbrick two-family house in the heart of Borough Park, a large neighborhood saturated with Orthodox Jews and tree-lined streets. Living amongst our own was one way—albeit not foolproof—of insulating the community from the "evils" of outside cultures. The way we dressed—generally dark suits and black hats for men, lengthy dresses and sleeves to the wrists for women—was another way.

The other half of the house was inhabited by my cousin Chaim's family. There was Chaim, his two older sisters, Sarah and Leah, Aunt Sheindy, and Uncle Zelig. Zelig worked as a salesman in a camera store on Forty-first Street in Manhattan. Sheindy sold dresses in a boutique on Thirteenth Avenue in the shopping district of Borough Park.

Zelig and Sheindy fought often, and loudly, usually about money. Their voices could be heard through the walls and sometimes even on the street. Despite their hardships, my parents—who agonized over being unable to have any more children after me—envied the size of their tribe.

Chaim was a year older than I and miles away in temperament. A stocky, short, but rough looking type, he was always in trouble in school and defiant with his parents. And he was my best friend.

My father attributed Chaim's problems to some form of heredity from my uncle Zelig, his brother-in-law, whom he tolerated only for the sake of his sister. It was no small feat for my father to tolerate someone he didn't like, for he was a man of little forbearance and much prejudice.

His antipathy list was extensive. At the top were non-Orthodox Jews, whether Reform, Conservative, or unaffiliated. He despised them all and referred to them with the same degrading Yiddish euphemisms that he used for Gentiles: *goyim* or *shkotzim* (from the biblical Hebrew word *sheketz*, meaning a detestable thing, or unkosher creature that crawls on the ground), which is plural for the infamous terms *sheigitz* (male) and *shikse* (female).

Also on my father's list, though not as high up, were some groups of Orthodox Jews; namely, those who disagreed with his particular leanings. There were, on one end, the more liberal types: those who dressed in contemporary clothing; indulged in modern forms of entertainment such as television, books, movies, and shows; sent their children to universities after high school; and lived in places like Woodmere, Long Island. And on the other end, there were the Hasidic Jews, for whom his dislike was a bit more perplexing.

It is said that only the Eskimo can differentiate among various types of snow. Likewise, only those within our community could fully appreciate the distinctions among the many factions of orthodoxy. To begin with, there were numerous Hasidic sects, and occasional conflicts—sometimes violent—between them. The reasons for these disputes could range from anything like whose meat was more kosher to whose leader was closer to God.

Another enmity, dating back to the very inception of Hasidism in the early eighteenth century, was the dispute between the Hasidim and the rabbis of the Lithuanian yeshivas. The issue centered on the teachings of Hasidism, its emphasis on the special spiritual powers of the Grand Rabbi, and its belief that devotion itself is greater than studying Talmud and observing laws.

The original Hasidim rebelled against the fundamentalism that dominated most of Eastern European orthodoxy. They appealed to the commoners, who lived in small, rural villages, who toiled hard and had little, who were unable to attend the aristocratic yeshivas of the gifted and privileged. They sought to create a religious experience that was not confined to study and strict observance. They were, ironically, the first reformers.

They revolutionized Judaism and, in so doing, incurred the wrath of the Jewish establishment, the Lithuanian rabbis of the renowned Talmudic academies in cities like Vilna and Volozhin, who waged their opposition with a vengeance. There were excommunications of Hasidic rabbis and their followers. The rabbis went so far as to try to convince the czar's police that one or another Hasidic leader was actually a spy against the government. The Hasidim were scoffed at and denounced as idolaters and infidels, but their movement continued to strengthen and grow. And now their descendants lived in America, side by side with their former adversaries.

My father, though American-born, was a proud bearer of the Lithuanian tradition. He was committed to the old grievances, but his feelings were tempered by the challenges of new, and more powerful, enemies: assimilation and secularism. American modernism posed a threat that united these bitter foes in a common struggle to safeguard the traditional way of life, a battle that made their own conflicts seem trivial.

My father taught in the Mirrer Yeshiva on Ocean Parkway,

the same yeshiva in which he had been ordained. It was reputed to be one of the most prestigious Talmudic institutions in the world and had been named after the European town of Mir where it originated. In the months preceding Hitler's march on the Baltic States, after Germany's conquest of Poland, the leaders of the Mirrer Yeshiva managed to transport almost the entire yeshiva to a safe haven in the city of Shanghai. My grandfather was among those leaders, and later, upon coming to America, he became one of the founders of the yeshiva in Brooklyn. It was fitting that my father was a teacher there, and he expected that I too would one day do the same.

When my father had his heart attack, he was hospitalized for about five weeks and then recuperated at home for the rest of the summer. My mother had to devote all her attention to him, so at the unsullied age of seven I was off to camp, leaving my home and family for the first time. Accompanying me were a trunk, a duffel bag, Chaim, and an acute sense of abandonment. It was also Chaim's first summer away. That I wouldn't be completely alone probably made it easier on my mother.

On the day of our departure, my mother and Sheindy drove us to the bus. When we arrived at the departure site, Chaim and I unloaded the car and put our stuff in the line of bags for the bus's luggage compartment. There was a good crowd, parents and children bidding farewell for the summer. I recognized several kids from the neighborhood.

When the counselors had finished loading the bags, the driver boarded the bus, took his seat, and started the engine. A counselor announced that we would be leaving in five minutes. My mother burst into tears. She hugged me and kissed me all over my face. I held onto her, but didn't cry. Crying was *muturnicht,* forbidden, for my father's son. My father often said that Jewish men shouldn't cry; life is filled with suffering and pain for the Jew and he has to be strong. At that moment I would have made him proud.

As the bus pulled away, I could see my mother wiping her eyes with her handkerchief. Aunt Sheindy stood beside her, holding her. Within seconds they were out of view.

Prior to that moment, my mother had been the one constant in my life. Her presence counterbalanced my father's absence; her tenderness offset his stoicism. I tried to keep her in my mind for as long as possible, to smell the scent of her perfume and hear the sound of her voice. I could almost feel the touch of her lips, the warmth of her arms, her cheeks as they pressed against mine.

She was regarded in the community as a woman of exceptional beauty. As with me, others often lauded her physical attributes, but in her case it was as if that were all she was, all she needed to be. Petite in stature, she was endowed with classic features, full lips, a perfectly proportioned nose, and light chestnut eyes. Her long, wavy, ebony hair was usually covered by a *sheitel,* a wig of similar color and texture, as a sign of her fear of heaven and devotion to her husband. She dressed modestly, but in style, and carried herself with an understated elegance.

Esther Eisen, the *rebbetzin,* the rabbi's wife. They saw her as a complacent hausfrau, docile and reserved, a mere shadow beside her husband's regality. But I knew otherwise. For just as she covered the true allure of her hair and body from the outside world, she also concealed much of her authentic self. In our home, she was a force.

She tempered my father's moods and, in her wisdom, understood his limitations. She never argued, but always spoke her piece. And the thing I remember most is that she had about her an air of sadness, the source of which was a complete mystery to me for many years.

CHAPTER 4

THE NIGHT AFTER my encounter with Rebecca, I couldn't sleep. I sat up in bed recounting to Chaim what had happened. He seemed disinterested until I came to the part about her father. "That man is nothing but a *putz*. He thinks he's so important and that he knows everything," was his only response to my story.

"By the way, you know Chani Berkowitz?" he continued.

"You mean that counselor you've been talking with?"

"It's a lot more than just talking. Man, is she something!"

"She's very pretty," I observed, hesitating, wondering what "more than just talking" meant.

He related that he'd been spending time with her in the evenings. It occurred to me how unmindful I had been of his whereabouts. We hadn't been seeing all that much of each other aside from work.

"Where have you been going with her?" I asked innocently, trying to disguise my curiosity.

"We've been taking walks, and some nights we go into town."

He was referring to Woodbourne, a small country village about two miles from the hotel. The town itself was only three blocks long and consisted of restaurants, stores, an arcade, and a dilapidated movie house. On its outskirts was the Woodbourne State Penitentiary, a source of employment for the year-round natives and probably the only reason the town was even on the map.

Unlike the larger towns of Fallsburg and Monticello, which were inhabited predominantly by blacks, Woodbourne was a hamlet for Orthodox Jews. Virtually all the eateries—the pizza place, luncheonette, ice cream palace, bagel shop, and bakery—were kosher. And the streets were crowded with the yarmulkes, black hats, and *sheitels* of the summer residents of neighboring bungalow colonies, hotels, or camps. A modern-day Anitevka.

Just a year ago, when we were counselors at Camp Yad Avraham, Chaim and I spent our Saturday nights together playing air hockey and pinball in the Woodbourne Arcade. We met up with friends from home who were working in other camps or hotels, and hung out until it was time to get back for curfew. Sometimes we even missed curfew and had to sneak back into camp. Chaim was an expert at such things and I followed along. We were never caught, a perfect team. Now things were changing.

As I listened to him go on about Chani, I thought about the two of us and how we ended up in this place. We had spent ten consecutive summers at Yad Avraham, and were ripe for a change. It was the same issue for each of us, though he was more adamant. He couldn't stand the restrictions of an all-boys Orthodox camp any longer. He argued endlessly with his parents, until, finally, they gave in.

My aunt and uncle were, no doubt, justified in feeling that Chaim still needed a structured environment. During the past year alone, he had been caught shoplifting, had been truant from school at least thirty times, and was suspended once for slashing the principal's tires. He would have been expelled altogether were it not for my father's influence.

I, on the other hand, was my same old self. An honor student, the pride of the yeshiva, playing my role to the hilt. I could do no wrong. It was becoming terribly boring, in fact. So

I decided to try something new, something completely out of character. An experiment.

Cheating on secular subjects was commonplace in the yeshiva. It was, in part, the by-product of the disdain that the students and rabbis held for secular studies, since they merely detracted from precious time that could be spent studying Talmud. It was also because it was something devious, something that the clever yeshiva student could get away with, a surreptitious form of defiance for young men who, in every other respect, were completely dutiful.

So for the first time, I decided to join the ranks of my peers and turned to Chaim for help. He was flattered and excited at the opportunity to corrupt me. It would, somehow, equalize us.

I chose chemistry because it was the most difficult subject. The method was simple. Chaim instructed me on how to prepare cheat-sheets, small pieces of paper containing volumes of information, and where to best conceal them. While the inside of a sleeve or belt were suitable, the yeshiva student had an even more inconspicuous place: the inner lining of his yarmulke. Playing with one's yarmulke by moving it from time to time to different positions on the head was not unusual, especially in warm weather. It was a habit that many yeshiva types, including my father, shared.

The key was to keep my cool. "Whatever you do," Chaim warned, "don't look nervous!" I should just remove the yarmulke, hold it in the palm of my hand, and put it back on my head. I would also have to study the cheat-sheets, know the exact location of each answer, because I would only get split-second glances.

The final exam was held on a scorching afternoon in the first week of June. There were thirty of us crowded into the chemistry classroom. All the windows, which comprised the upper half of an entire wall, were open. For safety reasons, these windows would only open from the top, and only about a third of the way down. There was no breeze.

We were all sweating. The air was heavy. At the front of the room, seated behind the teacher's desk, was Mr. Stern, the chemistry teacher. He looked just like any ordinary science teacher: short, thin, and balding, with wire-rimmed glasses, a button-down checkered shirt, and wrinkled tan polyester pants. He didn't seem to be paying much attention.

I managed to sneak only a few glances at my yarmulke before large beads of sweat began dripping from my head. The cheat-sheets were getting more smudged by the moment, until they were no longer useful. I had answered ten of fifty questions; the next forty would have to be educated guesses.

A week later I learned, not surprisingly, that I had failed my first exam in my entire academic career. Everyone else—my parents and Mr. Stern—was shocked. I wasn't. What did throw me, however, was that it was one of the few moments in my life when the notion of reward and punishment seemed unclouded.

That incident had been just a few weeks before Chaim and I arrived at The Pineview. Once his parents had decided to allow him to come, my parents soon followed. It wasn't easy, however.

My father had long been unhappy with my summer excursions. He felt my time would best be spent continuing to study in the yeshiva, especially during the summer months when there were no secular studies to distract me. He acceded only because he felt that Chaim needed *my* influence. Yankel the chaperone.

But when he heard that our plans were to work in a hotel, he blew his top. "At least in that camp you were able to spend some time learning Torah each day," he proclaimed. "But to work in a dining room of a hotel, that is not something for my son to be doing. You should be studying Talmud in yeshiva all day. You won't become a scholar serving other people food!"

He was right. I should have been spending the summer in the yeshiva brushing up on my Talmud. The upcoming year was to be a difficult and decisive one. I would be judged as a candidate for the honor of studying an additional five years for *smichah,* rabbinical ordination.

"Don't think that just because of my position you have it in the bag. You don't. No one does," my father pointed out. "If you continue to follow your cousin, you will eventually follow him to his father's camera store. Is that what you want for your future?"

My mother intervened and softened him up a bit, telling him that she had gotten used to the time that they had shared alone during the summers. This was bull—she, like me, never got much of him at any time of the year—but it worked. I also appeased my father with promises that I would study daily. He reluctantly consented to let me go.

He wasn't happy, though. And the last words he spoke before I left were, "Be careful how you spend your time. Remember Yankel, you can't always do what you want or have what you want. Sometimes you must make choices. *Sometimes you must sacrifice!"*

CHAPTER 5

THE FAINT SOUNDS of a Hasidic medley could be heard from a distance as the Moshe Kleinman Orchestra did its usual Saturday night gig in the hotel lobby. Rebecca and I were sitting on lounges by the outdoor pool under a clear, starry sky. The breeze was chilly and the usual odor of skunk filled the evening air, but neither of us was bothered.

"Do you believe in God?" I asked.

"What kind of question is that? Of course I do!" she responded.

"I mean, do you really believe that God cares about what we do as people and that we are rewarded for good and punished for evil?"

"Well, the way I see it, things are more complicated than that."

"How so?" I pressed.

"You really want to talk about this?"

"You're the one who said that you wanted to talk more about those 'light' subjects, didn't you?"

She hesitated, then replied, "I suppose I did."

"Okay, so what do you think?"

"I believe that the ways in which God rewards or punishes are mysterious and that we don't always see the whole picture. You know, the-forest-for-the-trees sort of thing."

"Why don't we take a specific example, say the Holocaust," I said. "If you believe that God runs the world, then surely He is as responsible for that as He is for anything else. So you believe that God brought about the suffering and killing of children and righteous people for some reason that we cannot see because we don't have the big picture."

"Boy, you really have a way of getting to the heart of the matter, don't you?" she reacted, almost angrily.

"Well, that is what you're saying, isn't it?"

"But you sound as if you don't believe."

"I asked you first."

"My, you're full of surprises."

"I know. I even surprise myself sometimes. But I really want to hear your thoughts," I said.

She pondered in silence for a moment. I waited and watched her. Then she began, "I admit that there are things like the Holocaust, or any time an innocent person suffers, that I don't understand. Sometimes they may even cause me to doubt. But I know that much evil is caused by human beings and that maybe God allows it because He created us with freedom of choice. If we can't choose, then there is no such thing as good either. If everything is simply predetermined by God, then everything just *is,* and there is no purpose for value judgments like 'good' and 'bad.' Things will just happen no matter what we do, and moral judgments and moral behavior make no difference. So we have to have the choice to do evil in order to do any good."

"But you've left out natural disasters such as illnesses, starvation, earthquakes," I said.

"I don't pretend to have the answers to everything. Faith is not knowing, it's believing. I do believe there is a reason for everything that happens, and that the reason becomes clearer as history unfolds."

"So now you're back to saying that everything that happens *is* part of God's plan. What happened to your freedom of choice? Either God's in charge or we're in charge."

"You'd make a great lawyer."

"My teachers say I'll make a great rabbi," I said sarcastically.

"A confused rabbi; a great lawyer," she replied with that smile.

"But we're off the topic; you didn't answer my question," I pressed again.

"Well, I know that I am, in some way, contradicting myself. But it may be that God is in control of some things and that we're in control of others. A system of checks and balances maybe, like the President and the Congress. How the powers are distributed, I have no idea. Maybe God guides us, gives us some challenges, intervenes when we go too far astray. I don't even pretend to know how it works, but I do believe that it does work."

"So the Holocaust wasn't 'too far astray'?"

"To you and me it certainly was, but the fact is that it didn't completely destroy the Jewish people, and that's important, too. We have suffered so much, it seems remarkable that we're even here today to talk about it. By every rule of history, we should have disappeared long ago. And with the State of Israel we're stronger and safer as a people than we ever were. It's not my place to judge or to say, God forbid, that the State of Israel is in any way worth the Holocaust. But its existence reflects as much godliness as the Holocaust reflected ungodliness."

"It sounds good, but there are still many contradictions."

"I agree, but I prefer these contradictions to the alternative," Rebecca responded.

"What's the alternative?"

"Well, if you don't believe in God then there is really no purpose to our existence. We're just here because of some random combination of chemicals and when we die that's the end. The world and history have no meaning. And there is also no standard for morality."

"What do you mean by that?" I asked.

"I mean that there really is no objective reason why one shouldn't murder or steal. The Nazis believed it was moral to kill Jews, Robin Hood believed it was moral to rob the rich, and cannibalistic tribes believe it is moral to sacrifice people and eat them. Who's to say they're wrong? I may disagree, but that's only a matter of opinion. Unless, of course, I believe in God. Then I believe that there is a universal standard of morality for all people in all times that says thou shalt not murder, thou shalt not steal. It gives purpose and moral structure to the universe."

"I agree," I stated, "and maybe that's why people believe. It helps them make sense out of their lives."

"Is this an argument for atheism that my ears are hearing?" she countered sarcastically. "Since you know why people believe in God, then maybe He's a figment of their imagination. That sounds like circular reasoning to me!"

"It seems that you've thought about these things," I said.

"Does that surprise you?"

"A little." It really surprised, and excited, me a great deal.

"Why?"

"Because I didn't think most people thought about these things."

"Is it because I'm a girl?"

And a very smart girl at that! "No." I hesitated, then continued, "Well, maybe."

"It seems that your ideas about girls are as off as your ideas about God."

"But you don't know my ideas about God. I haven't told you, I've only asked you questions."

"Oh, but I could guess," she replied, staring into my eyes.

We had ended up in this same spot a few nights earlier on our first of many scheduled rendezvous. We had walked around the grounds for hours, talking about our backgrounds, families, and just being flirtatious. Our legs had grown tired. We had found a secluded place to sit and continue conversing till well past midnight. We had returned for the past three evenings and had discovered much about each other. It was frightening, and exhilarating.

We learned that we were the same age and that we both had one more year of high school left. She told me of her plans to go on to college. She wanted to be a teacher. Of what, I asked. She didn't yet know exactly, only that she wanted to teach something. She would be an excellent teacher, I thought.

I told her that my fate had been decided even before I was circumcised. College wasn't in the cards for me. I would continue studying in yeshiva for another five years to receive rabbinical ordination. Then I, too, would be a teacher.

We also talked of our mutual curiosity regarding her father's acquaintance with my father. Rebecca had tried to ask her father about this, but each time she broached the subject he successfully avoided it. There was something to this, and somehow she sensed her father was concerned about our friendship. But for now he wasn't interfering.

CHAPTER 6

ONE EVENING toward the end of July, after we got off from work, Chaim asked me what time I was planning to go to sleep. An odd question. He read my face and explained that he was hosting a poker game in our room that night and wanted to make sure he wasn't inconveniencing me. I told him not to be concerned. I wouldn't be back before one o'clock.

Chaim had fallen in with a sordid group. Gambling, smoking, drinking. All kinds of mischief. I turned a blind eye and gave him the benefit of every possible doubt. The last thing I wanted was for us to relive the acrimony between our fathers.

I had no idea from this exchange that I was pledging my undying absence until the stroke of one. So when I made my way back about a half hour earlier than predicted, and saw from outside that the lights were off in our room, I naturally assumed that the game was over. I entered the building and climbed the stairs to the second floor. I came to the door of our room, which was shut, and opened it slowly so as not to awaken him in case he was already asleep.

As I turned the knob, I heard a loud thump from inside. I couldn't imagine what it was. I opened the door further and the light from the hallway entered the room just enough for me to see Chaim sitting up on the edge of his bed, shirt undone, hair disheveled, yarmulke missing. Next to him, frantically fastening her unbuttoned blouse, was Chani Berkowitz. They were stunned by my presence.

"Yankel!" Chaim whooped as he reached over to the night table, grabbed his yarmulke, and placed it on his head.

I stared in disbelief.

"You said you wouldn't be back until one!" he asserted.

Should I be apologizing, I wondered?

Chani finished with her blouse and just sat there, looking embarrassed, saying nothing.

"I think I'll come back in ten minutes," I remarked almost inaudibly. Without waiting for a reply, I turned on my heels and left.

I stayed outside and walked for a while. My mind raced with images, one after another. Chaim and Chani lying there half undressed. I imagined what they must have been doing, pictured it with as much graphic detail as my yeshiva mind could possibly conjure up. I pictured what I must have looked like as I barged in. And then, the faces changed. I saw myself, instead of Chaim, with Chani. She was quite appealing—long wavy blond hair, full figure, blue eyes, voluptuous lips. Our bodies were locked together, our lips pressing against each other. Suddenly it was no longer Chani. The body was more petite, the hair was dark. It was Rebecca. We were wrapped together in endless passion. And the face of the intruder in the doorway—it was the face of my father. My thoughts returned to Chaim. I was angry. Again, I was jealous.

When I finally returned, the room was empty. I said my evening prayers, undressed, and got into bed. The images returned, but with greater power. I could almost experience it—the scent of her hair as our faces merged, the taste of her mouth, the soft feel of her bare chest upon mine. I reached down into my underwear and felt the fullness of my erection.

The turn of the doorknob brought me back to reality. The door opened and blocking the light from the outer hallway was Chaim. He saw I wasn't yet asleep, but he still closed the door and entered quietly as if I was. He walked toward his night table, sat down on his bed, and stiffly gazed in my direction. I turned toward him and could see that he wore a look of embarrassment.

We remained silent for a while, him sitting up and me lying there in bed, until he began to speak. "I just want you to know that we didn't really do anything that bad. I mean we were just kissing and stuff."

"You really don't have to explain yourself to me," I said.

"Do you think there's anything wrong with kissing?"

"What difference does it make what I think?"

"I just want to know," he stated.

"Well, you know it's forbidden."

"But I want to know what *you* think, not what's forbidden!"

"I really haven't thought about it," I replied curtly, turning away from Chaim and pulling my blanket up.

"Oh, come on, Yankel! You mean to tell me that you never think about doing such things with Rebecca?"

I conceded. "So what's your point?" I was still facing the wall.

"I want to know what you think, not what the Talmud or the Torah or your father thinks. What *you* think!"

"What I think doesn't really matter. Who am I to defy the laws of the Torah?"

"You still haven't told me what you think," he pressed.

"We're not communicating here," I replied.

"Only because you're afraid to speak your mind. You're always afraid to say or do what you want. All you do is follow the books. That's the way you are!"

"And you don't seem to care what the Torah says! You're always doing exactly what you want. I guess that's the difference between us." It was getting more difficult to conceal my anger.

"So you would like to do what I did?"

"Why is it so damn important for you to know that? Does the fact that I might want to do the same thing absolve you in some way?"

"No, it just tells me whether you really think you're better than me or not."

The truth was unearthed. I was naive to think it could remain buried forever. The sins of the fathers being visited upon the children.

"I don't even know how to begin to respond to that." Defensiveness. "But, anyway, I'm very tired and want to go to sleep." Avoidance.

He seemed disappointed but didn't push the matter. He removed his yarmulke, and began disrobing for bed. Somewhere in the process he said, "Good night."

But it wasn't a good night. I tossed and turned for hours, ruminating over the same images as before. When I finally did fall asleep, it was only for a short time. And when I awoke, there was a cool, wet sensation permeating the crotch area of my underpants.

This wasn't a totally unfamiliar occurrence. In fact, the first time it had happened to me, several years earlier, I innocently confessed to my father. The rabbis in yeshiva had warned us about this most horrible of crimes, the killing of millions of innocent potential souls. I hoped he would reassure me that I wouldn't go blind or meet an early death. I was disappointed.

He was firm in admonishing me about the serious implications of what he termed "spilling one's seed in vain." He told me that despite my lack of control over what happened in my dreams, this was still a sign that I was harboring impure thoughts, and, in order to cleanse myself, I should wash my hands immediately upon awakening, recite special supplications for God's forgiveness, and study extra Torah throughout the day.

Such was the prescription I would obediently follow after every subsequent wet dream. And today was no exception. When I got out of bed I immediately washed my hands and prayed intently. Several times throughout the day I stopped, reminded myself what I'd done, and beseeched God's forgiveness. During my break in the afternoon, instead of my usual excursion to the river, I remained in my room studying Talmud. I tried to repent, to expunge myself of this hideous sin. And the only thing I truly gleaned from all this was a clearer sense of the prodigious power of guilt.

CHAPTER 7

THE FIRST SIN I remember committing was back when I was seven years old, at Camp Yad Avraham during the summer when my father was sick.

The camp was a pretty place, with lots of grass, trees, bushes, and wildflowers. It sat on a hill, off the shore of Sackett Lake, just outside the town of Monticello. The bunks stood atop the hill, twelve in all, in a semicircle. Halfway down was the head counselor's bunk, and about fifty feet below that was the dining room which also served as the canteen and recreation hall. Next to that was a smaller building with a large sign stating *Bes Hak'nesses* in front. This was the synagogue, or *shul.*

A pebbled road ran all the way from the camp entrance up past the synagogue, dining hall, and head counselor's bunk to the top of the hill. Across the road from the dining hall and synagogue was another large building that housed the main office and living quarters for various personnel. All the buildings were white with blue trimming.

It was an all-boys camp, in keeping with the ultra-Orthodox dictate of separating the sexes until they are of marriageable age. There were seven other kids in my bunk; Chaim was with kids his own age in the connecting bunk. Our two bunks shared a bathroom with two showers, three sinks, and three toilets.

I didn't know any of the kids in my bunk, but I did know my counselor, Ezra. He was a student of my father's in the yeshiva and had been to our home several times for *Shabbos* meals. Having him as my counselor made it all a bit easier.

He was eighteen years old, tall and heavy. He had a youthful, straggly beard, a crew cut, and a protruding nose upon which sat thick tortoiseshell glasses. Atop his head he wore a big black velvet yarmulke, which constantly stuck out from the back of his black fedora. Every day, he would put on a fresh white cotton blend, button-down, long-sleeved shirt and a pair of baggy black polyester pants. He had four pairs of the exact same pants and two identical black suit jackets. This was the usual uniform, regardless of the weather.

Hanging down over his pants, from the sides of his shirt, would be the fringes of his *tzitzis.* I also wore *tzitzis,* but my father told me it was permissible—indeed preferable—to tuck them in. He thought that wearing them on the outside was pretentious. It was immodest, in his view, to flaunt one's observance in this way. But many of the students, in their desire to outdo their own teachers, did it anyway. My father used to mock them, claiming that since having a *bris* was also a *mitzvah,* why not show that off as well.

Ezra looked like the type of person who, ten years later, would end up as one of those big fat teachers whom the kids would be afraid of. But in truth, he was gentle and compassionate. And of me, the son of his revered *rebbe,* he was especially protective.

Our routine was fixed. We awoke at seven each morning and the entire camp gathered in the synagogue for the morning prayer service. By eight, we were all in the dining hall for breakfast. Clean-up was from nine to nine-thirty. From nine-thirty till ten we wrote letters home, and from then until twelve we studied Torah. After lunch there were sports, swimming, nature hikes, and the like.

Showers were from four to five-thirty. After that, we recited the afternoon prayer service. Then there was dinner, the evening prayer service, and another two hours of Torah study before bedtime. On *Shabbos,* there were no sports or swimming.

It was by the third week of camp that the roots of my insurrection began to sprout. At first they were innocuous. I began arriving late for prayers, daydreaming during classes, and neglecting some of the blessings over food. I wasn't feeling particularly devout, and seemed to be coming down with frequent physical illnesses of one sort or another.

Ezra noticed all this and after a few days decided to intervene. It was on a warm, sunny afternoon. He asked Chaim's counselor to cover both bunks for a softball game so that he could take me aside for a walk down to the lake. When we got there, the waterfront was empty. A slight breeze came off the water. The lake was serene except for a few speedboats and water-skiers in the far distance. It was a sizable lake with another camp on the other side and several private homes. We sat down beneath a tree that stood about ten feet back from the shoreline.

"You know, I wanted to spend this time with you alone because I know that it is hard for you to be here when your father is sick," Ezra began. He adjusted his glasses as he spoke, a nervous habit he often displayed.

I listened.

"I've noticed that you have been thinking about him a lot?" A statement phrased as a question—the Jewish way of communicating.

"My mama writes that he is okay," I said.

"And I'm sure he is . . ."

"But I want to be home."

"I know you want to be home, Yankel, but it is best for you to be here. Your mama needs to spend all her time and energy on your father so that he can recover."

I paused for a moment to think about what he said. "Ezra, do you know what indigestion is?"

"Why do you ask?"

"Because that's what my mama says my *totti* has."

"It's when you have a problem with the stomach," he responded in a tentative tone. Again he adjusted his glasses.

I could tell he was uncomfortable answering me. I remained silent.

"Yankel, I see you've been getting lazy."

"What do you mean?" Defensiveness.

"You've been late the past three mornings for *Shach'ris,* morning services, and I've noticed that you haven't been making all your blessings before eating."

"I make them quietly, to myself."

"I don't even see your lips moving! You know you're supposed to at least move your lips when you say a blessing."

"I make them to myself." I was looking at the lake instead of at him. I wondered if the people on the boats moved their lips when they said their blessings.

He stared at me, figuring out what to say next.

"How come when I ask you questions during class you answer as if you don't know what's going on? It's like you're in a cloud," he continued. Again the glasses.

"Because I think about my *totti* sometimes."

"What kind of thoughts do you have about him?"

"I wonder why God would make him sick."

"No one really understands God's reasons for the things He does," he responded in a compassionate tone.

"But my *totti* is a rabbi. He does all the *mitzvahs* and learns Torah all the time. Why would God want him to be sick?"

Now Ezra was silent.

"I think maybe it's because I did something wrong," I added under my breath.

He responded, "Why would you say such a thing?"

"Because God only makes people sick when they do things wrong, but my *totti* never does anything wrong. So maybe I did something wrong."

"No, Yankel, you haven't done anything wrong," he explained as he put a hand on my shoulder. "I told you that we can't know why God does anything. We can only have faith that whatever God does is good in the end. Your father is a special person, a *talmid chuchum,* a great scholar, and God will make him well again, I'm sure."

I just listened.

"Now come, we have to get back to the others. I want you to think about what I said and to try harder on doing your *mitzvahs.* You do your part and God will do His, okay?"

I reluctantly nodded in agreement.

The real transgression didn't come until a few days later, on *Shabbos.* I woke up in the morning complaining of a stomachache. Ezra gave me an impatient look, but agreed to let me stay in the bunk while the others went to services. He would check on me before breakfast to see if I would be able to go to the dining room or if I needed to be taken to the infirmary.

I lay in bed for a while reading the latest Captain America comic my mother had sent. I was never allowed to read such things in my father's house, but when I had written home that some of the other kids had them, a whole bunch arrived in a package the following week. In the middle of the comic, I felt my stomach acting up. I got out of bed and walked to the back of the bunk, through the cubby room, and into the bathroom. I made it to the toilet just in time.

As I walked back to my bed, I felt myself overtaken by a strange feeling, a compulsion of sorts. It led me to the front door of the bunk, where I could look out the screen and gaze upon the quiet campus. Everybody was in services.

To my left, about six inches from the doorpost, was the light switch. It was in the off position where it would remain until the end of *Shabbos.* Unless, of course, someone accidentally turned it on. Then it would remain on till the end of *Shabbos.* Accidents were forgiven, of course, but the intentional use of electricity on *Shabbos* was a grave sin. It was an act of creation on the day of rest, and who knew what God would do to someone for such a violation.

I had always imagined thunder and lightning, or leprosy, or some such affliction. Imagined, and feared. Divine retribution, reward and punishment.

I stood there for a time, staring at the light switch, wondering. My hand reached out, just to touch it. My fingers rubbed it, almost caressing it. I was observing my own movements as if I were removed from my body. Still wondering, trembling with the fear of retribution, I was pulled by a force outside myself as my grasp tightened. I looked once more outside the screen. No one was in sight.

Suddenly my arm moved upward, my fingers glued to the switch. I looked at the lightbulb hanging from the rafter above my head, and as it went on I beheld my creation. I had made light. I had done the unthinkable. Then, after about two seconds, my arm returned the switch to its original position. I had made darkness.

I waited for the thunder and lightning, but there was none. There was nothing, not even guilt. I stood there for a while, looking out the door, waiting for something to happen. I thought about what I had done, whether I should try it again. I didn't. When I'd waited long enough, I returned to my bed and resumed reading about Captain America.

Perhaps God hadn't made my father sick after all.

A week later, on visiting day, my mother drove up with Zelig and Sheindy. They arrived late, well after all the other kids' parents, and I waited in the bunk alone until they came. My father was doing well and would be getting out of the hospital soon. I was assured that by the time I returned home, things would be back to normal.

I never repeated my little fiasco with the lights. I didn't want to test God's forbearance. I also began feeling better after visiting day and started behaving as was expected. By the time the summer ended, I was ready to return home and resume the acquiescent lifestyle I had left behind. But I still had a lingering curiosity about what to make of my little discovery.

CHAPTER 8

MOVIES WERE ON THE LIST of forbidden indulgences among the ultra-Orthodox. They were a poisonous influence, a waste of time, a senseless indulgence in modern culture. But watching them was one of Rebecca's favorite things to do. She had tried on several occasions to coerce me. She even resorted to teasing me, pointing out my contradictions with statements like, "I don't understand, on the one hand you're not even sure there's a God, yet you believe it's wrong to go to the movies."

"Are you the only one who's allowed to have contradictions?" I would counter.

She knew she was hitting below the belt and that my commitment to the lifestyle in which I was reared was about more than just belief in God. And she also knew that I was only playing around with questions, neither affirming nor denying God's existence. But she wanted me to go to the movies with her, so she used whatever ammunition was at her disposal. And so, eventually, I agreed.

The feature film at the Woodbourne theater for that week, and for most of the summer, was *The Exorcist.* Rebecca warned me it would be very scary. I didn't believe her. I just couldn't imagine how any intelligent person could be scared by something on a screen.

It was a rainy Wednesday evening, and a sizable crowd was lined up outside the movie house. We stood close together under an umbrella. We had never been this close; the scent of her perfume was getting to me. I paid for both of us. My first real date.

We entered an auditorium that hadn't been renovated since the days of silent films. It had antiquated wooden seats and paint peeling off the walls and ceiling. My sneakers stuck to the concrete floor as we walked down the aisle.

Within minutes of seating ourselves, the lights went out. The smell of popcorn and the sounds of candy wrappers filled the air. I wondered if there were any rats wandering around and asked Rebecca about that. She hit me on the arm.

It wasn't long before the thought of rats was completely out of my mind and replaced with other fears. I couldn't have been more mistaken about the movie. I should never have come. I wouldn't sleep for days.

The only good thing about it was the touching—or rather grabbing—that went on between us during the scariest scenes. It was quite innocent; I would have grabbed a stranger. But it felt good.

When the film ended, we acted as if the touching had never happened. We left the theater. It was no longer raining.

We walked about a block, and then crossed the street to go into the Lucky Dip ice cream palace. On the way we discussed the movie and the possibility of there being a force of evil, a devil, that could overcome people like that. We were petrified and tried to reassure each other that there was nothing to be afraid of. Judaism doesn't believe in that nonsense, I asserted, but I was feeling somewhat possessed myself, and I wasn't very convincing.

We entered the Lucky Dip and sat down at a table near the soda fountain. Rebecca ordered a banana split and I got a vanilla malted. As we talked and ate, I observed with meticulous detail her every movement. I watched as her lips parted and her tongue caressed the ice cream; the way she held the spoon and slowly dug into the scoops on the metal dish. Between mouthfuls, she would lick her lips, and then her hand would again rise from the dish with another spoonful. She was aware of the scrutiny, even enjoyed it.

We sat there until closing time, and then returned to the hotel. We found our lounge chairs by the outdoor pool and talked some more. Before we knew it, the sky was becoming light.

Parting was awkward. We couldn't kiss, embrace, or even shake hands. We both knew that intentional touching before marriage—not the "accidental" type in the movie theater—was expressly forbidden. We both probably wondered what the possible consequences could be. It seemed to me that she might be less concerned with the religious ramifications than I was. But I was certain that, for whatever reason, she did not take a physical relationship between us any more lightly than I did. To her it might not have constituted a grave transgression, but it was still no less of a responsibility. We said our good nights and shared a few suggestive glances. That was it.

I got back to my room in time to zip through the morning prayers and make it to the dining room in time to set up for breakfast. Chaim was already awake. He said nothing about my having been out all night.

The Kleinmans showed up for breakfast at their usual time, all but Rebecca. She was lucky to be able to catch a few hours sleep while I played the walking dead. Even luckier to miss those unsettling looks I was getting from her parents, particularly Benny. He didn't say anything out of the ordinary, but I could tell something was up.

After breakfast I quickly set the table for lunch, and went back to my room to nap for a few hours. I set the alarm so as not to oversleep. When it rang, it seemed as if only five minutes had passed. I made it back to the dining room but my body felt like it was still in bed.

I was walking over to my station when I heard my last name being called by the deep raspy voice of the head waiter. I turned to see what he wanted. He waved me over to him.

As I walked in his direction, he was busy talking to someone else, and his back was turned toward me. I approached and he turned around, looked at me, and said, "Eisen, your station is being changed to fourteen." Station fourteen was all the way over on the other side of the dining room.

"What?" I reacted with utter astonishment. "But the Kleinmans seem satisfied with my service!"

"It's got nothing to do with the Kleinmans. The waiter at fourteen needs someone better than he has now, and you're the best we got."

I gave him a look indicating that I knew he was full of it. Something had happened. Benny was behind this and I didn't understand why. But from the way the head waiter returned my look the matter was closed, period. He was a large, husky fellow with a round face, big hands, and big feet. Nobody messed with him; nobody argued. I wasn't going to start. My problem wasn't with him anyway.

When lunch came around, Rebecca was there, sitting with her parents. I could see, even from afar, that something was wrong. The entire family was unusually subdued; there seemed to be little conversation. Rebecca appeared sullen and defeated, and didn't once look my way.

I didn't want to make a scene there and then. I will see her later, I thought. I'll find out what happened and make it right. I couldn't stand the distance between us. Why wouldn't she even raise her eyes to find me? Why didn't she even look up from her food?

After lunch, she got up from the table and left with her parents. Their usual frolicking was noticeably absent. I looked over to Chaim for a signal. He shrugged his shoulders in confusion.

I no longer noticed how exhausted I was. I cleared and reset my tables in record time, and then burst out of the dining room into the main lobby. I searched the recreation hall, the grounds, and was even bold enough to knock on her bedroom door, all to no avail.

Then it hit me. Perhaps she would come looking for me. Of course she would. And I knew where.

I ran out to the road, hurtled across to the other side and into the woods, down to the stream. As I approached the edge of the water, I looked out at the rock, sure she would be there, only to find it empty. I froze, stared at the top of the boulder, and thought about all the times we had rendezvoused here since she had first discovered my secret. In the water I could see my tired reflection and the overcast sky.

I stood and waited. I sat down in the dirt and waited. No one came.

After dinner, when Chaim came back to the room, I was lying on my bed staring at the ceiling. He reported that he'd heard nothing during dinner. There were still no clues, but something was obviously wrong.

Chaim changed his clothes and told me he was going to town with Chani. I declined his thoughtful, insincere invitation. I had plans of my own. I knew that this time, for certain, she would show.

At some point I dozed off, and when I awoke again it was eleven-fifteen. Her parents usually went to bed between ten and ten-thirty. That should give her enough time to sneak away.

I went into the bathroom and washed the sleep from my eyes. The foreboding expression I saw in the mirror scared me. I looked down at the sink, filled my hands with cold water, and splashed it on my face. I returned to my room, combed my hair, put on a fresh shirt and pair of pants. I picked up the prayer book from the night table, turned to the evening service, and offered my perfunctory rendition. The words on the pages passed by my eyes automatically, but somewhere I inserted a personal supplication. Dear God, please don't let happen what I think is happening. There was no room for atheists in this foxhole.

By eleven-thirty I was ready. Instead of going through the kitchen, I walked around the main building. It was a muggy night, and the stars were hidden by the same clouds that had blocked the afternoon sun.

As I came around the building, I passed by the front door and made my way westward, across the lawn. I could feel the wetness of the dew seep through my sneakers. The visibility wasn't great, but in the distance I could make out Rebecca lying on her lounge by the pool. I walked up to the gate, stopped, and stood there quietly for a few moments, just watching her lie there. She was in a daze and didn't notice me until I opened the gate. The noise caught her attention. She jumped from the lounge and ran toward me. Her arms came around the back of my neck; her body pressed tightly against mine. I was stunned initially, but soon found myself holding her. Her head fell into my shoulder. She was crying.

"Yakov, I'm so sorry," she repeated several times. I stood there, held her, and tried to soothe her. Strangely, I felt no guilt. It all seemed natural.

"Sorry about what?" I asked as I leaned back and looked at her face.

"What my father's done. It's terrible." More tears.

"So he did have me moved."

She nodded.

"But why? What happened?"

"He won't tell me why. He won't talk to me about it. It's so unlike him. He never had any problem with me having male friends and I thought he really liked you and respected you. But now he says that we've gotten too serious, spending too much time together and all that, and he wants the whole thing to stop. And my mother's behind him. It's the strangest thing. My parents have always been so open . . ."

"I know," I interrupted. "Maybe I'll talk to him tomorrow."

"No!" she blurted. "That's not a good idea."

"Why?"

"Because he can't find out that we met and talked. He'll take us all home if I don't listen to him, I'm sure of it."

"I won't tell him we talked. It doesn't take a genius to figure out what's going on here."

"But he won't tell you anything either. I begged him. I cried, I even got hysterical. I've never had to act like that, and he just looked at my mother and insisted that I obey him."

"Well if I talk to him, he's got to say something. He can't just ignore me!" I said.

"I'm sure he'll be polite, but all he'll say is that he doesn't want you and me being together."

"So let him say it to *me!*"

I stopped, looked at her, my hands still around her waist. I released her and moved back a step. She reached out with her right hand to take mine, and led me over to the lounges. We sat down and continued peering at each other.

"I thought you would have gone to the stream this afternoon," I said.

"I think he was afraid we would try to meet, so he took us all out shopping in town for the day."

"Well, he knows that sooner or later . . ."

"He's not thinking rationally. That's the thing. It's completely strange. He even talked about having you fired if you didn't get the message."

I pondered for a moment. "This has something to do with whatever went on between him and my father, I just know it."

"That's exactly what I thought. I even said something about it, but he got very defensive and said that he doesn't have to explain his reasons to me. Even Moshe was shocked. He's never been like this before! It scares me."

"Well maybe he'll explain it to me."

"I still think it's a bad idea."

"What are we supposed to do, just roll over and play dead because he says so!" Infuriated.

"Yakov," she said softly as she took my hand again, "he's my father."

There was no response to be offered. I understood completely. I was the last person on earth to ask anyone to defy her father.

"I really have to go," she said nervously. "I waited here for you for at least a half hour, and I'm afraid he'll get up to go to the bathroom or something and check on me. That's how paranoid he is about all this. It's so strange." Each time she repeated how out of character his behavior was, I felt the dread inside me intensify. Something was very wrong.

"Can we meet here tomorrow night?" I asked.

"I don't think so." Her lips quivered as the words came out. She stood up, still holding my hand, and repeated in a whisper, "I don't think so." Tears fell from the corners of her eyes. She slowly released her grasp, backed away, and ran off weeping. I got up to go after her, but stopped myself. I stood there, frozen, watching as she slipped from view into the fog. And though she was gone, I could still feel the touch of her hand, her body against mine. I could still hear the sound of her crying.

I knew then that a part of her would always be with me.

CHAPTER 9

LEANING AGAINST THE FENCE, I watched the yellow ball go back and forth over the net. It made a hollow *ping* as it bounced off each player's racket, smoothly and speedily flowing toward a strategic position within the lines of the other player's side. The competition appeared fierce, the players so engrossed in the game that my presence was unnoticed.

It was four in the afternoon, the same time each day that Benny Kleinman was defeated by the youth, energy, and skill of his son, Moshe. It was the only time and place I knew that I would be able to find Benny without a lot of people around. In a few minutes, the game came to its conclusion.

They were walking off the court, in my direction, when they saw me. Benny had his arm around Moshe's shoulder. I could hear him offering fatherly praises of a game well played. He seemed to be pretending that nothing was wrong as they approached me.

"You see my star here, Yankel," he opened, gesturing to Moshe, "I really can't keep up with him anymore. I'm afraid he's going to have to find a more worthy opponent."

Moshe looked a bit embarrassed. I smiled. I was nervous, unsure of how to begin. "The game looked pretty intense, but I came here hoping to talk about something other than tennis," I said.

Benny was taken aback by my directness. So was I. He asked Moshe to go on ahead. "I think Yankel and I need to talk."

"Well," he continued after Moshe was gone, "I guess I owe you an explanation." Reasonable; open. I was certainly surprised. The curious look I wore preempted the need for me to respond. "Come, let's take a walk," he suggested, pointing toward the road at the bottom of the hill.

"I suppose you want to talk about why I've interfered between you and Rivki," he opened. Forthright, but friendly. I was silent.

We began walking and he continued, "I want you to know that I like you, Yankel; I have from the first day I met you. You're a sincere *Ben Torah,* a true *mensch.* In many ways, you resemble your father when he was your age."

"Is that what this is all about? Something to do with my father?" I interjected angrily.

"You're very smart, Yankel, and it's important that you understand that this has nothing to do with the way I feel about you. There is something that stands between you and Rivki that has nothing to do with either of you . . ."

"And what exactly is that?" I demanded.

"I'm very sorry, Yankel, but that is something I just cannot tell you."

"Why not?"

"Because it is something deeply personal, and it would be disrespectful and unfair to your father for me to share it with you."

"Then I will ask him!"

"I wouldn't suggest that." He paused for a moment. "I must warn you that if your father learns of your relationship with Rivki, it will cause more pain to more people than you can imagine."

"Pain about what?" I pressed.

"Yankel, I know this is hard for you," he said with genuine sympathy. "But a scholar like you should realize that there are things in life that we can never know, regardless of the frustrations that such ignorance brings. You and Rivki must both accept this. If you don't, the pain that you will cause will surely be much greater than any pleasure the two of you could ever have. You must understand me! I am speaking to you like a father, like a man who would be proud to have you as his son-in-law. But that can never be. It hurts me more than you will ever know to have to talk to you like this. But this is how things must be, and we can never speak of this again."

"So what am I supposed to do?" Desperation.

"You must somehow move on and forget about Rivki. This is a sacrifice you have to make. We all sacrifice. Your father has sacrificed much in his life. That's one of the things that makes him such a great Jew. Now it is your turn. Life means making difficult choices. *Sometimes you must sacrifice!*"

Familiar words. And through his obvious sincerity and firmness, I could discern an underlying anguish which, despite my desolation, made him all the more likeable. I appreciated and despised him at once, a not entirely unfamiliar conflict.

I couldn't stand seeing Rebecca, day after day, watching from afar as she came and went in the dining room. Between meals I kept to my usual routine, hoping she would sneak away and meet me by the stream. For a few nights I even showed up at the pool. But she didn't come.

There was really no point in seeing her. Nothing would be solved; nothing would change. But I needed to be with her.

After a few days I noticed that she began smiling again from time to time, but I knew in my heart that this was mere pretense. Unable to sleep or eat, with barely enough motivation to pull myself out of bed in the morning, I found my despair worsening. I couldn't take it any longer. I had to do something, and the only choice I was really left with—considering all the circumstances—was to flee.

So I quit, packed my bags, and went back home to Brooklyn. Chaim was sad to see me go, but probably glad to have the room to himself. I had worked out an explanation to my parents: I felt it best to have a few extra weeks to prepare for yeshiva. This would be most gratifying to my father.

On the bus home, many images passed through my mind. The most potent was the face of my father transforming into the face of Benny Kleinman, and then back again. From the lips of these interchanging faces came the same words: *Sometimes you must sacrifice.*

CHAPTER 10

CHAIM CAME HOME a few weeks later. He took his place working at his father's side in the camera store. I took my place, sitting in the *Beis Medresh,* the study hall of the yeshiva, laboring over texts of Talmud while also leaving time for things like science and math. The trick, with the secular studies, was to just get them done without taking them too seriously. Pick up the diploma in case you ever need it to get a job, but forget all the *nahrishkeit,* the foolishness, that you had to learn along the way.

For me, this attitude didn't wash. Despite the demanding schedule, I still devoted time to my secular studies. This kept me up late into the nights, and sometimes through the nights—a welcome distraction from my longing for Rebecca.

Another way I had of coping was by displacing my anger and breaking loose from my shell of complacency. I was becoming provocative, even confrontational, in discussions with peers and teachers. It was dangerous, but invigorating.

My preoccupation with philosophical questions about the mysteries of human existence was no longer a secret to those who knew me. With each passing day, I spoke more and more freely of the contradictions of faith, of the uneven balance in life between suffering and pleasure, of anything that challenged the assumptions I had always been fed. And it wasn't that I'd become a nonbeliever—for I hadn't—that got me into trouble, but that I'd become boldly inquisitive. I had a talent for formulating questions that always seemed to be far more edifying than any of the answers my teachers gave me.

My father received reports about my behavior, but chalked it up to the contentious musings of an adolescent mind. It didn't seem to strike him as odd or problematic—I would grow out of it. As long as I was doing well in Talmud and adhering to the letter of the law in performing *mitzvahs,* what I thought didn't much matter. He spoke to me about it once and advised me that while one cannot necessarily control one's thoughts, one can certainly control one's mouth. But it *did* matter to me, and after a few months of struggling with this in the yeshiva, I decided to do something that would make it matter to him.

It was on a Wednesday in the last week of December, the day after a major snowstorm had paralyzed the city. The storm had lasted through Monday and Tuesday, cooping us up in the house, and giving me ample time to devise my plan. When morning dawned, on this day when the rest of the city was getting back to normal, I was ready.

I awoke a half hour earlier than usual so as to have enough time to recite the morning prayers. Normally, I would *daven* with the other students when I arrived at the yeshiva. Today, however, I had a different agenda.

I was extremely quiet, being cautious not to disturb my father who had, for several years, taken to awakening early each morning in order to prepare his Talmud classes for the day. He described these early hours as ideal for eluding distractions, and I certainly didn't want to give him one.

By the time I finished *davening,* I was back on my usual schedule. I went downstairs, took my coat and hat from the front hall closet, and spurted into the kitchen where my mother had just finished preparing my lunch bag. She handed me a glass of orange juice with her right hand as I grabbed the brown paper bag from her left and swiftly kissed her goodbye on the cheek. As I was halfway to the front door, she offered her motherly overture: "Have a good and productive day, learn well, and don't forget to wear your snow-boots . . . and your scarf, earmuffs, and gloves too!" I reached into the closet for the scarf, gloves, earmuffs, and boots, and thought about just how productive a day it would be.

Unfamiliar with the subway trains, I simply walked to the nearest station, which was located on New Utrecht Avenue and Fiftieth Street. I took my place on line at the token booth, and when my turn came I handed the man my money, asked for two tokens, a round trip, and directions to Washington Heights in upper Manhattan. He told me to take the B train and transfer at Forty-second Street for the IRT Number 1 train, which would take me all the way up the West Side to 181st Street. Simple enough.

It was my first experience on a train during rush hour. Standing room only, and barely that. Suffocating. Especially in a winter coat, scarf, gloves, and hat. Everyone else was equally bundled up, but no one unfastened their jacket. I found that strange at first, but soon understood that the subway was a place where people purposely didn't want to make themselves too comfortable. It was written on their faces, each passenger bearing the same expression. They hated this place, a necessary evil. And keeping one's coat and scarf tightly bound was a symbolic gesture to render the trip as painless, as transient, as possible. I was tempted to undo my coat, but decided to blend in.

The entire trip took slightly under an hour. When I ascended the stairs from the 181st Street subway station, I came out on St. Nicholas Avenue, a busy street with commercial shopping establishments on the ground floor of old tenement apartment buildings. The signs on the stores were all in Spanish and the pedestrians on the sidewalk appeared as if that were their native tongue. I looked around, certain that I was lost, when suddenly I caught sight of an older man with a yarmulke and a briefcase who, I thought, must have been heading to the same place as I. I took a chance and followed him as he walked up St. Nicholas Avenue to 185th Street and then turned right, continuing two more blocks to Amsterdam Avenue. At that point the neighborhood was radically transformed. I found myself surrounded by large modern buildings and students with yarmulkes crisscrossing from place to place.

The building to my immediate right had a white brick exterior, institutional windows, and glass doors. Above the doors were protruding aluminum letters reading "Furst Hall, Yeshiva University." Beneath the letters was a triangular emblem with an open Torah scroll in the middle and the Hebrew words *Torah Umadah,* meaning "Torah and Science," inscribed over the scroll.

I continued northward on Amsterdam Avenue, passing on my left a large redbrick building that encompassed the entire length of the block. It was a strange structure: a barren facade, a few small windows, and a single little door in the middle. A sign to the side of the door identified it as the library. I would later learn that this was actually the back entrance, at least architecturally speaking, while the front entrance, which consisted of two diagonally merging staircases and several imposing glass doors, was on the other side around the back. A building built backward—most appropriate for a storehouse of Hebrew books.

Walking on, I crossed 186th Street. When I came to the middle of the next block, I stopped, turned to my left, and stood facing the oldest building of the lot, a European-style edifice made of earth-colored stones with an incandescent marble archway above the entrance. It was four stories high with broad, antiquated windows and a large green dome sitting on the roof. The windows appeared grossly inconsistent with its architectural character, which demanded something more ornate, and the dome—a complete anomaly considering its role as the hallmark of another religion—looked almost like a giant skullcap.

I decided to go in. I walked up the few short steps to the large brass-framed doors that flew open from the inside as students dashed out. Upon entering the lobby, I noticed a peculiar design on the floor depicting some sort of astrological chart, a conspicuous illustration with brass figures embedded in the marble. It all struck me as quite odd—the dome above my head, the iconography beneath my feet. Strange indeed.

I remained there for a while, observing the students scuttling by in all directions. They were a broad mixture, some in contemporary clothes, others in traditional clothes; some clean-shaven, others bearded; some with small, hand-crocheted yarmulkes, and others with bigger black velvet ones or even black hats.

I looked around for a while longer. After finding nothing but classrooms and a large study hall, I decided to seek out some of the other sights. As I exited the building I noticed, directly across the street, a storefront with a sign above the door, "Kosher Dairy Restaurant." It reminded me that I was hungry.

I crossed the street and went inside. It was a decrepit place that looked like a luncheonette from the thirties or forties that hadn't had a stitch of work done on it since. The green linoleum floor was eroding, broken, and peeling down to the wood underneath. The metal rimmed Formica tables were filled with cracks, and the old wooden chairs were padded with vinyl that was frail and worn. To my left there was a long off-green Formica counter bordered by a row of five tall swivel seats. In the far left corner were two antediluvian pinball machines.

There was only one other person there, a short but robust-looking elderly fellow standing behind the counter. He looked at me, smiled, and held his arms out wide, signaling that I was welcome to sit anywhere. I took a seat at the counter.

"Vhat can I do for you?" he asked in a discernibly Hungarian inflection.

"Is it okay if I eat my own lunch here?" I asked, pointing to the brown bag in my hand.

He hesitated for a moment, looked at the bag, and authoritatively inquired, *"Milchig or fleishig?"*

"Milchig," I replied, confirming that my lunch was dairy and not meat.

He stood pensively for a second. "Ve'll, normally ve don't allow any outside food, but since it's *milchig* ve'll make an exception." I wondered who *we* were. He must have felt that speaking in the plural, like a king, made the decision seem more monumental. And with this, he wore an expression of pleasure from the opportunity to do me a favor. "I can see that you're not from around here," he observed.

"How can you tell?" I asked as I took my lunch out of the bag. There was a tuna sandwich, a pickle, and a homemade brownie.

"How can I tell?" he exclaimed, "I know all the students around here, and I know that you're not vone of them." He looked at my lunch, noticed that there was no drink, and asked if I would like one. I surveyed the menu hanging on the wall behind him, reached into my pocket to count my money, and ordered a vanilla milk shake. When he turned around to make the shake, I noticed that he was almost completely bald. His overall vigor had prevented me from seeing this right away. I also noticed that the inside of his left forearm bore the remnants of a Nazi concentration camp.

He looked up and caught me staring. I was embarrassed. He made no mention of it.

I asked him where I could wash my hands. It is a *mitzvah* to wash one's hands and make certain blessings before partaking of bread. He pointed toward the back of the restaurant where there was a sink explicitly for this purpose. By the time I returned to the counter, my milk shake was sitting there next to my sandwich. I sat down, picked off a small piece of bread, and recited the *Motzi,* the blessing for bread, under my breath. Although he could not hear me, he could see I was done when my lips stopped moving, and he bellowed out a heady *Amen,* an acronym for *God the king is believed,* the traditional response offered when hearing another's prayer.

"So, vhat is your name?" he inquired.

I hesitated, pretending to finish chewing and swallowing a mouthful of food. "Yakov," I said as a chill ran through my body. Yakov, I repeated in my mind, Yakov is my name. Yakov is what I want to be called!

"I am Harry." His voice broke my trance. He held out his hand in front of me.

I took Harry's hand and shook it. His grasp was firm, forceful. His face was healthy with color, simple but genuine. His deep brown eyes—what they must have beheld throughout the years—were the only worn part of him. They looked tired, even close to death. But his smile, like the rest of his features, belied his eyes. It was a smile of innocence and youthfulness, or perhaps, deception. Putting the whole package together, including the lines in his cheeks and the cracks in the corners of his eyes, he looked to be in his mid-sixties.

"So, from vhere did you come from, Yakov?"

"Brooklyn."

"Brooklyn is a very big place."

"I'm sorry, Borough Park."

"Ah, I vould have guessed."

"Is it that obvious?"

"I'm afraid so."

Just at that moment I recalled the image I had seen in the mirror that morning and pictured what I must look like now. The peach fuzz patches on my face that made a poor excuse for a beard; the outdated wire-rimmed glasses; the shorter than short haircut; the big black velvet yarmulke sticking out slightly from the back of my black fedora; the dark suit; the white shirt with open collar; the white socks. Yankel, not Yakov.

"And what brings you to our yeshiva, *Reb* Yakov from Borough Park?" *Reb* is a title of respect amongst religious Jews, similar to *Mr.* or *sir.*

"I'm thinking about becoming a student here next year and I wanted to see what it was like."

At first it struck me as odd, his reference to *our* yeshiva, as if he were one of the students or teachers. But a few seconds later, when a group of young students came in, I understood that he was, in his own way, very much a part of this place.

"Hey, Harry!" one of them yelped in a friendly greeting

while the others headed toward the tables by the pinball machines.

"Vhat'll it be, young men?" he responded, standing up tall, arms crossed in front of his broad chest. He looked proud to be dealing with them, as if they were his own sons.

"The usual," another one called.

"The usual it is, four specials coming right up!" He then turned to me and said proudly, "Vone day you should try one of my specials, the best ice cream soda in all New York."

He wore a gleam of great pleasure on his face and hummed an unfamiliar tune while meticulously preparing each soda. When he finished, he placed all four on the counter and called, "Come and get 'em!" Two of the students came over. The others were busy on the machines. They jousted back and forth with Harry for a few moments as they picked up their sodas. There was a tone of genuine warmth among them.

Later I would learn that this man before me was the sole survivor of an entire family: parents, siblings, a wife, and two daughters—the handiwork of Hitler. He lived alone in a one-bedroom apartment around the corner from the store in one of the few buildings in the Washington Heights area, aside from the university, that still had some Jewish residents. This store and its patrons, the students of Yeshiva University, were his family. It was *their* yeshiva.

We chatted a bit longer. He was easy to talk to, a good listener, and wise as well. He hadn't heard of my father, but quickly picked up on my predicament from the scant details I provided. I felt that he could be my friend, that he would be my friend, if only I was able to somehow pull off my plan and end up here. If only.

He suggested that I go to the white brick building, Furst Hall, and try to see a Rabbi Goldstein, the assistant director of admissions. "Just tell him I sent you. He eats here all the time. A good friend of mine," he insisted. I reached into my pocket to pay for the milk shake. "On the house!" he asserted. "Next time I vill make you pay, vhen you become a student!"

The receptionist behind the desk was an unattractive middle-aged woman, dressed modestly with a kerchief covering most of her hair, save for a few bangs. "Can I help you?" she inquired, looking at the stranger before her.

"Yes," I answered nervously. "Is it possible to see Rabbi Goldstein?"

"Anything I can help you with?" A good secretary trying to run interference for her boss. Harry sent me, I thought to myself, so you'd better let me speak to Rabbi Goldstein directly or it'll be no more blintzes for you!

"Maybe, I suppose." I hesitated. She waited for me to continue. "I was hoping to be able to talk to Rabbi Goldstein about becoming a student here next year." Tactful, but it made the point.

"Okay, why don't you take a seat and I'll see what I can do."

She disappeared through a door on the side, and when she emerged again she told me that the rabbi would be available in about fifteen minutes. I waited. The time passed slowly.

When the door opened again, a heavy-set man in his early thirties, with thick brown hair and a neatly trimmed beard, came out. He wore a gray plaid suit and brightly shined shoes. His white shirt collar was perfectly starched and his tie was impeccably knotted. He looked at me and invited me to step into his office.

"So what can I do for you?" he said in a friendly manner as he seated himself behind his desk. He motioned for me to avail myself of one of the chairs on the other side of the desk. I complied and began my tale.

"Borough Park?" he remarked, "Mir? Eisen? Are you perhaps related to . . ."

"He's my father."

There was a moment of silence and a look of understanding on his face. "Does your father know of your intentions?" he queried.

"No." More silence.

He leaned back in his chair. "Tell me, what is your grade average?"

"Ninety-seven."

"What about in secular studies?"

"That *is* in secular studies."

He sat up straight. "Ninety-seven," he repeated, "and you earned that legitimately?"

For the most part, except for one stupid chemistry test. "Yes," I answered.

"And I suppose I needn't inquire about your religious studies?"

"I suppose not." Barely audible.

"Well, I guess the next question is why someone like you is interested in YU."

"Because I want to study philosophy, *regular* philosophy, and I also want to continue studying Talmud. So I guess, from what I hear, that this is the best place to do both."

"You know that you could still stay in Mir and study philosophy at night in Brooklyn College," he baited me.

"There's no real philosophy in Brooklyn College, at least not at night. The night students are all yeshiva guys, or people with daytime jobs studying to be accountants. I don't want to be an accountant."

"What do you want to be?"

"A teacher," a voice from within me answered. "I would like to teach philosophy."

"I wonder how your father would feel about that?" Sarcasm.

"No need to wonder."

He smiled. "Well, from our end I'm sure you would have no trouble getting admitted. But from your end, you obviously have a bit of a problem." He stopped and observed my reaction. It seemed as if he felt sorry for me. "Are there any questions that you would like to ask me?" he offered.

"Yes, there's one." I hesitated for a second, and then continued. "Do you really produce Reform and Conservative rabbis?"

He seemed humored for a moment, and then reacted. "Reform, never! Well maybe once or twice, a hundred years ago, one of our undergraduates went to study in the Reform rabbinical seminary, but no one who was actually ordained here ever became a Reform rabbi." Adamant. "Conservative is another matter," he continued, though a bit defensively. "Thirty years ago or so, there weren't many jobs for Orthodox rabbis, so some of our graduates who wanted to serve in pulpits had to find Conservative ones. Now, it's a completely different story. In the past ten years, the only time we've sent anyone to a Conservative pulpit was in a situation in which we felt that the congregation could possibly change to Orthodox with the right influence. And there are instances in which we've succeeded."

"Have there been any failures?"

"Yes, I suppose, if that's what you want to call them. But you're not interested in the rabbinate anyway. You said you wanted to teach . . ."

"Yes, but my father, as you must realize, is very interested in the rabbinate. And for me to have any chance of convincing him to let me come here, I will have to assure him that I will study for *smichah,* that I will become a rabbi whether or not I ever actually practice. And I know what he thinks of your rabbinical school, no offense meant. But if I can convince him that his information is wrong . . ." I stopped myself. "Well, I guess I'll work on my mother first."

"It won't be easy for you to become both a philosophy teacher and a rabbi. Our rabbinical program is very demanding."

"If I was looking for easy, I would never have come here to begin with. But the first thing I have to think about is getting back here in the fall. Then I'll worry about the difficulties of your rabbinical program."

"Well, it may be of some help if you ask your father whether any Mirrer graduates have ever become Conservative rabbis. I think the answer might surprise you."

The train ride back to Borough Park seemed much longer than the trip that morning, a distortion symbolizing an even greater distance between these two places. I spent it preparing for the inevitable. An unprecedented streak of nerve consumed me as I decided to abandon the idea of approaching my mother first. I would simply lay my cards on the table for both of them, together, at the first opportunity. It would be at dinner that evening.

I managed to arrive home at my usual hour, just in time to help set the table. As I came through the front door, my mother was busy in the kitchen. She called out my name, as she always did when I got home, and asked her usual question of whether it was a fruitful day in the Talmud texts. I offered my perfunctory response, "I learned a *velt,* a world, Mama," as I removed my boots. I rationalized my little lie by believing that I had, in fact, learned a *velt.*

I took myself straight to the kitchen, kissed her on the cheek, grabbed three plates and glasses from the cabinets, some silverware and napkins, and proceeded to get to work. As I did this, I thought about the famous biblical story involving my namesake, Jacob. It was the one in which he lied to his father, Isaac, about his identity, saying, "I am Esau, your first-born son." Yet the rabbis didn't see it as a lie. In fact, they claimed that he merely omitted a few key words between "I am . . ." and "Esau." And if that can be explained away, I thought, my little omission should be a cinch.

I sat through dinner, my usual voiceless self, while my father shared his daily diet, the litany of consuming problems. First, there was a young doctor, son of a prominent contributor to both the yeshiva and the synagogue, who refused to give his wife a Jewish divorce in order to coerce her into dropping her financial claims against him. Next, there was a member of the synagogue who was dying of a rare form of leukemia; the community's search for a bone marrow match had thus far proved unsuccessful. And last, there was the *Rosh Yeshiva,* head rabbi of the yeshiva and my late grandfather's closest friend, who had been struck with Alzheimer's and continued to deteriorate daily.

To this list would soon be added another crisis: the rebellious son who breaks his father's heart—already impaired by two major coronaries—by deciding to attend a modern yeshiva where he can also get a secular education and thereby fulfill his dream of studying philosophy and going on to become a teacher of the same.

I waited, and listened. And waited, and listened, until I could wait and listen no longer.

"Totta," I interrupted, "I have something I need to talk to you about."

They looked at each other with surprise. Then they looked at me. "Yes?" my father said softly.

"I don't know how to say this," I began nervously, "so I'll just say it as it comes out, but I think I don't want to go to Mirrer next year." Sheepish.

Now my father looked really surprised. Again, his eyes met my mother's, and the expression on her face was intended to tell him that she was just as shocked as he, that there was no conspiracy occurring here.

"What do you mean?" he asked. A tinge of anger.

"I took a trip today instead of going to school." Hesitation. More nervousness. "I went to visit Yeshiva University."

There was silence. His eyes expressed the building rage that his tongue withheld. My mother sat, stone still, watching, waiting for me to continue. I knew I had to change my tone, to be more definitive, to overcome this fear of his disapproval that had always overshadowed me. Yakov instead of Yankel!

"I don't want to go to Mirrer. It's not the place for me!" Better. "I want to go to Yeshiva University so I can get a secular education along with studying Torah!"

"A secular education?" he responded. "Who has been filling your head with such *nahrishkeit?*"

"It's not foolishness! I want to study—"

"Enough!" he yelled as he banged his fist on the table. "I will hear no more of this *nahrishkeit!* No son of mine will go to that unkosher place where they make Reform and Conservative rabbis! Not my son!" His face was red, his eyes were bulging. My mother appeared concerned but remained calm. "Esther," he declared in her direction, "what is going on here? Our son takes a trip without telling us and then comes home to inform us that *he* has decided not to attend the yeshiva next year."

"But I will attend a yeshiva," I proclaimed. "And it's not true that they produce Reform rabbis. I don't know where you get your information from but it's not true!" I left out the part about Conservative rabbis because it was more complex, and this was a time for simplicity. I also skipped the part about Mirrer graduates becoming Conservative rabbis. It wasn't a great idea to put him on the defensive.

"Yankel!" my mother finally interjected, reprimanding me for the way I was addressing my father.

"Yes, and this is now how you speak to me," he added. "Is this also what they will teach you in that university that you claim is a yeshiva?"

He leaped up from his chair and began pacing around the room. I was certain he was going to have another heart attack, right there and then. I tried to compose myself. This was not going as I'd hoped, although it was as I'd expected. "Don't you even want to know why I want to go there?" I asked while looking toward my mother.

"You've already told us," he declared. "You want to get a secular education. I hear what you say and I really don't care to hear any more. The issue is decided!" he added firmly, leaning over the back of his chair as he spoke.

"Duvid," my mother said while gesturing for him to sit again, "maybe we should listen to what Yankeleh has to say?" Back to "Yankele*h*." The perpetual voice of reason.

"Oh, so now *you* are interfering for him. My whole family turns against me!"

She rose from her chair, walked over to him, took both his hands in hers, peered directly into his eyes, and said softly, "Duvid, I want to hear what Yankeleh has to say."

He was instantaneously quieted, like a pacified little child. What power she had! He sat back down in his chair and stared into space as she turned to me and whispered, "Yankeleh, go ahead."

I paused, took in what I had just witnessed, and then continued. "I've been unhappy for a long time—I don't know how else to say it. I've worked hard in yeshiva and I always wanted to please you." I was looking intently at my father. "But there are things that *I* want to do, and I don't know how to do them and still please you." I stopped. My father was now looking back at me.

My mother prompted, "What exactly do you mean?"

"What I mean is that I've always had many questions about things. I never shared any of them with you, but they stayed within me. I haven't found answers to these questions at Mirrer, and I don't know if I'll find any at Yeshiva University, but I want to give myself a chance and study other ways of looking at the mysteries of the world, other philosophies. Yeshiva University is perfect for this because I can study these things and still continue my rabbinical studies as well. So I won't be losing anything, just gaining, at least as I see it."

"To study Talmud there, it is not the same as it is in Mirrer. The secular studies detract from the time you need to study Talmud properly. You can never learn as much Torah under those circumstances." He was a little calmer.

"Maybe not," I conceded, "but they do have excellent teachers, and some of the world's most famous Talmudic minds, like Rav Liebowitz. Even the rabbis in Mirrer speak of him with great respect." Rav Liebowitz was the *Rosh Yeshiva* at YU, and was universally regarded as an eminent Talmudist.

"There's just him and maybe one or two others," my father replied, "and, anyway, they're only in that place because of the money. They also think the place is a breeding ground for heretics!"

"How do you know why they teach there?" I had never before questioned any of his assumptions out loud.

"You think I don't know of Rav Liebowitz or have never spoken with him? He knows me and I know him. And we both know that place!"

"Then you must know that Rav Liebowitz also has a doctorate in secular philosophy, from the University of Berlin no less, and that he takes secular philosophy very seriously and often uses it in his Torah lectures and books."

"Of course I know this, but he is a very rare individual. Not everyone is a Rav Liebowitz. Not everyone can study such things and keep them in the right perspective. He is an exceptional *talmid chuchum,* a God-fearing scholar who knows everything about the Torah inside out and knows how to deal with heresy. He is on a special level where these things cannot affect his faith. But he will be the first to tell you how many students' faith has been destroyed by such ideas." He waved his finger at me. "Because they were not adequately prepared, because they hadn't studied enough Torah. He will be the first to tell you!"

I sat, restraining myself, thinking of all the counterarguments I could pose. I could question why one *has* to be a *talmid chuchum* in order to study philosophy; why one must be "prepared," or rather immunized from its consequences by prerequisite biases. I had heard these assertions so many times before, in one form or another—that I wasn't somehow schooled enough, or saintly enough, to delve into *goyishe* philosophy. My teachers and peers demanded, "Who are you to ask such questions? Who are you to think such things?"

Who was I? Well, I'll tell you. For starters, I was curious. I had these questions and thoughts. I didn't know where they came from—maybe God plagued me with them, maybe the devil; the one in *The Exorcist.* All I knew was that I had always had difficulty with the things I was supposed to accept. That's who I was, and I could not acquiesce any longer to the desires of people who sought to deny me the right to search for answers.

But I kept my mouth shut, for it would serve no purpose to share any of this with my father. He knew enough, was finally aware of how I felt, and was no doubt beside himself over the entire matter. So I would grant him the last word this time—a token of respect—and hope that eventually his wisdom would bend his obstinacy, that love would prevail over fear.

In a few weeks' time, with much prodding from my mother, it did.

CHAPTER 11

As my mother and I unloaded Uncle Zelig's station wagon, it was apparent that I'd taken everything I owned, all my clothes and books, and had left nothing behind. Silly symbolism, for I would be back in Borough Park in just a few short weeks for Rosh Hashanah. But I needed to feel as if I was being completely transplanted, especially considering the purgatory I'd been through in the past seven months since my acceptance to the university was made known.

Word had spread quickly that the son of Rabbi Eisen had become an apostate. I was regarded as a pariah throughout the community. The hallways of the yeshiva would turn silent at my presence. The stares and whispers in the synagogue were unrelenting. Even Chaim turned on me. I could understand his jealousy because he was destined to spend his life behind a counter in a camera store while I was going off to college. He was, nevertheless, one person from whom I expected hearty congratulations.

Perhaps there *was* a person who would have been proud, but she would probably never know. A year had passed since I had seen Rebecca, and with the time some healing should have come. But I was never so alone as during that year, and never so longing for her presence.

My mother had borrowed Zelig's station wagon. My father was unavailable; he had other commitments. So it was just the two of us. She helped me pack from start to finish, helped me schlep my stuff up to my dormitory room on the sixth floor of Rubin Residence Hall, and helped find places to put everything. Since I was fortunate to arrive before my roommate, she even helped me choose my bed. Normally women weren't allowed in these dormitories, but on this first day, when students were moving in, an exception was made for families, especially mothers.

When we finished, I accompanied her down to where we'd left the car. I walked with her to the driver's side. She opened the door, turned around, embraced me fiercely, and kissed me on the forehead and cheek as tears fell from her eyes. I felt a lump in my throat but, as usual, no tears. A true Jewish man.

She made me promise to call at least three times each week. I said I would. She said I'd better. The tenor of her orders was as soft as her touch.

Then she got into the car, started the engine, and rolled down the window. She reiterated her instructions to call and drove off. I stood alone, on the street, watching the car as it made its way down Amsterdam Avenue and then disappeared into a left turn onto the Harlem River Drive. The lump was still in my throat.

After a few minutes, I realized I hadn't eaten lunch yet. I felt into my pocket to confirm that I had a few dollars and then turned up the avenue to Harry's place. I walked past another dormitory, Morgenstern Residence, a newer and more imposing structure than Rubin. Here, the older students, juniors and seniors, and their families, were rushing in and out, everyone moving in for the college year. There were all types, just like on the day I came to visit. Still, I felt a bit uneasy wearing my black fedora, so I removed it and held it in my hand. Next time I would remember to leave it in my room.

The luncheonette was in the middle of the next block. When I entered, the place was much more crowded than my last time there. Harry was the only one working; he was too busy to notice me. I took the only available seat at the counter, and after attending to something else, he turned around and saw me.

Over eight months had passed since our brief encounter, but he recognized me right away.

"Hey!" he cheered. "Just look at who made it uptown!" He gave me a hearty handshake.

"So you remember me," I said with pleasurable surprise.

"Vhat you think, I got senile or something? This mind," he exclaimed as he pointed to his head with his forefinger, "is as good as the day it vas born!"

"How have you been?" I shouted above the noise.

"Baruch Hashem," he replied. "And I can see that, *baruch Hashem,* you're doing very vell, too."

His Hungarianism hurtled forth with every word. *Baruch Hashem,* blessed be God, is the typical response that Orthodox Jews offer when asked about their well-being. It is a custom that stems from the belief that God deserves our blessings whether life is wonderful or just the opposite. Either way, we say *baruch Hashem.*

"So, vhat vill it be?" he asked as he waited for my order. No time for conversation.

"I'll have a tuna sandwich on rye and"—I hesitated for a split second—"a special."

He grinned so wide I could spot a gold tooth that replaced his upper right bicuspid. "Vone tuna and special it is, coming up."

He turned away and started on my order. He spoke, or yelled, as he worked. "So vhat happened to your hat?"

It was sitting on my lap underneath the counter. I told him so.

"But that's not vhere it belongs!"

"It's as good a place as any for now."

"Listen to me, my friend." It was apparent he'd forgotten my name, but that was okay. "You don't have to change a thing about yourself to fit in here. Ve have all types, so just be who you are."

I'm not sure what that is just yet, I thought. "Thanks," I replied as he placed the sandwich in front of me.

Then came the special and, again, the smile. He placed it on the counter with such force that it almost spilled over. "Enjoy," he added as he reached over the counter with the arm that bore the concentration camp number and patted me on the shoulder. "And velcome to our yeshiva."

Our eyes met. "It's Yakov," I said to him.

"Ah yes, Yakov. Velcome to our yeshiva, Yakov."

Our yeshiva.

CHAPTER 12

WHEN I GOT BACK to the room, my roommate was there unpacking his stuff with his parents. His name was Barry Glasser, which I had learned from the roommate list in the front lobby of the dorm. I was standing in the hallway just outside the open door and had not yet made my presence known when I heard his mother complaining that I had already chosen the "better" bed.

"Hello, I'm Yakov," I interrupted as I walked in.

"Hi, I'm Barry." He held out his hand, we shook, and then he introduced me to his parents. He was of medium height—about five feet eight inches—and thin, almost emaciated. He had straight, greased jet-black hair, pronounced eyebrows of the same color, and a thick, well-trimmed beard covering his long face. His eyes were brown. One look at him and I instantly knew he was a *Bal T'shuvah,* a "born again" Jew who wasn't raised as Orthodox but became so on his own. It was evident from the way he dressed: blue jeans, T-shirt, sandals, colorful hand-crocheted yarmulke, and *tzitzis* hanging out.

The expression on his parents' faces when they first saw me was also a giveaway. They were unaccustomed to seeing Jews who looked so "Jewish," and they probably prayed that their son, who was already becoming more Jewish before their eyes, would never end up like this.

I stood there, dark suit and fedora still in hand. Barry's father, who was wearing one of those fake silk white yarmulkes that are given out at cemeteries and synagogues, managed to be affable enough. His mother, however, was another story, for her face and manner bore hostility. I looked down at my hat and felt embarrassed. I would have to lose it, and the jacket, too.

That evening, Barry and I began getting to know each other as we lay in our beds with the lights out. He apologized for his mother's hostility and explained that she was unhappy with his newfound religiosity, and particularly upset with his decision to attend YU. He had been accepted to several Ivy League schools, and his choice to become a cantor was extremely distressing to her. Although she had always pushed him hard as far as his music had been concerned—he was apparently a rather skilled pianist—it had never been her desire that he actually pursue a career in music, especially cantorial music. She had hoped and prayed he would end up in one of the more prestigious "Jewish" professions, such as law or medicine.

Barry related to me how he became a *Bal T'shuvah* when he visited Israel on a summer teen tour during his second year of high school, and how conflicts developed between him and his parents when he returned home and decided to eat strictly kosher and observe the Sabbath. He told me how his father, who had been raised Orthodox, was much more sympathetic than his mother, but too timid to be of much help. I was not surprised to hear this.

By the sound of it, the Glassers were affluent people. Mr. Glasser was in real estate and Mrs. Glasser taught sociology at Stonybrook. She was emphatically liberal in every way, religion and politics included. Yet she was completely intolerant when conformity to her mores was at issue.

But the most interesting paradox of all was that Barry and I had ended up together. Two students, struggling, tangled in the throes of rebellion against their respective pasts, yet moving in quite opposite directions. What we shared was the very thing that divided us—a bridge and a wedge at once.

By the first day of classes I was rid of the straggly beard. My jacket hung in my closet, next to my hat. I would save them for trips home which, for now, I restricted to holidays.

It took a few more weeks until I saved enough money from my allowance to buy a couple of pairs of jeans and some shirts from one of the Hispanic clothing stores on St. Nicholas Avenue. A few days after that I purchased a small, colorful hand-crocheted yarmulke from a Jewish gift shop on the Lower East Side. It looked good on my new head of growing hair. Yakov.

Harry was most amused by the weekly transformations. He said he could never predict what I would change next. Neither could I.

My daily schedule was divided in half: Talmud until three in the afternoon, and college classes from then through the evening. I took quick breaks for lunch and dinner, and was usually awake well past midnight studying. It was grueling, to say the least. No time for any socializing, and even if there was, I was too busy becoming the embodiment of the great synthesis between the religious and the secular. No time for thoughts of Rebecca.

I needed a role model, someone who had faced the complexities of reality and hadn't succumbed to the basic human need for definitude. Someone who was willing to recognize the value of uncertainty, who struggled with the contradictions between contemporary and traditional ideas. I searched far and wide, but found no one.

The sad truth was that after a while I began to see that this place was a battleground of divisiveness. On one end was a powerful right-wing anti-secular faction that gained ground each passing day. On the other end were students who tolerated religious studies only to be able to avail themselves of the well-reputed pre-med and pre-law departments that boasted some of the highest graduate school acceptance rates in the country. Yeshiva University was not quite what I'd envisioned.

I had thought Rav Liebowitz would fit the bill, and he did, but only to a point. Notwithstanding his incredible brilliance, he left me wanting, not completely mollified, for there was certain ground upon which he would not tread.

His Talmud class was very exclusive. Only the brightest rabbinical students gained entry. I would have to wait four years, until I graduated from college, before I could be eligible for the rabbinical school, and then I would have to take an additional test to qualify for his class. Fortunately, however, he needed extra money, so he also taught philosophy in the college. This was how I met him.

He didn't usually bother with freshman philosophy, but that year the regular teacher was on sabbatical. When word spread that he was to be the teacher, everyone rushed to register. I was lucky that preference was given to philosophy majors, of which there were only a handful.

It ended up that there were more than forty students in the class. Liebowitz was used to this. His Talmud class numbered somewhere in the fifties. Neither crowds, nor much else, intimidated him.

He was in his early sixties, short, slightly overweight, and had a limp from childhood polio. Despite this, he held himself like a prince. When he came into the room, all the students were already seated at their desks, eagerly awaiting his arrival. He removed his black Homburg, placed it on the instructor's desk, and surveyed the room. His face was as white as a ghost's, as if he were wearing makeup, and he had a full head of glowing wavy silver hair that matched his sharply trimmed beard. His eyes were a deep brown, the color of his stylish, double-breasted, pinstriped suit. His white shirt was neatly starched and his conservative light brown tie was impeccably knotted into a Windsor with a perfect crease in the middle. In all he looked more like a German aristocrat than a Talmudic scholar or philosophy professor.

But when he lectured, there was no mistaking him. He spoke with a thick German accent, and was often hard to understand. It only forced us to listen more closely.

As time went on, he had difficulty adhering to the curriculum. There were too many questions, too many minds to mold. So he allowed himself to digress into whatever he saw fit. The world according to Liebowitz.

And I quickly became one of the outspoken. Sometimes, just to flaunt my intellectual prowess; other times, out of genuine curiosity. It got to where he would look at me in the last row and anticipate my attacks. He was ready, forever brilliant in his analysis, able to draw from a lengthy list of thinkers regarding any issue. He was subtle and creative. And he never neglected to cite the exact title and page of whatever source he was referring to.

But then there was that treacherous territory, the questions about God, evil, and morality. It was here that his creativity waned. He became polemical, closed off, and removed from the likes of Sartre and Wittgenstein who, in every other context, were his idols. It was here that I became disheartened.

"But the Torah explicitly states that if the Jews observe the *mitzvahs,* God will be good to us, and if not, He will punish us. Doesn't this mean that the Holocaust and other sufferings are merely punishments?" I once heard myself blurt out during a discussion of theodicy, the problem of God and evil.

"We do not take the Torah literally," he began with his deep voice. "We are a bit more sophisticated than that." Sarcasm. "Maybe the Torah speaks of reward and punishment in reference not to this world, but to the world to come? And if there is reward and punishment in this world, maybe we as humans don't understand how it is meted out? God's presence is hidden in the world, and He doesn't have to reveal a damn thing to us! The humility to accept this is the real essence of faith."

"But what about our rationality? God created us as rational beings with five senses and our minds. He gives us this world, which doesn't look too great, and expects us to believe in Him and His Torah. He expects us to ignore what we see and accept what we don't see!"

"Precisely!" he responded. "The rationality of man can go only so far. It can accomplish great things, put men on the moon, cure diseases. But it cannot know God. Faith is the willingness to accept a reality beyond that which you can know or sense."

"But Maimonides tried to prove God rationally. Why would he do this according to your analysis?" I asked.

"An excellent question. And he wasn't alone. The Christian philosopher Aquinas also did this, although he came after Maimonides. True, Maimonides was one of the greatest Torah scholars in history. And he wrote *The Guide for the Perplexed* to help people who were influenced by rational atheism. So he spoke in the language of his time, in the philosophy of his time, to try to demonstrate everything rationally. And along came Kant, and he rationally disputed those rational proofs. So what are you left with?"

I sat, thinking about his words.

"Today, we are not embarrassed to recognize the limits of our rationality," he continued. "This is the essence of faith."

The limits of rationality, the essence of faith. Poetic, I thought, even interesting. Pretty much the same thing Ezra, my former camp counselor, and Rebecca had argued, just fancier. But no more compelling. At least not yet.

About midway through freshman year I began feeling uneasy about Barry. Our nightly bedtime dialogues about Judaism were becoming scarce, and he appeared to be losing both his passion and fascination for observing the commandments. Most troubling was the case of insomnia he was developing.

To begin with, he had a strange habit of taking lengthy

showers in the middle of the night while everyone else was either asleep or cramming for tests. When he finally did get into bed, the noise of his tossing and turning on the metal-framed spring bed would awaken me and cause me to toss and turn as well. And the rare occasions on which he actually did fall asleep were accompanied by seemingly horrible nightmares.

He remained in bed most mornings, missing both *davening* and religious classes. I tried to ignore it. I was too consumed with my own sleep deprivation to think about his problems.

The shower room was located off the middle of the hall and was shared by all the students on the floor. It was one large tile room with six showerheads. There was not much privacy. I suspected that this was the reason Barry chose to shower at those odd hours, but had no idea why he needed such privacy.

One Tuesday night, in the second week of February, my question was answered with an astounding discovery on the part of a dormitory counselor who just happened to shower late that evening. The nitty-gritty details were never completely divulged, but what was revealed was that two students had been found engaged in some sort of homosexual play in the shower.

When I left the room the next morning, Barry was still in bed. I had no idea what had transpired the night before. In fact, I didn't find out until late that afternoon when I heard some students talking in Harry's luncheonette. There were no names mentioned, just that two guys were caught getting it on in the sixth-floor shower of the Rubin dorm.

The late night showers, the insomnia, the loss of religious fervor. It all came together. But I didn't want to believe it.

A feeling of dread overcame me. When I arrived back in the room and saw Barry's bed stripped and drawers emptied, my heart beat so fast I thought I was certain to inherit my father's illness.

I sat down on my bed, tried to calm myself, and looked over at the empty half of the room. He had probably been expelled, I figured. Definitely expelled. I shuddered at the thought of what had happened.

There was a knock on the door. It was the dorm counselor, Yosi Katz, the one who had caught the perpetrators. He was a third-year rabbinical student and an outspoken leader of the right-wing faction on campus. A transplant from the likes of Mirrer, he wore his arrogance as proudly as he did his long beard, big black velvet yarmulke, and hanging *tzitzis*. A defender of the Torah. An enemy of secularism.

He was short, thin, and bald except for patches of brown hair on the sides and around the back of his head. His posture was shlumpy—it looked as if he had a potbelly—and when he walked, his feet dragged as if it were a burden to lift them. He never managed to keep his shirt tucked in for very long and usually missed at least one belt loop.

Yosi didn't care much for me and made no effort to hide it. He knew who I was and where I was from. And my present incarnation was regarded by him as a personal insult. He never looked at me, and whenever he spoke to me I could feel the anger. He had his favorites, those with whom he joked and toyed. They were all *frum,* strictly observant, very, very *frum,* from head to toe. They were his compatriots, zealots in the struggle against the Torah's opponents. Fellow soldiers in the army of God.

He came in and looked at me. I was silent, still in shock. He showed no concern whatsoever, and coldly said he had instructions to accompany me immediately to the dean's office. *Immediately.*

On the way the only thing he offered was the identity of Barry's partner, another freshman who lived across the hall, and who also was, strangely enough, the son of a rabbi. Another renegade, he must have been thinking.

I wondered why I had been summoned. Was I also a suspect? Perhaps. After all, I was a heretic who had shaved my beard, an infidel with a small knit yarmulke, a heathen in blue jeans. Of course I was involved! Would I be suspended or expelled?

We arrived in the reception area of the dean's office and Yosi told me to take a seat and wait. He knocked on the beige steel door that bore a small red sign stating "Dr. Abraham Stein, Dean" as he simultaneously turned the knob and slipped himself inside.

I sat there for what seemed an eternity, my eyes fixed on that steel door. It was a famous door, one that was generally closed to students. The prevailing campus humor had it that the dean never ventured beyond his quarters, and seldom did a student enter the inner sanctum. Yet, to my chagrin, I was soon to be one of the chosen few.

Ironic. I had resented closed doors more than anyone I knew, and now one that I would just as soon remain closed was about to open. What luck!

Yosi emerged and escorted me into the office. There was one man seated behind a large oak-stained desk and another hunched comfortably in a high-backed all-wood university chair off to the right in front of the desk. There were two more such chairs, empty and waiting for us to occupy them, also situated in front of the desk. Yosi introduced me to the others and we took our places. By design, I ended up facing all of them.

It was a spacious office. The walls were decorated with countless diplomas and pictures of founding fathers of the university. The man behind the desk was the dean, a tall, thin, elderly man with a clean-shaven face, a sharp nose, and fat lips. He seemed to be a nervous sort, constantly blinking his eyes. The other man was the university's provost, the infamous Rabbi Schacter. He was obese, middle-aged, and of medium height. On his upper lip was a Clark Gable mustache and upon his nose sat a pair of octagonal reading glasses. In his hands, resting on his lap, was a file of documents. Probably my file, I thought. He was the first to speak, and when he did so the words came out in a high-pitched timbre with a grating singsong intonation.

"How is your father these days?" he sang.

"You know my father?"

"I know of him, heard him lecture a few times. He is a fine

scholar." Dean Stein nodded in agreement.

Yosi looked impatient, wanting to cut to the chase. "I've told Yakov why you've called him here," he interjected. His eyes hadn't met mine for a second, not from the moment he had entered my room.

"This is a most delicate matter," sang Rabbi Schacter. The dean nodded again. I just listened.

"What we want to know, Yakov," Yosi inserted, "is your account of what happened with Barry." Still no eye contact.

"I'm not sure what you mean," I replied innocently.

Yosi looked at the others and waited for one of them to say something. A moment lapsed, and then one of them did.

"What we'd like to know is how long you think this has been going on," caroled Schacter.

"I have no idea," I reacted, trying not to sound defensive.

"You mean to tell me that you didn't know anything about this!" charged Yosi.

"That's exactly what I mean to say. Why would you think anything else?" Couldn't contain that defensiveness for long.

"Why?" He paused and looked at the others as if I'd asked a stupid question. "Because you lived with the guy, Yakov, and we find it hard to believe that you were completely unaware of what was going on."

"Well, I'm sorry if it disappoints you, Yosi, but the whole thing's a complete surprise to me. And to tell you the truth, I'm a little shook up by it. After all, I *did* live with the guy."

His eyes finally met mine. He was disarmed and motionless. The other two sat like spectators for a few seconds until Schacter broke the silence.

"So you never even had a suspicion of anything?"

"Well, Rabbi," I answered in a much more respectful tone than with Yosi, "we lived together but weren't very friendly. I guess because we came from such different backgrounds." I stopped to collect my thoughts and then continued, "We talked once in a while but we were pretty distant, especially as of late. I was just too wrapped up in my studies to notice that anything was going on. I suppose in hindsight I can see that maybe there were signs that something was wrong. But I surely wouldn't have suspected *this*. And the truth is I didn't suspect anything at the time. I was just too busy. If that's a crime, then I'm certainly guilty."

They all looked at one another. The dean and the provost appeared satisfied, but Yosi Katz, soldier in the army of God, was visibly upset by his failure to snuff out yet another infidel. It was his duty to purge the yeshiva of the likes of Sodom and Gomorrah, and his victory thus far wasn't enough to satiate his appetite.

Barry's side of the room remained uninhabited for the duration of the year. A memorial, I thought, each time I gazed upon the empty bed. I wondered what he must have been thinking all those times he saw me undressed. How imperceptive could I possibly have been?

I also speculated about his parents' reactions. His mother most likely breathed a sigh of relief—better he be gay than a religious fanatic! Mr. Glasser, true to form in the presence of his dominatrix, probably said little.

As for Barry himself, I was saddened. He must have suffered much in his confusion. He had come to the yeshiva, probably seeking help from the structure and discipline that orthodoxy imposes, and had left demoralized and disgraced. I wondered if he would survive such a blow—if anyone could.

One night I had a dream that I met up with him several years hence somewhere on the streets of Brooklyn. The details were scant, but it seemed to take place in Crown Heights. From the appearance of things, I was completely removed from religion—bare-headed, feeling free and autonomous. He, on the other hand, was bearded and garbed as if he had joined the ranks of the Lubavitchers, a Hasidic sect that actively proselytizes among the lost and unaffiliated.

I didn't recall the interaction between us in the dream, and wasn't sure of whether appearing as I did was my fate or my fear. As for Barry, things seemed clearer. He had apparently found his salvation, a way of dealing with his inner demons and throwing his parents a curve in the process. He had become a *Bal T'shuvah* par excellence. Another soldier in the army of God.

After four years, I graduated from the college with honors, magna cum laude. To please my mother, I applied and was accepted to Yeshiva University's rabbinical school. To satisfy myself, I also applied and was accepted to a doctoral program in philosophy at New York University. I would somehow manage to do both simultaneously.

I chose NYU because of the program's excellent reputation and the option of taking evening classes. There was also the small matter of the scholarship I was offered, which would cover my tuition and most of my living expenses. It wasn't going to be easy handling two full-time commitments at once. It was also, technically, a violation of the rules of the rabbinical school. But I was determined and, by this time, quite adept at keeping secrets.

My father, though, could not be appeased. On my rare visits home, he would lock himself behind the door of his study. Even on holidays—I never missed a holiday with my parents—our interaction at the table was minimal, and he always retired to his sanctum as soon as possible. The pain that my presence caused him was apparent.

He had managed, however, to find solace in Ezra, who had grown to become his most prized student and a surrogate son. Ezra sat with him in his study day and night, had married a girl from an important rabbinical family, and was teaching Talmud to high school students. His wife had become close with my mother and the two couples often joined one another for *Shabbos* and holiday meals.

Chaim still worked in the camera store and hadn't married.

He had been engaged for a short time, but it was broken off for some unexplained reason. When I saw him on holidays, we would talk superficially, usually on the way home from *shul.* Otherwise, there was no relationship between us. I was troubled by this, and even more troubled by a gnawing sense that something wasn't right about him. I just couldn't put my finger on exactly what it was.

PART II

CHAPTER 13

IT WAS THE MIDDLE of July and forecasters were already labeling it the hottest summer in decades. The latest heat wave had just begun its fourth day, and the worst possible place to be was on the Seventh Avenue IRT during rush hour. Grueling, but a fact of life I had to put up with.

The ride to New York University from the West Ninety-sixth Street station was twelve stops in all, about twenty minutes provided there were no delays. Usually, there were delays.

I stood, my hand clenched tightly around the handrail, bunched up against strangers on all sides. It was an old train with no air conditioning. It jerked as it began to move, creating greater intimacy among the passengers. A haven for perverts.

This took much getting used to. The heat, the crowds, the shoving, the noise. A far cry from those summers in the mountains where even the most torrid days were moderated by open spaces, breezes, and cool nights. At moments like this I longed for the past.

The train came to a shrieking stop. The sign outside read, "Christopher Street, Sheridan Square," my daily retreat from the underground's racket and clamor. But deliverance lay not just in fleeing the train, for there were still swarms of fellow commuters pushing and bumping against one another, a giant caterpillar with hundreds of legs making its way up the stairs.

It was at this point, ascending toward the daylight, that I usually began regaining my serenity. But not today. Not for the past several days of seething heat did any part of the city seem liberating. Nothing was spared. Even buildings with air conditioning were warm, their power drained from the enormous overload.

I walked over to West Fourth Street and then turned eastward. It was a short walk—usually about ten minutes—yet it seemed longer in the heat. A few blocks later I passed the law school on my right and Washington Square Park on my left. Immediately after the law school stood my final destination: Bobst Library, a magnificent, tall, deep red stone edifice standing prominently among the smaller structures of the area.

New York University was regarded as an auspicious institution since its inception. Among its many attributes was its location, the heart of Greenwich Village, an incredible contrast from the bowels of Washington Heights. I had just completed my second year at the Graduate School for the Humanities and was spending the summer doing preparatory work on my doctoral dissertation proposal. Two years remained for me to finish my course work and complete my thesis. I was also beginning my final year at Yeshiva University's rabbinical school, a year marked by extensive exams, both oral and written. Balancing these two commitments had worked thus far, but now I was worried.

I'd been having a hard time finding a dissertation topic. I wanted to write about the theological questions I'd struggled with over the years, but was having difficulty focusing. My latest idea, subjective morality versus organized religion, sounded good, but was still too broad. "You can't be so ambitious," my professor told me on several occasions. "This is a thesis, not a treatise." That was the problem—I wanted to write a treatise. I wanted to make my ultimate statement, the final wedge between what I would become and all that had preceded.

The dissertation was supposed to be a scholarly rather than a personal statement; that is, an analysis of the work of others as opposed to an espousal of one's own philosophical inclinations. Of course, a student could reflect on those thinkers whom were most closely aligned with his interests. What remained for me was to decide which of the illustrious masters suited my needs.

And so my days were spent perusing journals and books, covering thinkers from Aristotle to Sartre, attempting to formulate a precise question that would serve as a point of departure. It was a search for specificity, prompted by my professor, Dr. Paul Waldman, who seemed to take great delight in pointing out my surprising lack of focus in formulating ideas for this project.

The most fascinating thing of all, however, was where I sat in the library. Day after day I automatically proceeded directly to a quiet table behind some of the bookcases on the ninth floor, right smack in the middle of the Judaica section. And there I would sit for hours, musing over texts of secular philosophy, enveloped by voluminous shelves bearing the works of Jewish history, tradition, and culture—a fortress shielding me from the vile influence of my own endeavors.

There I felt I could be invulnerable, able to delve into the deepest chasms of heresy yet remain unscathed by its allure. Or so I thought. In reality, I was simply managing to hold onto a shred of my heritage, to maintain a faint sense of rootedness in the past while graduating to a new identity. Still uncertain of my own convictions, fearing I might disintegrate, I found comfort in these surroundings.

At about eleven o'clock in the morning, there was a sudden loud thump followed by a gust of cool air from the air-conditioning vent. It was already Thursday, and the system hadn't been working properly since Monday. I got up and walked toward the vent. I stood before it; the chilling draft blew sharply against the sweat dribbling down my temples and neck. Relief at last.

The worst part of the heat was my *tzitzis.* I was still wearing them daily, as is commanded, and because of that I also had to wear an undershirt beneath them to prevent them from touching my body, as is also commanded. This amounted to no less than three layers of clothing, regardless of the weather. Then again, suffering was the essence of being Jewish. *Sometimes you must sacrifice.*

I had been standing directly in front of the vent, obstructing the stream of air, in a pleasurable trance for quite some time when I was suddenly interrupted by someone tapping on my back. My first expectation was to be admonished by some stranger for filtering the air with my odious scent. Then I turned around and saw Rebecca's face. It was a face I hadn't seen in seven years. And it hadn't changed a bit.

She stood about a foot away from me, staring into my eyes, smiling easily, as though gratified by my obviously astounded expression. For a split second, I felt myself in a daze, about to awaken from a daydream. I reached out and touched her shoulder and squeezed it just slightly, reassuring myself that she was real. Unaware that I was actually touching her, I uttered her name, just audibly, and she immediately responded, "Yakov, it's been a long time."

"Yes it has," I replied, again faintly, still hardly conscious, still afraid to awaken from the dream.

Suddenly, I realized it *was* real and also took cognizance of where my hand was. I withdrew it. She ignored that and leaned toward me, kissed me on the cheek, and embraced me in a warm nonsexual manner, as one would an old friend. I didn't resist. Up to this time she had been the only female aside from my mother who ever touched me like this. Because I'd allowed it in the past, it seemed all right now. It seemed just fine.

As she stepped back, I noticed she was wearing shorts, a sleeveless T-shirt, and sandals, a comfortable outfit for the weather. Beneath such clothing, her shapely curvature stood out, much more so than I remembered from her days in long skirts and full blouses. Time had been more than kind to her. She was still petite and thin, but not to the detriment of any essentials. Her hair was still long and wavy, but showed more body and luster. I don't know for how long I just stood there and took inventory, but it seemed to be quite a while.

The skimpiness of her attire displayed a boldness rare among Orthodox women. I wondered how the years had influenced her. I wondered many things.

"What are you doing here?" she asked excitedly. She seemed comfortable now, more so than during our stilted caress.

"I'm, uh, writing my dissertation," I responded with a tinge of hesitation and a slight smirk, knowing that this answer would only beg a thousand more questions.

"A dissertation!" She seemed pleasantly amazed. "As in 'doctoral' dissertation?"

"What other kind is there?" I replied.

She paused for a moment, taking it all in. "Really!" she said with a smile. "And what are you writing about?"

"Well, it's a long story. I haven't exactly narrowed it down yet." Not wanting to go further with this line of conversation, I tried to interject a question of my own, "What about you, what are you up to these days?"

"I'll tell you in a minute, but I'm really curious, what are you writing about?"

She was unswayed by my attempt to deflect the conversation. We were both withholding. Perhaps we each had much to hide; or perhaps neither of us felt that a single explanation could possibly do justice to the complex courses our lives had taken. Before even waiting for a reply, she looked over to my table, about five feet away from us, and walked toward it.

This was typical of her. If I wasn't going to answer, she would find out for herself. I followed behind. Just as she was about to inspect the books, I jumped in. "It's about philosophy."

"I can see that," she replied softly. At that moment she was more interested in examining the texts than in conversing with me. She glanced at practically every title, seeming totally fascinated. So this is what the yeshiva boy from Borough Park has been up to, she must have thought.

I intruded. "They're on . . ."

"I can see what they're on," she interrupted, "but tell me, what exactly do you have in mind here?"

"That's a good question. To be honest, I haven't quite figured it out, I'm just sort of reading a lot of different things and trying to come up with an idea." Vague enough?

"But none of these deal with Jewish philosophy."

"I know. I'm not working in Jewish philosophy."

"I see that," she observed as she held up a copy of Feuerbach's *Essence of Christianity,* a classic work by the infamous atheist who attempted to explain religion in terms of the projection of human desires and fears.

I imagined what was going on in her head: What a shock! Is this the sheltered ultra-Orthodox yeshiva student who was destined to do nothing but study Talmud for the rest of his life? And look at him. Normal clothes, clean-shaven, knit yarmulke, and all these unkosher books.

Her smile reflected some pleasure in the discovery. She was quiet for a bit as she continued to peruse. Now was my chance to inquire, once again, about her. "So, what's been going on with you all these years?"

She glanced at her watch and responded, "There's so much, and I *do* want to tell you, but I'm meeting a friend in ten minutes and I'm going to be late as it is." Avoidance.

I made no attempt to press for more. Without even asking, she tore a piece of paper from my notebook, picked up my pen, and wrote down her phone number. As she placed it in my palm, she closed up my hand into a fist and squeezed it tightly. "Call me. I want you to call me! Will you?"

"Yes," I said weakly as I looked at her hand clenching mine. "I mean, of course!" Stronger.

"Can you call tonight? I'll be home after ten."

"Okay," I responded with disappointment, wishing she didn't have to go, afraid of losing her once again. Take control, I told myself. Grab her! Insist that she cancel whatever other plans she has! Don't be such a wimp! But I let it be, and we said goodbye. Some things never change.

I walked with her over to the elevator. It came within seconds, leaving no time to do or say anything. We just looked at each other. I felt completely paralyzed. "Remember, I'll be home after ten," she repeated as she stepped into the elevator.

I watched her disappear as the doors closed, and continued standing there for a few moments, her image still fresh in my mind. Her appearance—the shorts, T-shirt, and sandals. Her evasiveness.

I remembered the very first impression I ever had of her: *another person who wasn't playing exactly by the rules.*

CHAPTER 14

THE UPPER WEST SIDE of Manhattan had become a haven for the unmarried Orthodox. Between Sixty-seventh Street and Ninety-sixth Street, from Central Park West over to Riverside Drive, existed a gold mine of Jewish singles searching for suitable mates. Their ages varied, as did their places of origin. Many came from the suburbs, others from various reaches of the country, and still others from overseas. There were the divorced, the widowed, the wayward, and those who simply rejected the traditional demands of early marriage and family. They all flocked to this place so they could live in a community with others who shared their lifestyle. Here, they were free of the shame and reproach that their status sometimes engendered in the extended Orthodox world.

A popular gathering place for the hordes of single Jewish yuppies was the Lincoln Square Synagogue, a modern Orthodox congregation located on Amsterdam Avenue and Sixty-ninth Street. On Friday nights and *Shabbos* mornings, there would be standing-room-only crowds, women and men on display, decked out, looking as successful and appealing as possible. A veritable "meat" market. On special holidays, such as *Simchas Torah,* the day the completion of the yearly Torah reading cycle is celebrated, the attendance would enter the thousands, with people from all distances, traveling and staying in other peoples' homes—on couches, mattresses, and even floors—just to participate in the vast social gathering on the sidewalk and street outside the synagogue. There, in the evening and morning, they would network for hours, in search of their *basheirtes,* their predestined mates.

The main sanctuary of the synagogue was built like an amphitheater, with ascending pews rising about ten levels. The *bima,* the podium from which the cantor leads the service, sat on the bottom level in the middle facing the ark, which was about three quarters of the way up on the eastern wall. There was a wide staircase with a bright red carpet leading up to the ark and its adjacent chairs—two on each side—where the rabbi, cantor, and other prominent dignitaries sat. About halfway up the stairs, between the ark and the *bima,* stood the rabbi's pulpit.

The men and women, of course, sat in separate sections, but the design was such that they inevitably faced each other. While this, no doubt, defeated the very purpose of separating the sexes during prayer—it is believed that such a separation facilitates greater concentration on The Almighty—it certainly satisfied many other agendas. And so Lincoln Square Synagogue was appropriately coined "Wink and Stare Synagogue."

I was twenty-four years old, six years beyond the time I should have been slated for marriage, and still very much single. None of the matchmakers in Borough Park would consider me. A genuine pariah.

My parents, whose last hope had been that I might meet a nice religious girl, had long given up. Over the years my mother had attempted a few introductions through friends or relatives, and I even played along. But nothing panned out.

I'd been doing some dating on my own, but the results were always the same. The very *frum* women were interested in men who wore black hats, studied Talmud day and night, and were going into family businesses. The modern Orthodox women were looking for would-be lawyers and doctors. Things did not bode well for me.

The year before, I had decided the YU dormitory no longer suited my needs, and had found a place on the Upper West Side. Not that I was particularly motivated to go on the hunt for an eternal partner, but I was ripe for some company.

My apartment was on Ninety-fourth Street, just west of Broadway. Though the area easily outclassed Yeshiva University's Washington Heights, the immediate neighborhood was wanting in comparison to the more gentrified realty of the Seventies and Eighties. In any case, this was all I could afford. It was a small studio, and despite my father's objections to the whole idea—by now, his disapproval was generally expected—he still helped me secure the place through a favor from one of his congregants, who owned several buildings in upper Manhattan.

The street itself was serene. There were two large apartment buildings across from each other on the corner of Broadway, while the remainder of the block was distinguished by brownstone houses and tree-lined sidewalks. My studio was in one of the brownstones on the south side, about a third of the way up from Broadway. Each morning, walking to the subway, I would turn that corner and join the bedlam of crammed walkways, honking cabs, and screeching buses. Upon returning home in the late evening, however, the very same corner took on a markedly different character, serving as a popular spot for the street people—the prostitutes and drug dealers.

While most of the lower blocks of the West Side had been cleansed of these elements, those above Ninetieth Street were still fertile ground. And despite the efforts of community organizations, regularly proliferating literature in their battle to rid the neighborhood of such industries, the action continued, night after night. Some of the hookers were regulars, faces I passed just about every evening, each becoming more familiar with time. They didn't seem to make much trouble; they would simply walk along the sidewalk propositioning men on foot, or stand out on the street waving down passing cars. The drug dealers, for the most part, were also innocuous. They maintained as low a profile as possible, quietly approaching pedestrians and offering their goods as if there was an unwritten compact to maintain the peace. After all, this was supposed to be a classy neighborhood, and if one chose to traffic his contraband in places such as this, one best do so with some measure of professionalism.

The night after I met Rebecca in the library, I arrived home around ten-thirty, as usual. I held the door slightly open with my foot to allow some illumination from the hallway, while placing my books on a small table immediately to the right of the entrance. I flicked on the light switch just above the table and let the door close behind me. I secured the three locks on the door, and then looked at the answering machine on the other side of the room to see if anyone had called. The little red light was blinking.

It was a humble apartment, reflecting the financial means of its tenant. The favor to my father included a significant rent reduction, and between the money my father provided, student loans, and my scholarship, I managed to make ends meet. There was one large room with a small kitchenette and a bathroom. The floors were bare except for a small rug at the entrance, and the furniture included a full-size bed and couch left by the previous tenant and an old dining table and chairs that had been gathering dust in my mother's basement. Covering two of the walls were bookcases I had made with bricks and planks of wood.

The only real luxury I had was an antiquated air conditioner that had been sitting in Uncle Zelig's garage for years. It worked, but made a loud grating hum that took some getting used to. Actually, the hum did block out the even more annoying sounds of traffic from the street below. It was one or the other. City life.

The message on the tape was, as I'd anticipated, the usual daily salutation from my mother, telling me she loved me, wishing me a good day, and asking me to call home to speak to my father. I picked up the phone and began dialing their number, but stopped in the middle and replaced the receiver. I thought to myself that it was just as well if I waited until tomorrow—why spoil a perfect three-day streak of avoidance?

I eyed the phone, reached into my pocket for the crumbled piece of paper on which Rebecca had scribbled her number, stared at it for a few seconds, and picked up the receiver again. I started dialing.

Rebecca answered on the fourth ring as if she had just walked in or was involved in something else. She seemed a little remote, probably perturbed at my not having called the night before. I began by apologizing and offered some lame excuse about having gotten home too late.

"Well I guess that explains it," she remarked indifferently. It felt good to know that she was upset. The plan had worked. I wanted to establish that I wasn't going to jump at her beck and call. Take control!

"I was really surprised to see you," was my next comment.

"I was surprised also. I mean, you were just about the last person on earth I would have expected to find there."

"Yeah, I've been full of surprises since the last time we saw each other and, I suspect, so have you."

A pause. She knew she would have to come clean sooner or later. "Well, what exactly do you want to know?" Her tone was warming up a bit. But her open-ended question was an obvious ploy. She was going to make me work, make it my task to tease things out of her.

I was a philosopher, adept at breaking things down, at moving from the general to the particular. This game I could play. "Why not start with right now? I mean, what are you doing presently? Are you a student? Are you working? What's happening?" Let's see her get out of this one!

Another pause. "I guess you get the idea that I'm having trouble telling you what's going on, or what's been going on."

"Well, I would have had trouble telling you, too. But I was at a disadvantage, under the circumstances. You know, the books and everything." Some empathy to loosen her up.

"Can't we wait till I see you? Then I'll answer *all* your questions, I'll tell you everything you want to know."

"Does that mean we're going to see each other?" I asked.

"I hope so." Hesitation. "If you want to."

"Of course I do!" No pretense. "I've wanted to for a long time. I mean, I've thought about you a lot over the years."

"Then why didn't you call last night?"

"I guess I was scared. I wasn't sure what would happen, and I thought a day or so might put some distance between us, give me some perspective."

"And now?"

"I'm still scared," I confessed. "But here we go again; I'm talking more than you. How do you do that, just turn things around like that?"

"Not very well, obviously."

The next question I phrased with deliberate force. "At least you can tell me where you're living."

"On the Upper West Side," she replied.

"Well there's a coincidence!"

"You're kidding!"

"Definitely not. So where exactly are you?"

"On Eighty-second, between Columbus and Amsterdam. What about you?"

"Ninety-fourth, between Broadway and West End."

I wondered why I never ran into her at the synagogue. Even with all the people there, she would have stood out. But I wasn't going to ask about that just yet. I assumed the answer would be tied, somehow, to all the other things she was withholding.

I shifted the focus. "By the way, how are your parents and Moshe doing?" Innocuous enough.

"Oh, they're pretty much just the same as you remember them. My father's still a principal and my mother still teaches.

And Moshe, as you must know, has been very successful in Jewish music. He's made quite a few albums."

"Yes, I do know. I even have one or two of them. He's become very popular in yeshiva circles, sort of like a Hasidic Bruce Springsteen."

"I don't know if he'd appreciate the analogy, but he's had a lot of *mazel.*"

"Anyway, when are we going to get together so that I can finally learn the nitty-gritty details of the life of Rebecca Kleinman?"

"Well, how about tomorrow night? For dinner, maybe?"

I, of course, agreed and suggested a particular restaurant I favored among the numerous kosher establishments in our neighborhood. She suggested instead that she cook something at her apartment. "Restaurants are too noisy," she said.

I agreed and didn't think twice about the implications, about the prohibitions against men and women being alone in a room unless they are married. In fact, I was incredibly excited about the idea. It was Rebecca. I couldn't believe it, no matter how many times I repeated it. It was Rebecca. And we were going to be together, alone.

My mind went wild with fantasies. I had waited years for this, and never thought that it would actually happen. Rebecca. I pictured her then and now. I pictured us together in the future. I imagined so many things.

And then there was reality: the reality of who she was today, and whether we could ever truly have a relationship; the reality of those things that had separated us in the past, of that haunting secret that had once ravaged our lives. I tried to erase these intrusions from my mind, to think only of my hopes and wishes, but her father's old warning kept playing over and over again: *The pain that you will cause will surely be much greater than any pleasure the two of you could ever have.*

I sat by the window, staring at the night, hearing the echoes of the past.

The next day it finally rained. The storm had begun sometime in the early morning hours; I was awakened several times by resounding booms, the howl of wind and clamor of rain crashing against the windows. Not even the old air conditioner could drown out such raucousness. By the time the radio-alarm went off, I'd already been out of bed for over an hour.

I was standing beside the table, donned in my *tallis* and *t'fillin,* the prayer shawl and phylacteries that Jewish men wear when reciting the weekday morning prayers. The *t'fillin,* given to me by my father at my *bar mitzvah,* were two small black leather boxes containing parchments inscribed with special passages from the Torah. They were worn on my left arm and around my forehead, fastened by long black leather straps that were wrapped in a prescribed manner. This was the way we fulfilled the biblical commandment to bind the words of the Torah "as a sign upon thy arms" and "as frontlets between thine eyes." And the reason *t'fillin* aren't used on the Sabbath is because the Sabbath itself is enough of a sign of God to obviate the need for any other signs.

The *tallis* was an heirloom; it had belonged to my grandfather. It was a full-body shawl which draped well below the back of my knees and enabled me to sheathe myself completely. It had once been immaculately white but had yellowed slightly with time. For my grandfather, this was his special *tallis,* the one he reserved strictly for use on Sabbaths and holidays. His regular *tallis,* which had been severely worn and frayed from sixty some odd years of daily use, was the one in which he had been buried. This was another requirement of Jewish law, that a man be interred in the same garment with which he offered supplication during his life.

For most Jewish men, the obligation to wear a *tallis* refers to after marriage. I, however, was joined to a unique tradition, prevalent generally among Jews of German descent, that required the wearing of the *tallis* after one's *bar mitzvah.* The custom descended from my paternal great-grandfather who had originally come from a small village outside the city of Berlin before he went to serve as a teacher in the Lithuanian yeshiva of Mir.

This was supposed to be a special time of day. This hour, each morning, was supposed to be the time to connect with something beyond myself. The corporeal qualities of the *tallis* itself, its soft texture and distinctive smell, were supposed to merge me with an ancestry that I had known only through stories. The very act of praying, the experience of entreating one's maker, was supposed to strengthen my faith and foster a sense of humility. But I never felt these things.

For me, the prayers were perfunctory. Every morning was the same, just going through the motions. No passion, no fervor. No great revelations or spiritual experiences.

Usually my mind would wander onto some philosophical problem, an unfinished paper, an upcoming test, a recent argument with my father, or something of the sort. But today it was on Rebecca. I was completely oblivious to anything other than the upcoming evening. I envisaged all sorts of details, from what she would wear to what she would serve. I planned my attire, something I had never paid attention to before, and even pictured us together sexually. Yes, there I was, shrouded in my *bar mitzvah t'fillin* and my *zayde's tallis,* imagining myself enveloped in the arms of a woman, a naked woman no less. And it wasn't difficult for me to picture the contours of her body, how she felt pressed up against me. The only thing that was difficult was trying to erase these lustful thoughts from my mind while *davening,* trying to eradicate the guilt stemming from having an erection at a time when I was supposed to be focused on spiritual rather than physical matters. I wasn't making much headway.

This, no doubt, wasn't the first time my mind had wandered in such directions, either during prayer or any other activity. But it seemed that these days the tendency was burgeoning.

This fantasy had a power all its own, a draw so compelling it frightened me. In the past, I'd managed with relative ease to separate thought from action. Now I was no longer confident of my ability to do so.

The weather report called for showers and thunderstorms all day. While normally I would have been inclined to remain at home—I had enough research material to keep me quite busy there—I felt I needed to get out. So I forced myself to travel downtown to the library to spend my time searching through card catalogues and bookshelves, and even went out for lunch. I hoped that being somewhat active would help free me from these arousing images.

It didn't.

By evening the rain had stopped, and with it the heat wave. When I got outside, the block was unusually deserted as if everyone else was still unaware the storm had ceased. The downpour had effectively reduced the humidity, but the wetness of the streets left a musty smell in the air. The pavement glittered from the sun shining through the trees. It was six o'clock, about an hour and a half before sunset, and I thought how fortunate I was to live on this street that had few tall buildings and generally enjoyed sunlight into the late hours.

As I turned the corner onto Broadway, the atmosphere remained noiseless. The walkway was literally barren; the riffraff hadn't yet arrived for the nightly frolic. I could have hailed a cab, or even taken the subway, but I chose to walk, to enjoy the stillness. And to release some nervous energy.

When I got down to Eighty-second Street, I crossed Broadway going east and then continued for a block and a half. I stopped in front of 165, her address, and looked at my watch. I was early. Definitely not a "cool" thing to be. I would stop and look around for a few minutes to waste a little time.

The surroundings appeared much the same as on my street, except there were fewer trees and more buildings. Immediately inside the entrance to her building sat a doorman who seemed oblivious to me despite my having stood right outside the door for at least ten minutes. I could hear the sound of the baseball game from a radio near the switchboard behind his tall chair. Perhaps he was engrossed in the game, or half asleep, or simply inured to vagrants hanging out in front of his building. After all, this was New York City, a place where one has to do something incredibly ludicrous in order to be noticed.

I disturbed his stupor by pulling open the door. He swiftly rose to his feet to lend assistance, politely greeted me, and asked what apartment. When I said "10-F," he responded, "Oh, Ms. Kleinman. May I say who's calling?"

"Mr. Eisen," I replied.

He was a tall, thin, bald, middle-aged man with long, wide sideburns and a Fu Manchu mustache. His intonation and physical mannerisms were effeminate, and he addressed me as if we were well acquainted. "Oh, she's such a wonderful lady, I hope you have a pleasant night," he remarked. And as I walked onto the elevator he continued, "She always gets the good-looking ones, you know."

I came off the elevator on the tenth floor and found her apartment. There wasn't a split second between my ringing the bell and her opening the door. She looked exactly as she had the other day, except, of course, for her clothing, a black skirt that fell just below her knees and a long-sleeved white silk blouse. Black and white—ironic for an evening that held the promise of so many shades of gray.

The very first thing I offered, even before hello, was a comment on my reaction to the doorman. "You know, the guy downstairs is a bit strange."

"Do you mean Sandy?"

"I guess that's his name."

"What's so strange, that he's gay?"

What was really on my mind was his comment about the men in her life. Not wanting to bring that up, I replied instead, "A bit flamboyant, wouldn't you say?"

"Does that bother you?"

"Does it bother you?"

"No, not at all. Actually, I think he's quite nice."

"I'm sure he is, but . . ."

"Oh, by the way, hello," she interrupted. "Quite a nasty day. Is it still raining?" A nonchalant change of subject.

"No, it stopped before I left home."

She took me by the hand. "Come, let me show you my place."

She led me into the living room of what was a small one-bedroom apartment. Again, she didn't hesitate to touch me; I didn't hesitate to let her. It was a well-lit room, modestly furnished, with a stained wooden floor and a large area rug. The decor, like mine, was hand-me-down.

She sat me down on a comfortable but worn light-brown velour couch and asked if I wanted something to drink. I politely declined as she excused herself, stating, "Okay, make yourself at home, I have some last-minute things to do," and left for the kitchen. I sat there and continued examining the surroundings.

Directly across the room was a large wall unit that, except for a stereo set taking up a shelf in the middle, was filled with books. I got up to examine the contents. Now it was my turn to see what she was into.

The collection was diversified. On one shelf, John Stuart Mill's *Three Essays on Religion* stood beside Heschel's *God in Search of Man.* There was also a fair amount of traditional Judaica, editions of the Bible, Talmud, and various commentaries. The subjects seemed to be mostly philosophy and religion, with a smattering of literature, anthropology, and psychology. And the bindings of just about every book, especially the paperbacks, were sufficiently worn to indicate that they'd been well read. I was struck by how this could easily have been my own library.

"Oh, I see you're searching for clues," she remarked as she entered the room with a bowl of salad in her hands. She smiled as she looked at me and placed the bowl on the table. As with most New York apartments, the living room and dining room were one. The table was against a wall, directly across from the windows, which looked out on the street. I wondered if she had seen me standing outside before I came up.

She came and stood next to me. "Have you figured me out yet?" she asked.

"I don't think so. I have more questions than answers."

"Ah, spoken like a true philosopher."

"I'm not sure if I can qualify as a philosopher quite yet. Maybe you should just consider me a student of intellectual history." Feigned modesty.

"Details, details. You know we're all philosophers of some sort, trying to figure things out, make sense of the world, that type of thing."

"Why do I always feel as if you're baiting me, or teasing me?" I asked.

"Always?"

"Okay, I mean since the other day. Anyway, you know what I mean, you're just doing it again."

"Doing what?" she queried.

"Doing just that, that upper-hand thing. Being evasive. You know!"

She paused. "I'm sorry," she said repentantly, "I really am. I guess it's what I do when I'm nervous."

She finally seemed genuine. And while I had her defenses down, I figured I'd go for the kill. "What are you nervous about?"

"Come on, you already know the answer to that. Now you're playing the same game," she responded with an alluring, vulnerable look in her eyes.

"Maybe so," I replied, feeling strangely comforted by our mutual anxiety about the evening.

"Look, why don't we take it slow? Like, let's start by sitting down to dinner," she suggested as she gently took my hand again and led me to the table.

She then dimmed the lights, struck a match, and lit two tall candles that sat in small disk-shaped crystal candlesticks before disappearing into the kitchen. I offered to help but she insisted I remain seated. It was her show. She emerged from the kitchen with a bottle of dry red wine and a corkscrew, which she handed to me, saying, "I'll let you do this."

I opened the bottle and poured the wine while she served the salad. We ate silently, and then she returned to the kitchen and came out with dinner. It was a homemade meal and as good as any I'd ever had. The veal dish had no name but she said it was one of her mother's recipes. The trimmings included roasted potatoes and steamed asparagus with a hollandaise-type sauce. The wine added just the touch needed to make everything perfect.

The intensity of the dialogue before dinner had quelled somewhat, and for a while that was fine. The topic became, as one might expect, food, a favorite Jewish pastime. The meal was so good I couldn't help talking about it. Rebecca, of course, welcomed the reprieve and filled me with details about the recipes and what she did all day to prepare. I was pleased that she had spent an entire day doing this for me. It felt even better knowing that she was willing to share that fact.

About halfway through dinner, with the help of about three glasses of wine, she began feeling comfortable enough to open up. In fact, she took the lead.

"So, you want to know about my life."

"Well, you could start by telling me what you do right now."

"Well, you see, that's the hardest part. Why don't I start with college? After all, that's close enough to where we left off, anyway."

"You majored in philosophy," I observed.

"Yep—that's sort of obvious enough."

"Were there any men?"

"Now, there's a dicey question." She paused and stared into space for a moment. "There were some."

"Anyone consequential?"

"There was one who seemed so at the time, I guess." She appeared pensive about this topic.

"You don't have to talk about it if you don't . . ."

"I don't," she interrupted me again. "And you really don't want to hear about some late adolescent romance that doesn't mean anything in the grand scheme of things. What you want to know is if there's anybody now." She gazed at me for about five seconds and then said, "And there isn't."

"What made you think I wanted to know that?"

"Now *you're* playing the game."

"You're right, I'm sorry. I did want to know, and I'm glad you're not."

"I'm glad I'm not. And I'm glad you're glad."

We smiled simultaneously. We were comfortable. I wondered if it was the wine or if we had merely used the wine as an excuse to allow ourselves to be the way we really wanted to be. I was completely at ease, unlike any previous experiences I'd had with women. I sensed she felt similarly.

"When was your most recent relationship?" I asked with a natural, almost childlike curiosity, not feeling at all threatened by her possible response.

"I don't know if I can count that far," she said. "It's really been some time."

"I don't understand. I mean, you're so beautiful, surely you must have to beat them away with a stick."

"Not quite. You see, there's a slight problem, sort of related to what I've been doing with my life the past two years. It scares men; they don't know how to react."

"So that's why you're reluctant to tell me."

"Bingo, Sherlock, you've got it! But it's going to be even harder with you." Pause. "Oh yeah, with you there are gonna be *big* problems."

"What is it? Are you studying to be a mafia hit man or something?"

"No, a little bit worse than that, at least in your eyes."

"In my eyes?" I repeated.

She took my left hand, held it in both her hands, and squeezed tightly. "Yakov, I'm studying to be a rabbi."

I sat in dead silence for a few moments, looking at her and not knowing what to say. She broke the silence—probably because it was making her even more nervous than me—by asking sarcastically, "Didn't you hear me?"

"Yes, I, uh, I heard you. I, um, I just don't know how to respond. I've heard of women becoming rabbis but it's very unfamiliar. I mean, I've never known one."

"I only want to know how you feel about—"

"I'm not sure. Don't get me wrong, I'm not without my own conflicts and problems when it comes to Judaism. Hell, I'm still not even sure about God. But this, this is just so different."

"But don't you see? I *am* sure about my Judaism and I'm sure about God." Tears were forming in her eyes as she spoke. "I've lost so much by making this decision. My father, my so-called enlightened father, is embarrassed by me. And my mother, Mrs. Home Economics, can't even begin to fathom where I'm coming from. But I'm sure all right. I'm sure that Jewish tradition doesn't offer a place for someone like me, so I have to make my own place. And that's the hardest part, because I don't feel completely comfortable with Reform either. But they're the only ones who will accept me. I'm sorry, I'm just rambling on."

"No, you're not," I replied tenderly. "And I do know how you feel, not having a place where you fit in; I know how it is to be different; and, boy, do I know how it feels to be rejected by your father. I know these things only too well."

"You still have those old conflicts?" she asked as she wiped away her tears with her napkin.

"It's a long story. But let it suffice to say that I often think about giving up the whole thing: hook, line, and sinker. I'm not sure about it all or why I do it anymore. I don't think I was ever sure. You, on the other hand, are different. You want to challenge it, to change it, to affect it. You're much more of a threat than I am. If I ever decided to stop practicing, it might break my parents' hearts. But you wouldn't break their hearts; no, you would incite their rage."

"Am I inciting your rage?"

"No, of course not. I just believe that they'd be happier if I ended up with someone who had no beliefs at all than with someone like you."

"You keep talking about what they would think, but what about what you think?"

"What I think? You want to know what I think? I think I'm as confused as I've ever been, and that's pretty confused. I have to tell you that during the past seven years not a single day has gone by without you somehow coming into my mind. And here you appear, out of the blue, just like that, studying to be a rabbi of all things. It's just so foreign. And why? Why not an accountant, or doctor, or professor, or something else? Why this?"

"Because I believe it is my calling. Why are you becoming a rabbi? Because it's expected of you. You don't even really care to. It's just a compromise to keep your father happy, and it doesn't even work. Why should it be that I, who genuinely want this, am not permitted to have it, while you, who couldn't care less, gets it? And as for it being foreign; well, you say that only because you've never experienced it, that's all. If you grew up in a synagogue where the rabbi was female, it would be strange for you the first time you encountered a male rabbi."

"The way you argue, *you're* the one who should become a lawyer," I said with a sneer, recollecting the time that she'd made such a suggestion to me. She didn't seem to appreciate the humor. "Just kidding," I hedged.

"The way I argue, I should be a *rabbi,*" she rejoined.

"Yes, a rabbi," I resolved.

The depth of her commitment was apparent and I, not really being committed to anything except not being committed, felt plainly inadequate to argue with her. Beyond that, we were both beginning to grow weary from the effects of the alcohol and the lateness of the hour. Again, she took my hand from across the table, this time caressing it gently, and said, "I want very much to see you again, soon."

"You will."

CHAPTER 15

IT WAS *Shabbos* on the Upper West Side of Manhattan. It was *Shabbos* all over the world, but sadly, only few places actually enjoyed the sense of harmony and peace that the Sabbath day should bring. The Upper West Side, with its incessant raucousness, wasn't one of them.

Rebecca was expecting me for lunch. It had only been three days since she last enticed me with her cooking. I attended Lincoln Square Synagogue that morning but, as usual, was unable to concentrate on the prayers. So lost in the excitement over my impending lunch date, I wasn't even distracted by the multitudes of lissome women in clear view. On previous occasions, I had marveled at the brilliant design of this stadiumlike structure in which hundreds of single men and women gathered to praise God, and I often participated, in the innocuous game of reciprocal glancing. But today I was oblivious.

I imagined Rebecca in the Reform synagogue just a few blocks away. Having never seen the interior of such a place, I pictured it as much the same as many of the modern-Orthodox synagogues I'd been to: large, ostentatious, impersonal.

In my mind I could see her wearing a yarmulke and a *tallis* similar to mine, praying with an enthusiasm I could never muster. And despite my awareness that most Reform Jews wear neither skullcaps nor prayer shawls, I still imagined it that way. She seemed to have left much room for interpretation, not having actually defined herself as belonging to any particular camp, and portraying an air of detachment from all camps. In fact, we didn't exactly get down to discussing specific practices, and I wasn't sure if I was ready to either. It was enough, so far, to picture her like this, imposing my own set of references. She appeared as I thought a rabbi should, in a manner that, thus far, I had only associated with men.

Suddenly I realized that the rabbi, Shmuel Roth, was speaking. He was a physically unassuming person, short in stature and slightly overweight. Always impeccably dressed, he wore perfectly tailored fashionable suits, stylish wire-rimmed glasses, and freshly shined shoes. His yarmulke bore a colorful, hand-crocheted design—a symbol of the modern-Orthodox—and sat upon a full head of jet-black hair. His face bore neatly trimmed sideburns, but no beard. Not even a mustache. Clean-shaven, almost baby-faced, and somewhere in his mid-forties, Roth's appearance struck me as unusual for an Orthodox rabbi.

When he spoke, the flavor was quite dramatic. His piercing tone filled the room, each well-enunciated syllable was joined by perfectly orchestrated hand gestures and bodily movements to strengthen the impact of his message. He positioned himself behind the podium and repeatedly rose up on his tiptoes when reaching a point of emphasis. This gesture also made him appear taller and more authoritative. He would frequently wander from the podium, walking from side to side as he spoke, approaching the congregants sitting in the rising pews on either side of him, using physical closeness as a means of effecting influence.

Roth was perfectly suited to his upper-crust West Side audience of doctors, lawyers, financial advisors, academics, and the like. He knew that it took much to impress them, so he often embellished his speeches with Latin phraseology or contemporary neologisms. To me, his orations were creative and refreshing, especially compared to what I had been accustomed to hearing in the shrines of Borough Park.

Coincidentally, he happened to be speaking about the issue of women becoming rabbis when his words so rudely intruded on my fantasy. Perhaps that was what caught my attention. No customary exposition of the Torah reading this week, not after the recent announcement that the Jewish Theological Seminary, the rabbinical school for Conservative rabbis, was proceeding with plans to join the Reform in ordaining women. I was struck by the timing of it all and, for a fleeting moment, was tempted to see some divine hand in it.

For Rabbi Roth, this was a particularly sensitive issue. It required very delicate handling because of the demographics of his congregation. He had developed a reputation in the community for being a proponent of expanding women's roles within traditional Jewish life. At times, it even appeared that he was stretching *Halacha,* Jewish law, and pursuing far-reaching conclusions to accommodate the needs of those egalitarian-minded types who attended his synagogue. One such decision, for example, was to establish a women's *minyan,* a service exclusively for women. In this setting, women would conduct and lead every aspect of the prayers. The catch? No men were allowed. For this, Roth was vociferously denounced by most of his Orthodox colleagues.

For someone like Rebecca, of course, women achieving parity only through the absence of men was merely skirting the issue. For Roth and his followers, however, it was a bold step, a statement that Orthodoxy could move forward in addressing the ever-changing needs of contemporary society while maintaining its fealty to *Halacha.* For the ultra-Orthodox like my father, it was an anathema, an indication of the deterioration of Jewish tradition and the poisonous influence of modernity.

"In this decision," Rabbi Roth was saying, "the Conservative Movement has followed the lead of Reform in making Jewish law secondary to contemporary values. This is a pivotal deviation from the way they have dealt with such issues historically. Until now, if there was conflict between modern and traditional values, they would attempt a resolution that respected both, but put the integrity of Jewish law first and foremost, above all other considerations. Now, they achieve resolution by dispensing with Jewish law altogether, just as the Reform Movement has done from the onset. And in doing this, they have opened the door to a host of other problems that will come to haunt them.

"Yes, my friends, by ignoring *Halacha* in favor of the modern ethic of egalitarianism, of total uniformity of gender roles, the Conservative Movement will be forced to follow that line of reasoning to its logical consequence. And, that is, that they too will eventually decide, as the Reform already have, to allow fathers to play an equal role in determining the religion of children.

"Yes, my friends, the inevitable conclusion of such a philosophy is total and complete uniformity for men and women in all ways. And this means *patrilineality,* that the father should determine the religion of the child just as strongly as the mother. And what will this do to the Jewish people? What are the ramifications of this? In years to come, there will be people who believe they are Jewish even though their mothers were not. And *we* will not regard them as Jews, we cannot. For to us the mother determines the religion of the child! So, in the end there will be two separate Jewish peoples who *really* cannot marry one another or pray together.

"Now, the Conservative Movement will deny adamantly that they are going in this direction, that they are joining the Reform Movement in dividing the Jewish people forever. But on what basis can they say this? If egalitarianism is now their only standard for making decisions, and *Halacha* is secondary, on what basis can they deny fathers an equal say in the religion of the child?"

An interesting argument. I wondered how Rebecca would respond. It certainly could make for a stirring lunchtime conversation, if it weren't for the fact that she'd invited other guests, close friends whom she wanted me to meet. I was curious to know who they were, anticipating, perhaps, other female rabbinical students, or at least folks of the same ilk. And I had no intention of getting into a discussion on a topic about which

I had no real opinions, only feelings. Especially in an atmosphere where I would be outnumbered and perhaps even stereotyped.

I arrived at Rebecca's apartment about five minutes late; the rabbi's speech was longer than usual. She escorted me into the living room. Another couple was already seated on the couch. They both stood up to meet me. She introduced them as Bob and Stephanie.

"Bob goes to school with me and Stephanie is a nurse. I've told them all about you," she remarked. Cute.

"Well, I hope it wasn't too terrible," I jested.

"Why don't we all move over to the table. I'm ravenous," Rebecca said.

The table was decorated traditionally, with an embroidered cloth covering two *challahs,* a silver *Kiddush* cup, and two candlesticks coated with the hardened drippings of the candles that had burned the night before. I tried to survey subtly, when I looked up and caught her eyes. She wore a slight smile, indicating her awareness of my approval.

We stood around the table for a moment as Rebecca put a yarmulke on her head. I was not surprised. The silver cup was directly beside her place setting. She filled it to the very top with red wine, placed it in the palm of her hand, and began to recite the special benediction for *Shabbos* afternoon. After she had completed the blessing, Bob and Stephanie responded with *amen.* I had never seen a woman say *Kiddush* before, and it took an effort to appear comfortable. I was not going to be opposed to something simply because it was outside my usual realm of experience. After a moment of hesitation, I too said *amen.*

"This is all new for Yakov," Rebecca remarked, smiling to the others. They, too, smiled, and looked at me warmly. Bob wasn't wearing a yarmulke. Oops, neither was Stephanie. "Come, let's wash," she said as she stood up and made her way to the kitchen.

Washing one's hands after *Kiddush* is the customary way of preparing to make the *Motzi,* the blessing over the bread. The purpose of this is to emulate the biblical practice of offering animal sacrifices, for which the washing of hands was also a prerequisite. By likening these two acts, eating—a purely physical and essentially self-serving endeavor—is elevated to a lofty spiritual plane.

Rebecca took a brass washing cup from the cabinet above the sink. She removed her pinkie ring from her right hand to fulfill the requirement that there be no impediment between the water and any part of the hand, and poured the water over her entire hand twice. She then refilled the cup and repeated the same procedure with her left hand. Immediately after, she took the towel, and just as she was about to dry herself, recited the peremptory blessing.

Bob and Stephanie were next. I was last. When I got back to the table, I found that Rebecca had placed the two *challahs* and the cutting board directly in front of my place, an indication that *I* had the honor of making the *Motzi* for everyone. I looked at her and smiled. I took the salt shaker in my left hand and sprinkled some salt on the board beside the *challahs.* This, too, mimicked the practice of the sacrificial offering. I then took both *challahs,* placed one atop the other, and made a slight cleft in the top *challah* with the knife as I recited the blessing over the bread. I proceeded to cut one piece from the top *challah,* dipped it in the salt, and took a bite. As I chewed on my piece, I cut three other pieces, dipped each in the salt, and distributed them.

After she took a bite of her *challah,* Rebecca stood up and excused herself to the kitchen. She refused all offers for assistance, which left the three of us alone. I was a bit uneasy, but Bob and Stephanie seemed friendly enough. Stephanie was a striking sort, with looks I would normally characterize as classical non-Jewish. She had natural light blond hair, long and straight, and a slender face with high cheekbones, a pug nose, and thin lips. Her eyes were sky blue, perfectly coordinated with the color of her dress, which contoured to a sticklike figure. Bob was a drop shorter than I, seemingly well built, with thick curly brown hair, even thicker eyebrows, and handsome features. A good-looking couple.

We talked for a short while about the weather and the rabbi's sermon at the Reform synagogue that morning. It seemed Bob took issue with something the rabbi had said. Stephanie gazed at Bob intently as he spoke, taking in every precious word like a pearl of wisdom. True love.

She was quiet as he did most of the talking in his distinctive Midwest accent. I was fine so long as I wasn't the focus of the conversation, but that didn't last for long. "I understand that you're studying to be an Orthodox rabbi," Bob said as Rebecca returned to the room with a bowl of salad.

"Yes, and I'm also doing a doctorate in philosophy at NYU."

Rebecca smirked at me. She was quite aware of my obvious attempt to emphasize my secular credentials and downplay the religious stuff.

"You're doing both of those at the same time?" asked Stephanie with wide-eyed innocence.

"Well, it's not as hard as it sounds, at least not till this year." The last six words came out as a sigh. "And anyway, I have to study something else because I don't plan on being a professional rabbi."

"Then why are you in rabbinical school?" Bob asked.

"Well, it's a very long story."

"That's okay—we like long stories," Stephanie interjected.

"Well, where I come from, I mean, in my family, it's expected that I will become a rabbi. My grandfather, and his father, and even several generations before that, were all rabbis."

"But they were professional rabbis?" Bob interrupted.

"I suppose you can call them that. They were mostly teachers, Talmudic scholars."

Bob, it was becoming more apparent, was from a very different world. I was guessing his place of origin as somewhere in Wisconsin, but soon learned it was Topeka, Kansas. To me, they were the same. I didn't even know there were any Jews in places like that. Quite ironic, that as a boy I had thought the entire world was Jewish, yet as an adult I had trouble imagining Jews anywhere outside of this city.

Bob's naiveté was refreshing. I spent much of the meal explaining to him and Stephanie how in the Orthodox world one doesn't necessarily study for *smichah* to serve in the professional rabbinate; how, in fact, the majority of my classmates did not intend to work as rabbis at all; how many, after earning their *smichah,* would go on to careers in law, business, and medicine.

They seemed to find this revealing, different from what they'd understood. Rebecca's beautiful face bore another reaction. She was angry. Angry at the men who had the right to be whatever they wanted, had the right to become rabbis and then go on to something else. Everything so easy—no struggles, no conflicts.

Bob began to enlighten me on many facets of the Reform rabbinate. He talked of his desire to work on a university campus, to reach out to the unaffiliated, to bring a sense of Jewish identity to young people who had graduated from Judaism at their *bar mitzvahs.* He spoke passionately about how he, who came from a totally secular background, felt uniquely qualified for this task. And as he spoke, Stephanie's eyes never left him.

Rebecca's uneasiness with the conversation was apparent. She said very little, but I knew that she saw herself as ill-suited to either world. When I first arrived that afternoon, I thought she had invited Bob and Stephanie to show me that there were others like her, a "strength in numbers" tactic to bolster her credibility. But now I realized that her intentions were just the opposite: she wanted to bare her peculiarity. She was, for all intents and purposes, an Orthodox woman living an Orthodox life in a Reform world. It was easy for me to feel her pain.

At the conclusion of the meal, Rebecca started humming a tune I recognized from one of Moshe's albums. Like many Jewish melodies, it had no words. Bob and Stephanie quickly picked up on it and joined in. I observed for a few seconds and suddenly I, too, was singing. Then, I saw a small tear escape the corner of Rebecca's eye. She nonchalantly wiped it away with her hand. No one else noticed. I wondered if she had any contact with Moshe, or her parents for that matter. Had they cut her off completely? How much pain did her choices bring her?

We sang a few more *Zemiros,* specific songs for the Sabbath table, and recited the *Birchas Hamazon,* the prayers for after meals. There is a special introduction to these prayers that is only supposed to be said, according to strict Orthodox law, if there is a quorum of three males. I remembered how Rabbi Roth, in his limitedly innovative style, had once argued that it could be said by three women, but, again, only under the condition that there were no men present. We were four, two men and two women, but we said the special introduction anyway. This time, I participated fully.

After lunch, we sat around for a while and continued talking. We covered topics ranging from philosophy to sports to current events. It wasn't until late in the afternoon that Bob and Stephanie left. I stayed to help Rebecca clean up, and to be alone with her.

"You seemed to have gotten along quite well with them," she observed.

"They're both very sincere people. He's committed to his goals and she's committed to him."

"And *you,* Yakov?"

"And me what?"

"What are you committed to?"

"I'm committed to finishing my doctorate, but beyond that, I really don't know. What about you, what are you committed to? You're a complete paradox to me. You're not like him, and you're not like me."

"Like you, I'm certainly not. I have a deep-rooted faith in God; I have made choices of consequence. I would imagine I'm much more like him than like you. I *am* committed to a great deal."

"To what?" I asked, feeling a bit put off by her comments.

"To Judaism, or can't you tell?"

"Frankly, I really don't get it. You keep a kosher home, you observe *Shabbos.* Where do you draw the line?"

"What line?" she asked, not quite understanding my question.

"The *rabbi* line!"

"It's simple. For me, there is no such line. You're the one who makes that line, not I. So, tell me, where do *you* draw it? Why do you bother drawing it at all? And tell me, how much do you actually care about it? You, who aren't even sure if you believe in anything, why do you become the great defender of the tradition?"

"I didn't mean to get into an argument about it."

"It's not an argument, just a heated discussion. And now you're trying to avoid it. Let's face it, Yakov, I think what bothers you most is that I've been daring enough to follow the strength of my convictions regardless of the outcome. And you aren't even sure if you have any convictions in the first place."

"Why did you invite me over today?" I asked with discomfort.

"Because I feel close to you and I wanted you to see me in my habitat, with people like me."

"But, you're so different from them! You're not Reform like they are!"

"Different and the same. Sure, Bob and I don't practice similarly. But what we have in common is far stronger than what divides us. I may choose to observe certain things and he may choose not to. You, on the other hand, make no choices.

"It's not your fault," she continued. "It's the way you were brought up. Like most Orthodox Jews, your choices were ready-made for you. You don't have to struggle with them. All you have to do is consult your rabbi or your books. And if you don't buy the whole system, that's okay, too. Just so long as you go through the motions and don't let anyone know how you really feel.

"I am Reform, Yakov, whether it pleases you to hear that or

not! And for me, that means that I have to make choices. There are some rabbinical students in my school who won't tear toilet paper on *Shabbos* and there are some who eat ham. Each makes his or her own moral decisions, and each is ready and willing to accept the responsibility for those decisions. *That's* what Bob and I share."

"So what you're saying is that you observe because you want to, and not because it was commanded by God?" I asked.

"Listen to yourself! Do *you* do what you do because it is commanded?"

"Sometimes." Tentative.

"And what about other times? The times when you're not really sure but you do it anyway because that's what you've been taught, what you've done all your life. And most of all, because that's what's acceptable to your parents."

"And what's wrong with that? What's wrong with compromising what you want, with surrendering your own will for something greater?"

"And what's greater?" she asked.

"The tradition, the community, the family."

"And how much of yourself do you give up for that? Where do you draw the line? Where does your individuality begin?"

"I don't really know. But I can't help feeling that it would be much too brazen of me to just make my choices and forget about everybody else," I said halfheartedly.

"If you can live that way, then fine. But I never could. I don't see myself as abandoning the tradition or the values that my parents taught me; I see myself as reshaping them, making room for new ideas, fighting rather than acquiescing. And I will fight, and struggle, until someone hears me."

"And what if no one hears you?"

"Someone will." She paused. "Someone already has."

I smiled.

Perhaps we'd reached a point of mutual understanding.

Deep inside, I knew she was the heroic one. For her choices entailed not compromises, but commitment and sacrifice. For this, she had won my respect.

We talked well into the night. She told me of the turmoil in her relationship with her parents, the anguish that their disapproval had caused in her. I offered some anecdotes of my own. She was not alone.

Yet despite the closeness we were forging, I couldn't shake the gnawing sense that some day our destiny would be to part, just as we had before. For if I ever gained the courage to make a choice, to decide between faith or apostasy, *we* would lose. There could be no room for her in my life if I were to return to the way of my fathers. And there could be no room for me in her life if I were to venture down the path of disbelief.

For me, it was simple. There were only two alternatives: a Borough Park black-hatter or an absolute defector. I couldn't seem to find a satisfying compromise. If I believed, I believed all the way, and if I didn't, there was no reason for pretense. The problem I had with Rebecca was that she didn't fit into any of my neatly contrived categories. The problem I had with myself was another matter.

I was walking home from Rebecca's. It was a murky night and on the corner of my block the prostitutes were out in their summer lace. As I turned onto Ninety-fourth, in the shadows stood a young lady in typical hooker get-up. She seemed attractive, but the darkness and her makeup precluded a fair appraisal. I had seen this woman many times on the same corner.

I noticed her only briefly as I walked by. She smiled, fell in line next to me, and said, "Looking for someone, honey?" I tried to ignore her and continued on my way. She seemed amused. "Are you a rabbi or something, honey?" she asked, seeing the yarmulke on my head.

"No," I chuckled as I replied. I also looked around, feeling quite uncomfortable that someone might see us and recognize me.

"Then, why don't you want any company tonight?" she asked as she took me by the arm.

"I've already had all the company I can handle for one evening, thanks." I continued walking; she continued following, her hand still on my arm.

"But honey, you haven't had all the company you can handle till you've had Tina. And I would just love to get my claws into a good-looking man like you, so whad'ya say?" She aggressively thrust forward to position herself in front of me and met me head on, her breasts touching me.

Now, as we stood practically breath to breath, I could examine her close up. Beneath the facial paint was a worn, tired face, probably the result of years of drugs. But attractive nonetheless with olive-colored skin, wide brown eyes, and large sensual lips. Her lengthy perm of auburn hair fell just to her shoulders. And her shapely, almost perfect figure was bursting out from her skimpy lingerie top, pants, and black-ribbed stockings.

"So that's your name, Tina," I said as I took a step back to create some space between us.

"Uh-huh," she replied. "So rabbi, what's yours?"

"I told you I'm not a rabbi, and what's my what?"

"Your name, silly, or should I just call you John," she mocked with a giggle.

Suddenly, it dawned on me. I was standing there having a conversation with a prostitute.

"I'm sorry, I think I have to go. *Alone,"* I asserted.

"Suit yourself, Rabbi John. I'll see you around."

As I walked away, I thought about her, the way she looked in that outfit that left little to the imagination. She couldn't have been more than eighteen. I wondered how she ended up on the streets. From where had she come? What were her dreams? Where was her family? I had an urge to turn back and engage her as a human being, offer her a meal, some conversation, and friendship. Maybe I could help somehow.

"What, are you crazy?" I said to myself. "She's not homeless; she's a hooker! She lives in a world of dollars and cents, and that's what it would take to have any friendship with her. Or anything, as long as you're willing to pay the price."

Suddenly, my mind descended below my belt. Sex for money, no complications, no conflicts, no deep philosophical conversations on values and compatibility. Just lay your money down and undo your pants. No one gets hurt.

I couldn't believe what I was thinking, but couldn't help thinking it either. If I can't help her, I wondered, maybe she can help me. At the moment, I had to admit, the idea had its appeal.

CHAPTER 16

I HAD FINALLY settled on a dissertation topic by the last week of August, just in time for the beginning of the new school year. When I explained the details to Rebecca, a forlorn expression came over her. The thesis would explore the origins of atheism in the writings of Freud, and demonstrate the influence of philosophy, as opposed to science or psychology, on his ideas regarding religion.

"That sounds like an awfully ambitious project to me," was her first response.

"I know, but my heart's in it, and I think I can handle it."

"What about Waldman, will he accept it?"

"I'm pretty sure. It's certainly focused enough for him. I mean, I've narrowed it down to only one thinker and one particular aspect of his work."

"I understand that, but Freud isn't even a philosopher, at least not in the formal sense."

Freud was an extremely controversial figure, and Rebecca was aware of that. He was an adamant atheist, and beyond that, a severe critic of the Bible and Jewish tradition. In his writings, he claimed that Moses was an Egyptian and was killed by the Hebrew pagans who resisted his monotheistic proselytizing. He also regarded religion as a regressive force, neurotic in nature, and contrary to rationality and science, the true panaceas for humankind.

"That really doesn't matter. I'm looking at definite philosophical influences on his theories. That should be philosophy enough for Waldman. He loves this stuff, taking scientists, artists, or historians, and showing what philosopher they really were. That's what he means by intellectual history. He thinks it's better than philosophy; it encompasses philosophy, and just about everything else."

"And you really have to write about *that* particular topic," she asked. The thought of me spending the next two years totally immersed in Freud actually frightened her.

"And you really have to become a rabbi," I responded in kind.

We had seen each other almost every day for two weeks straight but never ventured beyond casual touching or inadvertent brushing up against one another. Nothing overtly sexual; no kissing, extended hand-holding, lengthy hugging, or anything of the like. Despite endless suggestive glances, and certainly enough lust to fill a star system, neither of us was prepared to make the first move. Me, because that was a line I had never crossed. She, because of her obvious reservations about our future.

The following weekend was Labor Day and I was contemplating visiting with my parents. I hadn't spent a *Shabbos* there in several months. Rebecca hadn't been with her family for a *Shabbos* in over two years and, somehow, when I told her of my plans, a spark ignited within her to do the same. It wasn't that she was completely estranged from her parents; in fact, she spoke with her mother at least once weekly. It was her father, his staunch disgust for the life she had chosen, that kept her at a distance. This was all surprising to me, for I had remembered him as more enlightened than that. But then I thought about my father and Barry Glasser's mother, two people who couldn't have had less in common but reacted similarly when their children veered. Now Benny Kleinman was keeping company with them. Perhaps intolerance is infectious when it comes to one's own.

When Rebecca told me that she was also planning to go home, I felt a mixture of delight and fear—elated that I'd inspired her to reconnect with her father and afraid of the consequences of his knowing about our relationship. She had already told her mother that she ran into me in the library and had invited me for dinner, and I was sure that Benny's ear was not far off. All that was left to tell them was the extent of our involvement.

I knew that there was little Benny could do to stand between us at this point. Things were very much different now. What I didn't know was whether he would come clean and divulge exactly what it was that we were facing, whether he would reveal the terrible secret that had once so heartlessly broken us apart.

For me, there was another matter as well. Beyond the mystery, and the anticipated results of its uncovering, there was the fact of *Rabbi* Rebecca. And however fierce Benny Kleinman's reaction to this may have been, I was convinced it wouldn't hold a candle to my father's. Especially once he learned of my involvement with her.

On the Friday before Labor Day I took the subway to Brooklyn. I sat in a stupor, reflecting on all the suffering I had already caused my father in the brief twenty-four years of my existence. I thought of his broken dreams and my yet unfulfilled dreams. I thought of his failing heart, which had suffered yet another attack a few years back. And I thought of my mother, of her gentle power, infinite patience, and forbearance, and wondered if she too could weather the storm that was to come.

When I arrived home, my mother was in the kitchen, still in the throes of preparing an elaborate *Shabbos* dinner. A redolent aroma immediately hit me. It was the scent of homemade *chal-*

lah, gefilte fish, chicken soup, *kugel,* and a host of other delicacies she was planning to stuff me with. Bribery to inspire more frequent visits.

Upon hearing me enter the house, she called out to see if it was my father. Without answering, I walked into the kitchen and then said, "No, Mama, it's me."

She stopped what she was doing, turned around, and stood silently for a second just looking at me. She appeared exactly as she had on my last visit about three months earlier, almost the same as she looked when I was a child. The years had not stripped one iota of her fairness.

She came toward me, a pot holder still dangling in her hand. She took both my shoulders, drew me to her, hugged me intensely, kissed me hard on my right cheek, and said into the same ear, "I'm glad you've come." The pot holder was wedged between her hand and my body.

"I'm glad too," I responded, almost sadly.

"Come, come and sit here"—as she walked me over to a chair—"and tell me how you are."

"But Mama, I just spoke to you yesterday and everything is the same."

"Well, how was your trip."

"What trip?"

"The trip coming here! What else would I be talking about?"

"Mama, that's not exactly a trip. It's more like a ride."

"Opp, there's my Yankeleh, a Talmudic scholar and philosopher all in one, making differences between trips and rides. Tell me," she continued humorously, "do they teach you anything else over there in Manhattan?"

"Oh, many things, Mama," I responded with a smile, "and I would like to share them with you," I said more seriously, "but, tell me does *Totta* know I'm here?"

"Of course he does, and he would have been here to greet you except he probably got caught up in something or other at the yeshiva."

She seemed a bit disturbed at having to make excuses for him. But that was her vocation, forever the peacemaker. And before either of us could say anything else, we heard the sound of the front door opening.

"There he is right now," she declared excitedly. "Duvid, is that you? Come in here! Yankeleh's here with me."

He appeared in the entrance of the kitchen. Unlike my mother, he had aged in the past three months. His face looked worn, almost lifeless. His cheeks seemed to droop more than before, his wrinkles seemed more pronounced, his eyes were red and tired, and his hair was completely gray. I thought of how the long intervals between visits had afforded me the displeasure of witnessing a deterioration that more continuous contact would most probably have masked.

"Yankel, you look well," he stated.

"You don't," I responded truthfully, intimating enough concern to erase what otherwise might be interpreted as disrespect.

"I'm fine," he reacted plainly, "I just need to go upstairs, take a quick shower and shave before *Shabbos,* and then I'll even feel much better."

He asked my mother if there was anything she needed him to help her with and when she declined, he excused himself. I, too, went upstairs to unpack my bag, change, and shower, to prepare to go with my father to *shul* for Friday evening services. On my way to my room I passed the closed door to his study. Always closed, whether occupied or not. I stopped for a second and just looked at it. I have never been able to pass that door without noting its existence.

Just before leaving the house, the three of us gathered in the kitchen where my mother lit the Sabbath candles. She wasn't wearing her *sheitel,* so instead she took the pot holder and placed it on top of her head for a covering while reciting the blessing: "Blessed are You, Lord our God, Who has sanctified us with His commandments in commanding us to kindle the Sabbath candles." As she spoke these words, she took her hands and waved them gently in a circular motion over the flames three times as if she were trying to bring the warmth closer to her body.

When she was done, we all turned to one another to say *gut Shabbos.* My mother and father kissed; my mother kissed me on the cheek; my father and I looked at each other and nodded. Then we left for *shul.* It was a short walk, only two blocks. The silence made it seem much longer.

The *davening* was perfunctory: the usual tunes, the annoying chattering amongst the men in the back, and my father sitting up on his podium, seemingly oblivious to the world around him. I sat in the pews with my uncle Zelig who explained his son's absence as the result of a bad cold. On the way to *shul* my father had informed me, in a suspicious tone, that Chaim had been under the weather for several weeks. "But it seems to affect him only when it involves coming to *shul;* otherwise I see him all over the place," he related.

At the other end of the row sat Ezra, with his eyes glued either to the page of his prayer book or my father's face. He had gained much fame in the community as a young rabbinical scholar, a true follower in his teacher's path. On the rare occasions on which my father and I spoke, Ezra's name inevitably came up. I was constantly reminded of his marriage to the famous Rabbi Sharfman's daughter, his success in teaching in the yeshiva, his popularity with the young students, and the plans for him to become the assistant rabbi in my father's synagogue.

And what did Ezra know of me? Nothing from my father, I was certain; but a great deal, nonetheless. After all, he had had the sole privilege of bearing witness to the genesis of my incredulity. And for this, I had always felt okay with him. Despite the absence of any real relationship between us, the past had left us with a bond.

I was never jealous of him; in fact, I had grown to be sort of thankful for his presence. He was a stabilizing influence in my father's life, bringing him pleasure to ease the heartache I had created. In some ironic sense, it was Ezra's existence that allowed for mine. His obedience permitted my defiance; his loyalty enabled my irreverence. As long as he was there, I could be who I was without fearing my father's extinction. But now, with Rebecca in the picture, I was no longer sure that this would be the case.

At the conclusion of the service Ezra came over to greet me. We shook hands and he inquired about recent events in my life. Keeping matters superficial, I spoke of my upcoming *smichah* exams and life on the Upper West Side, all in the most general terms. Polite and boring. As I talked, he stared at me intently, showing extraordinary interest in whatever I was saying. He was undoubtedly sincere.

He joined us on our walk home, exchanging ideas on the weekly Torah portion with my father. It was a warm, still night. The sky was clear and the stars were visible, even from these Brooklyn streets. I kept up with them, pretending to listen. But my thoughts were really of Rebecca, wondering how her *Shabbos* was going, curious about what she was doing at this very moment. Suddenly I heard Ezra say, "What do you think, Yankel?"

Think about what, I asked myself. "I'm sorry, I wasn't listening," I explained abashedly.

"Your father and I were talking about the Torah reading tomorrow in which God says that we have a choice between 'life and death' and 'the blessing and the curse.' It's a problem, you know. I mean, if everything is predestined by God, then how can He also give us a choice? It's a contradiction, do you get what I mean?"

My father kept walking silently as they awaited my response. "Yes, it does sound like quite a contradiction," I said almost patronizingly. "Do you have a solution?"

"Well, Maimonides says that a person can spend his entire life trying to solve this problem and never come up with a solution."

"Is that your answer?" I queried, a bit more curtly than intended. I saw my father's face begin to anger at my subtle impudence.

"Actually, I heard an interesting answer from my father-in-law. He said that God is not bound by the notions of past, present, and future. He even quoted Einstein's theory that time is dependent on space and matter, and since God is pure spirit, time and space don't exist for Him as they do for us. So, for God, the question of predetermination isn't really a question."

A surprisingly sophisticated analysis, I thought, and one that was not entirely unfamiliar to me. But in truth, with abstruse questions such as these, one can answer with just about anything. There's simply no way to prove an answer as either true or false. That's why many modern philosophers have come to regard discussions about metaphysical matters as basically meaningless.

I chose not to share that with them, however. Not only because it wouldn't be wise under the circumstances, but also because—notwithstanding the sneering of my graduate school compatriots—I was still very much preoccupied with metaphysical problems of my own. It would have been disingenuous of me to advance a position that I didn't find compelling.

"That's an interesting answer, but it really doesn't address the question of freedom of choice," I responded. We had arrived in front of our house.

"Well, I guess we won't be able to solve all the problems of Judaism tonight," my father intruded.

"I guess not," I murmured under my breath.

Ezra just smiled, said *gut Shabbos,* and continued on his way.

It was during dinner that I had planned to tell my parents about Rebecca. I was hesitant, only because of my father's frail appearance. But by the time dessert came around, the three of us were just sitting, waiting for him to start the after-meal prayers, and it seemed as good a time as any.

"I met a girl," I stated plainly.

They had both long abandoned any hopes of finding me a *shiddoch* from amongst their ranks, so I thought at least this piece of the news would be well received. I was partially correct. My mother smiled enthusiastically, but my father remained reserved. He would wait to hear the entire story. That made me even more nervous.

"Where is she from?" was my mother's first question. Natural enough, but with the hidden agenda of finding out if Rebecca was from a community where Orthodox Jews lived.

"Her family lives in Woodmere," I answered ardently, hoping that the remaining probes would be as easy to satisfy.

"What's her name?" she asked. My father still sat silently, observing.

"Rebecca."

"*Nu,* Yankeleh, tell me about her, or do we have to sit here and play twenty questions all night?" she pleaded.

And so I told them the story of how we met originally—keeping it all extremely innocent—and how we ran into each other again. I told them what she looked like, what her family was like, and of some of the things we had done together over the past few weeks. I made it all sound quite proper, and artfully avoided any problematic details such as last names and vocational plans. I hoped I could get away with it.

"So what is her family name?" my father finally injected. Nice try.

"Kleinman," I responded without a moment's pause, feigning ignorance of any problem. Seek and ye shall find, I thought to myself.

"Kleinman," he repeated as he looked toward my mother. The excitement on her face suddenly turned to apprehension. "Is she related to a Benjamin Kleinman, perhaps an uncle or a cousin?" he inquired softly.

"Her father, actually," I responded. "Why, do you know him?" Not a bad performance.

"Oh yes," he said, again softly, with eyes fixed on my mother.

"From where?" I continued.

"It's getting late, I think we should *bench* already," my

mother agilely interrupted, referring to the recitation of the prayers for after eating.

"But I want to . . ."

"Yes, we should *bench,"* my father reflected, cutting me off.

"Wait, what's going on here?" I shouted. "Is there some family secret that I'm the only one not to know?"

"Does her father know about you?" he asked.

"Yes." At least he did in the past, and probably would again soon, if not already.

"And he's never let on that there's a connection?" he probed.

"The truth?" I paused, and he nodded affirmatively. "He's mentioned it but has refused to elaborate."

"Uh-huh," he mused.

"So, what's the big secret?" I pressed.

"Tell me, Yankeleh, you love this girl?" my mother asked abruptly.

"I . . ." obvious lack of conviction, "think so."

"It's not important, what has happened in the past. It's done and over with. What's important is how the two of you feel," she continued.

My father seemed to ignore us both and began his prayers. It was so typical for him to finagle his way out of the conversation like this. I was about to disturb him when she signaled not to. I complied, knowing I wasn't going to win, not then.

Leaving well enough alone was, of course, partially to my advantage. If they didn't want to talk about their little secret, then I didn't have to divulge mine. *Quid pro quo!* Spiteful, but reasonable. And anyway, there was the chance that Rebecca had run into better luck than I, that her parents had been more forthcoming. If so, I could delay telling them the whole story indefinitely.

The next day at lunch, it was as if I'd never made mention of Rebecca at all. The three of us were surprisingly adept at playing make-believe. My father hummed a Sabbath melody while he ate, spoke with my mother about the latest synagogue business, and even indulged me with some conversation.

"So, what do you *really* think about Ezra's analysis regarding freedom of choice?" he asked as he stroked his goatee.

"I'm sorry," I responded, not having heard him because my mind was elsewhere.

"Ezra's analysis last night on the way home from *shul,* you remember it, don't you?"

"Um, yes . . . what about it?" I was caught totally off guard. Of all things to talk about from last night, and he chooses this.

"Well, what did you think of it?"

"I thought it was interesting, as I said, but that it didn't really answer the question." I could feel the nervousness in my voice. What was he up to with this? My mother sat there, observing us, taking pleasure in the fact that we were interacting, a sight she so seldom witnessed.

"And you think there is a better answer to this question?" he asked with a mildly arrogant smirk.

"No, in fact, I think there is *no* answer to it."

He stared at me intently, his fingers twirling the ends of some beard hairs much as one would a frayed wire, waiting for me to say more. I was still confounded by the entire line of questioning.

"The problem, as I see it, is a contradiction, plain and simple," I began. "Ezra seems to have a need for a solution, but there is none. If God is all-knowing and, as such, can see the future, then there is no such thing as freedom of choice."

"Then why did you ask Ezra for an answer? Were you baiting him?" Insightful.

As you are doing to me now, I thought to myself. "I was just making conversation." Defensive.

He paused for a moment. "But what about what Ezra's father-in-law, Rabbi Sharfman, says?" Now, his tone seemed genuinely curious. He must have been testing me, using this issue to probe my mind, to see where my head was at these days. Was I so far gone as to have the audacity to criticize an esteemed scholar like Rabbi Sharfman? That was what he was after. I wasn't sure how honest to be, but decided go for broke.

"Truthfully, I don't understand what Rabbi Sharfman means. To me, it seems like a form of linguistic trickery to get around the question. And, as Ezra himself pointed out, Maimonides says that one could ponder this question for a lifetime and never find an answer."

"But that doesn't mean that there is no answer," he reacted quickly.

"I guess not," I responded, unsure of how far I could take this.

"It seems that you have learned some things in that university of yours," he observed, half sarcastically, half admiringly.

I was wordless, even more confused.

"Perhaps you are right, perhaps there is no answer," he added. "After all, what does it mean to say that there is an answer but we can never know it. Then how is it an answer? It is self-contradictory to speak of answers that cannot be known." His voice became low, introspective. "When they are known, they are answers. Until then, they are only mysteries. You agree, Yankel?"

I sure did, but I was too dumbfounded to respond. It was shocking to discover that my father was much more the philosopher than I'd ever thought him to be, that perhaps there was some common ground for us. It was humbling to have been mistaken about his motives in this conversation. He wanted, it seemed, only to chat. Utterly uncharacteristic of him, yet so wise under the circumstances.

He gave me a knowing look, and then stared off into space. His mouth opened again to break the silence, but this time a melody came out. It was the same slow, soft tune that he usually sang at the *Shabbos* table, the same tune his father and grandfather had sung at their tables. It had no words, but his gentle, melodious voice filled it with meaning. I had been used to hearing him sing over the years, but never so much as now was the sweetness of his voice apparent. It was incongruous for such an austere man to be able to sing like that, but at this moment it seemed fitting.

My mother sat and watched as he disappeared into the song, his eyes closed, his body swaying casually from side to side. Usually at this time, she and I would be clearing the table. Not now. She sat still, her eyes fixed on him lovingly. I could see tears welling up in them, but she kept her composure.

How little I knew of their relationship, how little I understood of what went on between them. I'd always thought their union was guided by tradition and responsibility, and never imagined that she was actually in love with him. But now I could see I'd been mistaken, that there was much more. Much more to him, much more to her, much more to this little world I'd once believed I had figured out.

After the evening service, my father and I returned home to recite *Havdalah,* the concluding ritual for the Sabbath. He sat in his chair, at the head of the dining-room table, and my mother held up a candle with three separate wicks, forming a robust and lustrous flame. He held the wine cup in his hand—filled to the brim to represent an abundance of felicity—and recited the blessing, acknowledging God for separating the Holy from the Profane, light from darkness, Israel from other nations, and the seventh day from the six days of creation. After completing the blessing he drank some of the wine and spilled the rest into a silver plate for my mother to use for extinguishing the candle. After she did so, he stood up, took each of his pinkies, dipped them in the wax-tainted wine, and rubbed them on his forehead and chest before placing them in his pockets. This customary gesture represented the hope that the *Havdalah* wine would bring with it wisdom, health, and affluence.

This had always been a special time; the three of us would sing a melody, wishing each other a good week, a week of peace and prosperity. We would pray for strength and hope that God would guide us through until the next *Shabbos* came. But tonight it was different. A dispirited look filled his eyes as he rendered the blessings. A sadness pervaded the air as we sang together. I watched the two of them in the light of the flickering candle, gazing at each other. They knew that I would soon be returning to the world outside, to that something from their past that had come back to haunt them.

The next morning I took the train back to the Upper West Side. Rebecca and I were scheduled to meet early that afternoon, so I used the hours in between to purchase some materials I would need for school. Both graduate school and Yeshiva were scheduled to start the day after Labor Day, as was Rebecca's rabbinical school. A day and a half for us before returning to the rough-and-tumble of our normal schedules.

The walk to her building was fraught with as much trepidation as the first time I had done it. When I arrived, Sandy the doorman was sitting up on his bench in full gear, and another baseball game was playing on the radio. A gay guy so enamored with baseball. Strange, I thought. Maybe he just enjoyed hearing about the boys running around the bases or something. It seemed that every time I encountered him I felt a need to undermine him.

He was his usual convivial self, fervently greeting me and probing about how things were going with "Ms. Kleinman." Obvious flirtation. He was always this way with me, and seemed to get quite a kick out of it. Once again, I was unnerved. But I responded politely until rescued by the elevator. I bid him goodbye with a sigh of relief as the doors closed.

As I entered Rebecca's apartment, the first thing I expressed was my exasperation at the "inappropriateness" of her doorman.

"Oh, lighten up!" was her reply.

"Lighten up? It's he who needs to lighten up. The guy's got a freaking crush on me!"

"So what? He's gay. He's got good taste," she jested.

Feeling both flattered and renewed in my manliness, I was able to let go of the anger. "Okay, let's forget that. Tell me, how was your weekend?"

"Do you really want to know how my weekend was, or do you want to know what I found out?"

"Did you find anything out?" I asked, not bothering to address her question.

"You mean you didn't?" Clever.

"God knows I tried. I told them about us and they admitted that they know your father, but beyond that they wouldn't budge. There must be some story there."

"There is. And a very unhappy one at that."

"Then you know." Well, tell me, said my expression.

"Come and sit down," she motioned as she led me to the couch.

"Okay, I'm sitting. So what's the big secret?"

She saw I was getting annoyed. "It's an amazing story, Yakov. The world is full of coincidences; the hand of God is everywhere."

"Rebecca," I said as I took her hand, "I don't want a lesson in theology. I want you to tell me straight, What's going on?"

"Okay," she began, stroking back the hair on my temples. "Our fathers were once the best of friends. From what I was told, they were friends from when they were children." By the strokes of her hand, I could tell this was going to hurt. She continued, "You know your father's heart problems, they didn't just start when he was forty."

I replied without words, only a look of complete bewilderment.

She went on. "Actually it all began when he was very young, just a child. He suffered from rheumatic fever and it left his heart damaged. My father tells me, though, that his mind was extremely strong, and while other kids were playing ball and running around, he was always inside studying and learning. My father stayed with him a lot. You have to understand, Yakov, they were really best friends," she said with tears in her eyes. "I think they loved each other deeply."

She stopped for a moment, gained her composure, then continued. "My father admitted that he could never keep up with your father in learning, and of that he was always envious. But the fact that he was physically healthy prevented him from feeling entirely inferior. He said that almost everything he learned about Torah was taught to him by your father, his closest friend, and that your father even made the rabbis look silly."

"They were best friends!" I reacted. "Unbelievable! And how could your father have kept such a secret when he knew who I was?"

"Let me finish the story and you'll understand everything." The look on her face told me that she really didn't want to be telling me any of this.

"Okay, go ahead," I muttered impatiently, "I'm sorry for interrupting."

"Don't be sorry for anything, Yakov," she continued. "When they were in their last year of high school, your grandfather arranged a *shiddoch* for your father. After meeting the woman a few times, I guess he believed he loved her, so they were to get married." At this point her voice started trembling.

She hesitated again, took a deep breath, and blurted out, "Yakov, the woman was my mother."

"What?" I shrieked.

"Your father was supposed to marry my mother."

"But that's . . ."

"I think you should let me finish the whole story."

She waited another moment and then continued, "About two months before the wedding, your father became very ill. It was something to do with the rheumatic fever; I think it was a heart attack."

"This is just impossible. There has to be some mistake, some misunderstanding!"

"Yakov, there's obviously a lot they didn't tell you. And a lot my parents didn't tell me. Until now. I guess they tell us only what they think we need to know."

"And they expect us to tell them everything! Well, go on!"

"Are you sure you want me to?"

I nodded. "Yes."

"It seems that my mother's parents called off the *shiddoch* because of your father's illness. He was in the hospital for almost two months; they didn't know whether he was even going to live!" Her tone was at once emphatic and apologetic.

"How did she end up with your father?" I asked.

"She had already known him through your father and after he got sick, they saw each other often at the hospital. They started talking and seeing each other, and I guess you can figure out the rest."

"And when my father got better?"

"By the time he was released from the hospital, they were already engaged. It was a scandal throughout the community. Your grandfather was so angry that he refused to allow my father to study at Mirrer any longer. That's how he ended up going to Yeshiva University."

"My poor father, it must have destroyed him. I never imagined that he had to endure such pain," I lamented.

She looked at me and squeezed my hand tightly before continuing. "My parents also know your mother from those days, and they tell me she's quite exceptional."

"You're trying to console me," I responded cynically.

"No I'm not. I really mean it. Your mother had to be quite special to have married your father and built a life with him knowing of his affection for another woman. I also understand she's quite beautiful and could have had her pick of the lot."

"This is really amazing," I reflected, completely stunned. "And to think, you could have been my sister." A touch of levity.

"I am your sister," she responded in all seriousness, "your soul sister. Don't you see? This was all part of God's plan, to bring us together like this, as lovers. We could never have ended up this way if things hadn't happened as they did. Our relationship is the phoenix that rises from these ashes," she offered dramatically. "It's God's hand! Everything has happened just as it was meant to happen."

"You sound exactly like a rabbi."

"I intended to."

"And you really believe that there's a divine plan behind this?"

"I believe there's a divine plan behind everything."

"And what did they think about us being together?" I asked.

"At this point, they're not against it like they were years ago. Too many things have changed since then."

No doubt about that, I reflected privately.

She continued, "They were worried about how your parents might react, but as far as they're concerned, I think they're even relieved that I'm with you. After all, you're 'Orthodox.' " She laughed as she said that.

"That's a good one," I countered.

I sat quietly for a few minutes—there was much to digest. My thoughts focused on my father, the anguish he must have experienced, and the inevitable reliving of this anguish that was now to haunt him all over again. All because of me. I, his only child—another undeserved affliction—was never destined to bring him even a morsel of pleasure. Only pain. Over and over again. And my mother, with her unbounded love and acceptance, would I finally bring her to the brink of collapse as well?

And then there was the image of the great Rabbi David Eisen, caught up in a love triangle, betrayed by his closest friend to whom he lost his betrothed. The saintly exalted scholar brought down by the world of carnality, tangled in a web of romantic strife and perfidy. This was a twist I would need much time to absorb.

Last of all, I pondered the term *lovers,* Rebecca's chosen description of our relationship. A designation that I knew in my heart was accurate, but felt uneasy with. Not wanting to open that can of worms, I let it be. There were too many other things I had to settle inside myself. And by my silence, I hoped she was able to glean an impression of acquiescence.

Suddenly, she reached toward me with both arms, brought her hands to the back of my neck, and drew herself closer, her face approaching mine. The next thing I knew, our lips were touching. It was a gentle and short kiss, but infused with passion. Afterward, her face was about four inches from mine, just enough distance to gain focus, and we stared at each other for a few seconds. She then moved toward me again, and this time the kiss was long and deep.

We stayed there, kissing and hugging. That was all we did, for doing anything more than that would have most definitely undermined the tenderness of the moment. It was simple and nice. It was what we both needed at the time.

CHAPTER 17

PROFESSOR WALDMAN sat at the head of an empty long rectangular table in a seminar conference room on the fifth floor of the humanities building. He was in his mid-forties, a short man about five feet four inches with a slightly bulging potbelly, puffy cheeks, swelled lips, deep brown eyes hidden behind circular wire-rimmed glasses, and thick curly black hair atop his head. As usual, he was sucking on a Corona, the stench of which was but a mild discomfort to his devoted students.

In keeping with the customary visage of professional intellects, Waldman's early autumn garb was most informal: a faded cotton mesh polo shirt, lightweight baggy khaki jeans, and dirty white deck shoes without socks. When the weather cooled off, he would change to one of his more authentically academic Harris Tweed jackets over an oxford button-down collar shirt, a knit tie, pleated sport slacks, and suede shoes with rubber soles. And yes, argyle socks. The Professor, to a tee.

I was the first student to enter, about five minutes before the scheduled time of the class. Waldman was so engrossed in what he was reading that he didn't notice me. I placed my briefcase on the table in front of one of the chairs, and the vibration caused him to look up.

"Mr. Eisen, my friend, long time no see. How was your summer? Productive and elucidating, I hope?"

"So do I," I replied. "I think I have something for you," I

mentioned, referring of course to the dissertation, the same matter he was inquiring about.

"Then we must set up an appointment to meet as soon as possible," he offered enthusiastically.

His manner was pleasant, but beneath the veneer of amiability endured a difficult and neurotically exacting temperament. I wondered what stumbling blocks yet waited along the way, what new analyses and demands he was still to conjure up. He was a tough man to please; no doubt, one of the qualities that most attracted me to him.

"And how was your summer?" I asked.

"Very nice, thank you, and quite fruitful I might add—as you will, no doubt, see. I spent many tedious hours in preparation for this very seminar, and I think I have some unprecedented insights to offer, perhaps even publishable. But I will have to let my students evaluate that; they're always the best judges of this sort of thing."

"I'm glad you have such faith in us," I said with a smirk.

"Oh, most certainly I do. Especially you, my friend; I expect great things from you," he stated emphatically.

Wonderful, I thought, another person to disappoint. Before I could say anything else, three other students entered the room and his attention automatically shifted to acknowledging their arrival.

"Good, it looks like we're all present, so now we can begin," he enjoined.

It wasn't unusual that there were only four students in this seminar. There were very few students in the philosophy program altogether, and among them there was a distinct paucity of those who were disposed to take a seminar with Waldman. I was the only one crazy enough to choose him as a dissertation advisor.

The subject of this class was a critical evaluation of Friedrich Nietzsche's *Beyond Good and Evil,* the seminal work in which the noted philosopher put forth his ideas regarding the source of ethics and the influence of religion in society. Waldman had a particular affinity for Nietzsche, arising from the controversy concerning the philosopher's influence on the emergence of Nazism in Europe. Waldman believed Nietzsche had been given a bum rap and was misunderstood by historians who connected the rise of the Third Reich with the philosopher's notion of the *ubermensch,* the superman who creates his own morality, a "master morality" as Nietzsche called it. He argued that while Hitler might have believed himself to personify the *ubermensch,* this was a gross bastardization of Nietzsche's intention.

For Waldman, Nietzsche was a hero. The philosopher's exoneration had been, in fact, the topic of his own dissertation twenty years earlier at Harvard. And to this day, almost all his seminars dealt with Nietzsche's ideas in one form or another.

But the matter ran much deeper. Waldman's own parents had been survivors of concentration camps, and in his work on Nietzsche he found an opportunity to extricate himself from the severe emotional constraints that his childhood must have imposed. By successfully exercising objectivity over even a single historical aspect of the Holocaust, he afforded himself the freedom to rise above it, to somehow gain a semblance of control over what to a child of survivors would have seemed insurmountable.

In a larger sense, this was the essence of his persona. The painstaking efforts he took to analyze virtually all aspects of his experience were merely neurotic means of defending against the anguish of his past. In this, I found him to be a kindred spirit.

"Let us not waste any more time, because we have only one semester to arrive at a true understanding of Nietzsche," he began. "And the purpose of this seminar is to learn how to read him, a difficult task indeed. In fact, some of the most well-known, self-proclaimed experts haven't yet mastered this basic skill, and we have but four short months. Are there any questions?"

No one said a word.

"Good, then let us begin. Mr. Eisen, how would you encapsulate Nietzsche's view of morality?"

"I would say he was amoral," I answered tersely.

"And why would you say that?" he solicited.

"Because he rejected morality as we understand it. He believed that democracy was a morality for slaves because it advocated that all men were created equal. He rejected the morality of Christianity because it had too much pity for the downcast."

"So now that you've told us what he didn't believe, enlighten us as to what he did believe."

"That's where it gets unclear to me. He speaks of a division in humanity, between the weak and the strong, or between 'supermen' and 'slaves.' He seems to indicate that morality should be determined by the strong, and the weak should be compelled to comply."

"Sounds like fascism to me," Waldman said snidely.

"To me, too," I replied.

"But that's where the mistake lies. You cannot just read what a man writes without knowing *how* to read him. First, Nietzsche wrote polemically. He purposely phrased himself provocatively, to stir up severe reactions among readers. He wanted to infuriate, to disturb, so he often exaggerated. And he obviously has succeeded in your case, Mr. Eisen.

"As philosophy scholars, we know that beyond the veneer there is much subtlety. We are not misled by appearances. True, Nietzsche rejected the morality of his culture, but this did not make him amoral. True, he sought the emergence of a master race, but only for the purpose of creating an even more rigorous code of ethical behavior. He believed that the *ubermensch* should be the purist representative of morality, not a Nazi barbarian."

"I know that *you* believe that," I responded, "but where in this text does it say what you claim?"

"Ah, good question, Mr. Eisen, and that is precisely what I will show you."

The others in the room remained silent.

"Now, Ms. Avery," he said, referring to the only woman amongst us, "why don't you begin reading on page one."

The other students exchanged looks of exasperation; this was going to be a page-by-page, even word-by-word reconnaissance. I, on the other hand, being well schooled in Talmudic exposition, was most comfortable with this technique. Sharon Avery began reading, and the search for truth commenced.

CHAPTER 18

THE JEWISH NEW YEAR came late that year. For Rebecca, this was to be a particularly special Rosh Hashanah. She had been invited by the rabbi of her synagogue, who was also one of her professors, to apprentice with him over the high holidays by serving as assistant rabbi. A distinct honor considering that many of the students competed for such prominent internships.

For me, however, it presented another major conflict. She had extended the invitation, or rather the challenge, to me to attend the services. The synagogue was within walking distance, so the only excuse left was the problem of not going home to my parents. Although I'd never missed a Rosh Hashanah with them, using that excuse at this point would have been an obvious cop-out. I could also have invoked some principle forbidding me from participating in a Reform service, but Rebecca would have taken me to task on that as well. So I was left with one option: to accept.

The compromise I had conjured up in my mind was to wake up sufficiently early, so I could *daven* at home first. Thus, I would exercise my obligation as an Orthodox Jew first, and then go to her temple to try out the part of a Reform Jew. So I woke at seven, donned my *tallis,* and began reciting the morning service for Rosh Hashanah. The prayers are replete with references to God as "King" and to the holiday as a Day of Judgment. The liturgy is, of course, much longer than usual, containing special poems and supplications devised specifically around these themes. The overall message is that God watches over each individual and that there is accountability for *all* our actions; that there is a judge and ultimate justice; and that we have ten days to repent for our transgressions, starting with Rosh Hashanah and culminating on Yom Kippur. While I neglected the traditional reading of the Torah, a ritual that requires the presence of a *minyan,* ten men, I did make provisions to borrow a *shofar,* a ram's horn, from a friend, and blew the obligatory hundred blasts. I was surprised not to have incited any neighborly recriminations for the piercing howls emanating from my premises.

It took me two hours to finish the entire service without an omission. It was the first time I had prayed these particular prayers outside the walls of my father's synagogue, and, moreover, it was the first time I had actually thought about the meaning of what I was saying. Unsure of the extent of my credence, I went through all the motions obediently and, somehow, felt relieved at having done so.

I arrived at Temple Israel at about nine-forty-five; the service was scheduled to begin at ten. The sanctuary, at first glance, seemed enormous, but after looking closer I noticed that there was actually a movable wall that had been opened to create one large auditorium out of what had originally been two separate rooms. I learned later, from Rebecca, that the back half was a catering hall and that the expansion was used only on the high holidays to accommodate the overflow crowd. This was an odd concept to me, having grown up in a synagogue where the same number of people attended all year round.

The sanctuary itself contained about twenty-five rows of wooden pews with an aisle down the middle. The pews were padded with maroon-colored cushions that matched the carpeting. In the front was a podium, three steps high, and in the middle of the podium, against the wall, was the ark. It was the most majestic ark I had ever seen, about fifteen feet tall and ten feet wide, made of hammered bronze and shaped into a giant image of the tablets of the Ten Commandments. On the doors of the ark, also in bronze, were forged the Hebrew abbreviations of the commandments, five on each door in the traditional manner. To the left of the ark were four large wooden chairs and a few feet in front of these, facing the congregation, was the rabbi's pulpit. In the chair closest to the ark sat the rabbi, and next to him sat the president and vice president of the congregation. Rebecca sat in the last chair. On the other side of the ark was a similar arrangement, with the cantor's *bima* in front, again facing the congregation. Off to the left of the *bima* stood a large wooden organ with rising silver pipes and several layers of keyboards.

The wall behind the podium was a glistening brown marble, with three narrow stained-glass windows that ran from ceiling to floor on either side of the ark. As I faced the ark, the wall to the left was the same type of marble and covered with memorial plaques. To the right, upon a white wall, was a resplendently colored collage symbolizing the seven days of creation.

As I was looking around, an usher approached me and offered to help me locate my seat. I handed him the ticket Rebecca had given me. Fortunately, I was escorted to a most desirable location in the pews, fifth row, center, in front of the rabbi's pulpit.

As I was about to sit down, I caught sight of Rebecca glancing in my direction. She threw me a smile and I returned one in kind. Seeing how uncomfortable I must have appeared, she mouthed the words "just relax," and discretely winked an eye. I mouthed back, "okay," and winked as well.

I looked around and noticed that there were a handful of individuals among the hundreds present, who like Rebecca and me were actually wearing yarmulkes. The rabbi wasn't one of them. He was distinguished, however, by the majestic white robe that covered him down to his ankles, and the thin silk replica of a *tallis* draped around his shoulders like a scarf. This was in sharp contrast to the traditional full-body shawl which Rebecca wore. I wondered why he chose to wear any sort of *tallis* yet no yarmulke, but resolved on this day of judgment to be more concerned with my own inconsistencies than with those of others.

Suddenly, the rabbi rose from his chair and approached the pulpit. Silence magically descended upon the audience as he simply stood there and looked outward. After a brief moment, he leaned toward the microphone and announced, "Our Rosh Hashanah morning service will now commence, and the cantor will begin chanting from the *Gates of Repentance* prayer book beginning on page seventy-nine." His deep resonant voice filled the hall almost as if God himself were speaking from on high.

The cantor, an imposing, overweight gentleman with a perfectly round face, and also in a long white gown—but no scarf—stood behind his *bima*. A loud chord rang out from the organ, which he then matched with his voice as he began to chant. The first words he sang were familiar, a Hebrew hymn from the Book of Psalms. In addition to the organ, he was accompanied by a choir of eight, four men and four women, all dressed in white gowns. When his rather lengthy rendition was concluded, the rabbi led the congregation in responsive reading of English prayers. As the service continued, the rabbi's English portions alternated with the cantor's Hebrew highlights.

The congregants, for the most part, participated actively in both the Hebrew and English. There was a familiarity with the melodies and prayers that impressed me. But most extraordinary was the decorum. Unlike the *shuls* I was accustomed to, there were no conversations in the back and the rabbi never had to stop the cantor to wait for quiet.

The service progressed in this manner, abbreviated Hebrew segments from the traditional liturgy mixed with English compositions, both traditional and contemporary. The Torah reading was abbreviated as well, but that didn't bother me too much. Alas, I felt like a full-fledged Reform Jew—I was accepting scattered bits and pieces of the religion with the justification that it is better to have *some* than none.

After the Torah reading, the rabbi delivered his sermon. He was a powerful speaker, charismatic with a sharp wit. He spoke of the universality of the message of Rosh Hashanah, and how, in his view, the *shofar* represents the calling of humankind to awaken to its moral responsibilities and obligations. As an allegory, he used the biblical story in which God provides a ram for Abraham to sacrifice instead of Isaac, the horn symbolizing the abandonment of evil, the abdication of the commonly practiced ancient ritual of sacrificing children. And then, in brilliant homiletic style, he spoke of the ways in which we sacrifice our own children every day in our society.

His speech was unlike the bookish, esoteric orations I was accustomed to. He used text not to prove his point, but rather to illustrate it. He did not speak of parochial and exclusive Jewish interests, but rather of universal and inclusive ones. On the other hand, I wondered about the implications of his message. Maybe I was being too much the philosophy student, but what exactly did he mean by moral responsibilities? Whose morality should be practiced—his? Mine? Marx's? Hitler's? Of course, he was referring to so called Judeo-Christian morality, an ambiguous notion considering, for example, the practice of polygamy among many Sephardic Jews and Mormons. I made a mental note to take this up with Rebecca later, wondering if she too was perplexed by this.

At the conclusion of the speech, the rabbi asked all to rise, and the service for the sounding of the *shofar* began. It was here that Rebecca performed her rabbinical function, taking the rabbi's place in leading the English portions while he blew the horn. At first she seemed nervous. Her voice trembled ever so slightly, but after a few moments she gained her composure and went on like an old pro. I even managed to make fleeting eye contact with her a few times during the recitations; we exchanged faint smiles. I knew she was happy that I was there, and that made me happy as well. I wasn't sure, however, of my own feelings about being there.

When the service ended, I tried to make my way toward the podium where Rebecca, the rabbi, and the cantor were surrounded by a bevy of well-wishers. It took a few moments to get through the crowd, and as soon as I was within arm's reach, Rebecca grabbed my hand and pulled me in to stand beside her and the rabbi. He was busily greeting the congregants, but she nevertheless put her hand on his shoulder to get his attention. When he turned to us she opened her hand, gesturing toward me, and said, "Rabbi Samuels, this is Yakov Eisen, the friend I've been telling you about."

"Ah, yes," he responded, "the rabbinical student from Yeshiva. Welcome to our temple; this must be a big change for you," he continued in an inquisitive tone.

"It's a first," I answered politely.

"Well, I'd like to hear your impressions. I don't know whether Rebecca told you, but I'm also a graduate of Yeshiva University," he said with an innocent smile.

"No, she didn't," I remarked with an astonished look.

"Not the rabbinical school," he clarified, "but the college."

"Oh," I said, relieved that my father's words had not been borne out. The crowd continued to surround us, with several congregants bidding for his attention.

"Well, I'd like to speak with you more, but as you can see, duty calls." He held out his hand to shake mine; we exchanged the traditional greeting, *shannah tovah,* for a happy new year. He smiled at Rebecca and planted a New Year's kiss on her cheek—for a job well done, no doubt—and then turned back toward the crowd.

Rebecca watched him disappear into the gathering, turned to me, and said, "I do hope you get to meet him again under better circumstances; he really is a very special man. The two of you would have so much to talk about. He is incredibly brilliant and interesting, you know."

"Yes, you've told me that," I remarked impatiently.

"Well I just wanted to tell you again," she added with a smile, "in case you didn't hear me the first time."

She took my hand and escorted me down the steps and through a doorway immediately off the right side of the stage into a beautiful office, the rabbi's study. It was a large room with bookshelves covering every wall, deep brown carpeting, a huge mahogany desk, and several pieces of black leather furniture including an impressive soft black leather executive chair and similar couch. There was also a private bathroom which Rebecca used to freshen up and change out of her frock while I sat alone in one of the chairs facing the desk.

As I sat there, I looked around and noticed several plaques and frames hanging from the wood-paneled walls. Some of the frames contained certificates and awards from various community organizations, but the ones that caught my eye were pictures of the rabbi with such notables as John F. Kennedy and Martin Luther King. These photographs not only dated him, they also revealed much about his preferences and why Rebecca was so enamored of him.

When she emerged from the bathroom, she was wearing a simple black wool dress that ended midway between her knees and ankles and covered her arms just below the elbow. As usual, the modest style couldn't disguise the contours of her figure. Around her neck was a long strand of pearls falling neatly below her breast line. Draped over her elbow was the white gown.

"Don't you feel a bit silly in that?" I remarked, referring to the robe.

"Why, no, it's my *kittle,*" she replied, smirking. A *kittle* is a white gown, symbolizing purity, that Orthodox men customarily wear on the high holidays, at the Passover seder, when they get married, and when they die.

"I should have known," I reacted.

She smiled at me, lifted her hand to my face, and caressed my cheek. I raised my hand to meet hers, moved it around toward my lips, and gently kissed it as I wished her a *shannah tovah.* She then stood up on her toes, and kissed my lips ever so softly.

"Shannah tovah, and thank you for coming to watch me today. I know it wasn't an easy decision," she said as the rabbi and a group of other dignitaries entered the study.

"I hope I'm not interrupting anything," he declared with a friendly smile.

"Oh no, we were just leaving," Rebecca said.

We were off to her apartment for lunch. It would be just the two of us. No company. She had originally invited Bob and Stephanie, but they had a prior commitment.

On the way, we walked close to each other. A breeze blew her hair into my face. I was captured by the sweet scent. She took her hand, straightened her hair, and looked intensely into my eyes. We kept walking, brushing up against each other, both of us quiet, not allowing words to intrude. I had completely forgotten about where I'd been just a few minutes earlier. The temple, the service, the rabbi's speech—all the things I had so wanted to discuss with her—didn't matter.

CHAPTER 19

I WAS FORTUNATE during my first two years in rabbinical school to have qualified for Rav Liebowitz's exclusive Talmud class. Under his tutelage, in a large classroom on the fourth floor of Furst Hall, I and my fellow students gathered daily to explore the world of the Talmud. It was special, for Rav Liebowitz possessed an uncanny ability to elucidate passages that had previously seemed quite unintelligible. In contrast to his occasional reticence when he had taught secular philosophy, he always approached the Talmud with the full prowess of his creative energies and boldly traversed the outer limits of interpretation.

At the end of my second year, Rav Liebowitz had announced that he would not be returning in the fall, but would be taking a sabbatical to teach in Israel and finish writing his latest book. He hadn't known who was going to replace him, but had assured us that it would certainly be a suitable substitute. He couldn't have been more mistaken.

In his stead, the administration chose to promote Rabbi Eliezer Trachtenberg, one of the younger teachers in the rabbinical school who had gained prominence among the right wingers. It was indeed an odd choice considering the attributes of his predecessor, but it was a clear message of the direction in which the administration was moving. For me, it was disastrous. Trachtenberg would not only prove to be the most eccentric human being I've ever encountered, he would relentlessly torture me with his dogmatism and spurious sense of reality.

He was called "the *shoichet,*" or slaughterer, a title bestowed upon him because of his fame for failing students. It was also a pun on the subject matter he chose to teach; namely, a detailed analysis of the rules pertaining to the slaughtering of animals and proper preparation of kosher meat. For him and others of his mind-set, this was the most relevant area of Jewish law for rabbinical students to study. Matters such as medical or business ethics, family counseling, and the like seemed of little importance. It was how to slaughter an animal properly—the appropriate size and sharpness of the knife, how to soak and salt the meat—these were Trachtenberg's essentials for rabbis of the twentieth century.

Not to imply that Trachtenberg was actually of the twentieth century, for his entire *weltanschauung* was clearly of another time, at least several centuries earlier. His uniform consisted of a long black caftan and a wide-rimmed felt black hat, both of which had certainly been stylish in Poland during the 1600s. The buttons on the caftan were deliberately placed on the left side, symbolically representing a rejection of the Gentile world, in which buttons for men's jackets and coats are typically sewn on the right. Looking at him, I could readily imagine his sense of satisfaction at having defied the couturiers of France, Italy, and Taiwan.

His polyester tie and pants were also black, his shirt and socks were white, and his beard was a combination of the two. He was a large man—about six feet, two hundred and fifty pounds—making him even more overbearing. When he removed his hat, a large black velvet yarmulke sat upon his otherwise completely barren scalp. His beard, which had never been trimmed, descended well below his chest and camouflaged most of his face up to the natural line above the cheekbones. This was fortunate for him because it made him seem older than his forty-three years, an age far too young for the position he held. Most of his colleagues in the rabbinical school were at least a decade beyond him, and it was known that some resented his presence for that reason. Usually, scholars in their forties or early fifties taught only in the undergraduate school, for it was believed that wisdom, and the privilege of teaching in the rabbinical school, came with age. But Trachtenberg was special because he'd been recognized as a Talmudic genius of great distinction, and very few, regardless of their years, could match his intellect. He was also a favorite among the religious zealots.

And he did just about all he could to foster this image, not only with his appearance and ideas, but even with his accent. For while he was born and raised in Boston, he worked hard at emulating an Eastern European inflection. It wasn't very good.

And who was he really? Rumor had it that years ago he was pretty much a regular guy who looked and behaved in tune with his times. In fact, he had graduated at the top of his class from Yeshiva University and was accepted to Harvard Law School. The story goes that he actually attended the law school for two years. Until, one day, God spoke to him. Then he dropped out, married, moved to a very religious neighborhood in Monsey, New York, became a rabbi, and fathered nine children.

The true details were unknown, only that somewhere along the path a radical transformation occurred. Not that he simply grew more religious in appearance or observance, but that his integrity became vested in the total repudiation of his previous being. Leaving law school had become the proudest moment of his life. It was the power of this repudiation that fueled his extremism, and made him even more fanatical than his vaguely similar replicas from my days in the Brooklyn ghetto. The first time I met him I knew that he was going to outdo all the others. Not just another soldier in the army of God, but a general; perhaps even commander-in-chief.

It was the first day of classes. Trachtenberg entered the room at exactly one-thirty, carrying a large volume with his left arm while his right arm drooped down by his side. He stood erect and walked easily, much like a king, as he proceeded toward the gunmetal institutional teacher's desk at the head of the room. He placed himself in his seat behind the desk and looked out into the audience, scanning the faces of each of the fifty-three students, muttering "uh-huh" under his breath, with an approving nod as his eyes traversed the length and width of the classroom. Before saying a word, he motioned with his hands, signaling us to move our desks up closer to his, and continued this gesture until the most obedient respondents were literally touching his desk and surrounding him. I remained somewhere in the farthest rows, but—as I was yet to learn—not completely beyond his reach.

Without further delay, he opened the book, announced the page, and proceeded to recite the first legal dictum concerning who is fit to perform the *mitzvah* of slaughtering an animal. The verse read, "Anyone is permitted to slaughter, even women."

"But boys, are women really, eh, permitted to do this? Of course not! So why does the *Mechaber* say that they are? It is, eh, a very complicated matter, as we shall see."

I hated when he referred to us as "boys," which was just about all the time. There was some obvious pleasure he derived from this, from reminding us that we were not yet men in his eyes.

He continued his introduction, pointing out that the *Mechaber,* the author of the text—Rabbi Joseph Caro, who lived in Safed in the mid-sixteenth century—was a brilliant and complex man who, in keeping with typical rabbinical style, deliberately employed words and phrases that begged interpretation. And, no doubt, it was he, Rabbi Eliezer Trachtenberg, coming some four hundred years later, who would elucidate the faultless meaning of the text. Hearing this reminded me of Waldman discussing Nietzsche.

"His brain was like, eh, one of those, how do you say, electronic boxes that have knowledge?" he asked, pantomiming the form of a computer, and looking out into the class for a response.

Immediately, some *tuchus*-licker in the front row called out, "Computer, *rebbe,* computer!"

Thus was the introduction to my final year of rabbinical school. Rav Trachtenberg's feigned ignorance of modern technology would be displayed again and again as he tried to prove himself a child of the pre-modern era. But he was not to be underestimated. For he was only too keenly aware of precisely what he pretended not to be aware of, and behind his feeble masquerade lay an obvious agenda; namely, to inculcate an appreciation of antiquity through mocking modernity. And the sad truth was that some of my colleagues bought it, undermining all the things that our former teacher, Rav Liebowitz, had stood for. They chuckled when Trachtenberg denigrated contemporary ideas, not because it was humorous, but because they concurred. And I would sit and wonder why I had ever come to Yeshiva University. For this, I could have stayed put in Brooklyn.

The class concluded exactly at three o'clock. I quickly gathered my books and my jacket, and dashed out into the hall to catch the elevator. I couldn't help thinking that Trachtenberg's eyes observed my brisk exit. I thought about it until the elevator reached the ground floor, and then another idea took its place. I was hungry.

I entered Harry's restaurant and all appeared exactly as it had been almost three months earlier, the last time I'd been there. All except one crucial detail: Harry was nowhere to be seen. Behind the counter were two men who seemed to belong neither to the restaurant nor to the prevailing local subculture. They looked like Hasidim. When I inquired as to Harry's whereabouts, one of them informed me that Harry had sold the establishment to them during the summer. I probed to find out where he went, if he moved or got sick, but they had no information and even seemed disturbed by my questions.

I knew that Harry had lived in one of the four buildings on a very short stretch of 187th Street between Amsterdam Avenue and Laurel Hill Terrace, so I decided to see if he was still there. On the way, my mind raced with thoughts of Rav Trachtenberg, the two Hasidic men in the restaurant, and Yosi Katz, the infamous dorm counselor. This place was becoming inundated with black-hatters. What were they all doing here? Why didn't they stay in Brooklyn, or Europe, or wherever? Was there not anyplace I could find refuge from the images of my past?

The four buildings were identical, redbrick apartment houses built probably some time between the first and second world wars. This had been a flourishing Jewish community then, but all that was left were these few blocks adjacent to Yeshiva University, and the people who inhabited these buildings were either students, teachers, or shopkeepers like Harry. I wasn't quite sure how to go about finding him. I didn't know his last name; I had never bothered to ask.

I entered the first building and instinctively rang the buzzer for the super's apartment. An Hispanic voice came over the speaker. It was difficult communicating through the intercom, but I was able to persuade him to allow me into the building. I took the elevator down to the basement where the super lived, and when I got there, two large German shepherds who were tied to a railing barked furiously at me. The hallway was dark and musty. The stench of compacted garbage filled the air. Suddenly, a door opened at the end of the hall, and a man stuck his head out, ordering the dogs to silence. His voice was the one that had spoken to me over the intercom. He turned in my direction and inquired, once again, what I wanted. I tried describing Harry to him. It was a laborious effort; he spoke broken English, and I spoke no Spanish. Finally, after about five minutes of my using creative hand gestures to supplement my words, he nodded with a smile indicating that he figured out who I was referring to. He told me that the man I was looking for lived in apartment 5F in the building directly across the street. I wondered how he knew that, so I diplomatically asked him if he was certain. He told me he was the super for that building as well.

There was no need to ring the buzzer because other people just happened to be walking out at the same moment I was going in. I looked innocent enough, and assumed that was the reason they didn't stop me as I caught the door before it closed. I took the elevator to the fifth floor of what was a seven-story building. I came out into a dimly lit hallway with faded brown paint peeling from the ceiling and walls. Pieces of the falling paint covered the deteriorated white ceramic tile floor. The elevator door closed behind me with a loud thump that echoed through the corridor.

I decided to go to the right first, and passed a series of dark brown wooden doors, each with three or four locks, until I stood before 5F. I reluctantly pressed the buzzer. My heart started pounding. More racing thoughts. Was I intruding on the man's privacy? Maybe he didn't want any visitors.

"Who is der?" a voice from behind the door interjected.

"Yakov Eisen," I said hesitantly, coughing and clearing my throat from the nervousness.

"Who?" the voice repeated.

"Yakov, you know, Yakov from Brooklyn."

"Oh, yes," he responded and unlatched three locks.

He opened the door and when he looked at me it seemed as if he understood why I had come. He motioned for me to come in, and as I did he asked, "And vhat is it can I do for you, young man?"

"I just came," I hesitated, speaking softly under my breath, "to see how you are."

"Ah, I see," he responded, suspecting there was much more behind my visit.

He led me into his living room. The apartment was large, with tall ceilings and arched entrances to the kitchen, dining, and living rooms. The walls were abundantly decorated with paintings and photographs, all reflecting a world long before my birth. The people in the pictures looked to be family members, everyone appearing very European, and very religious. The poor lighting and the deep gray faces made darkness the dominant motif. The living room floor was covered by a frayed Persian area rug. The furniture was antique. Even the television was of substantial vintage.

As I looked around I saw how the surroundings reflected the life of the man who dwelt within. This was his existence, or what was left of it. The figures, the eyes, all peered out at him, communicating in a language I could never comprehend. The darkness was frightening and comforting at once.

The couch I sat on was covered by a wool blanket, probably to protect the already corroding upholstery. He sat across from me on a large chair that seemed big enough to seat three of his skinny withered torsos. The robustness of just a few short years ago had wilted, but I hadn't really noticed until now. He offered me some tea. I declined. Then we talked.

"I came to see you because I heard that you sold the store and I wanted to make sure everything was okay," I opened.

"Okay? Vhat couldn't be okay for an old man who is alone and tired." All the vitality had been stripped from his voice.

"Are you well?"

"As vell as can be expected."

"Do you need anything?" I was beginning to feel intrusive.

"As you can plainly see, I don't need much." He gestured to reveal his surroundings.

His spirit seemed completely crushed. At least with the restaurant he could feel he had a purpose. It gave him energy. Now, his appearance reflected the misery that he used to be able to hide, the anguish, and the pain. He had become one with the walls around him.

I glanced at a picture sitting on the end table. It was of a young woman, a beautiful innocent face, well rounded, full lips, dark eyebrows, and long wavy hair. I figured it was his wife.

"So you find my Anna pretty?" he commented with a trace

of the levity that used to accompany his words.

"I find her remarkable," I said with certainty.

"Yes," he hesitated with a deep breath, "That's vhat she vas." He stared into space.

"Harry," I interrupted his trance, "why did you sell the restaurant?"

He looked at me and paused once again. I said nothing more. Silence. After about thirty seconds he responded, "It was time. I am a tired old man."

I searched my mind for a fitting reply, but there was none to be found. He was completely depressed, and nothing I could offer would change that. I guess he had good reason. And he had fought so hard and so bravely for many years. But now he was tired, and it had all caught up with him. I accepted my helplessness and, in so doing, caught a glimpse of his experience.

After a few moments of more silence, I shifted into small talk. "The men you sold the restaurant to, isn't it strange that they would want a business here?"

"Not really. It's a very good business. Vhy should they not vant to make money from our yeshiva. Our money is green also."

"I guess I made more of it because I feel that things are changing around me."

"They are," he interrupted delicately. "Our yeshiva has been becoming a different place for quite some time, becoming probably like the place you came to us from."

I was not surprised that he remembered from so many years ago. His memory, after all, was all he had.

"And I have changed too," I proposed.

"Everything changes, Yakov from Brooklyn," he asserted with a faint smile.

"I feel as if I don't belong here."

"You don't belong here, you don't belong there. Vell, vhere exactly is it that you think you do belong?"

"I don't have an answer to that. That's the problem."

"This is no problem. You vill find your place. God vill help you, you vill see." Confidence.

"Do you really, honestly believe that?"

"Believe vhat? That you vill find your place, or that God vill help you?" He seemed proud of his cleverness; shades of the old Harry.

"The part about God."

"I believe both," he replied with utmost seriousness.

I watched him speak those words, and was moved by the conviction that accompanied them. He, who was stricken and abandoned by God in ways I could not even imagine, expressed his credence unquestionably. Who could argue with such a statement from such a man? Maybe the faces in the pictures on the walls, but not me. In his simplicity, I found the most compelling exposition of faith I'd heard to date.

We sat for a while longer. Again, in silence. It was beginning to seem like an appropriate time to leave. "Is there anything I can get for you?" I offered as I got up from the couch.

"I'm retired, not dead," he responded. Another hint of his old self. "But if you should maybe vant to visit again, that vould be fine."

"I will."

"God villing," he responded.

"God willing," I repeated.

He escorted me to the door and as I left he turned to me and said, "Buchenvald, that's vhere my Anna died."

CHAPTER 20

WALDMAN LEANED BACK in his tall cordovan leather chair as he puffed on what remained of his putrid cigar. "This has potential, Mr. Eisen, not bad at all," he remarked. I sat in silence as he perused the remaining pages of the proposal.

He placed the papers on his desk, removed the stogie from his mouth, turned to me, and asked, "Okay, so let's cut to the chase. In English, skipping all the psychobabble and philojargon, what exactly is it you intend to focus on?"

"It's all there, just as I have written it," I responded defensively.

"Yes, I know that. But I want you to put it into words that a common person could comprehend so that I am sure you, yourself, understand completely what it is you're doing." It seemed like an insult to me.

I looked at him nervously for a moment, and then responded. "I want to demonstrate how Freud's view of God and religion was influenced primarily by philosophical considerations, and that his psychological and scientific understanding of humans was only secondary."

"How could you ever demonstrate such a thing? How can you honestly divide these three disciplines so neatly? Don't they overlap in complex ways that are almost impossible to dissect? Do you see what I'm getting at?"

"I think so," I said tentatively.

"Maybe his position was influenced by all three of these variables equally? What affects the human mind and influences our ideas is a very complicated matter. My point, Mr. Eisen, is that you can't always reduce things to singular explanations. The true scholar understands this." He took a puff on his cigar, a sign of victory.

Suddenly I felt that I wasn't a true scholar in his eyes. He was so clearly correct that I didn't even bother trying to argue. Instead, like the sheepish little boy I had always been, I asked, "Well, what do you suggest?"

"As I said, you've got something here, but you need to rethink it. It's overly ambitious, maybe even unrealistic to prove that philosophy carried greater weight than psychology and science in the mind of a man who was so devoted to all three. Perhaps, instead of trying to reduce things to one single common denominator, you might consider thinking in terms of synthesis. *That* should be your topic, to show how all three disciplines contributed to his view of God, to demonstrate the interdependence of different fields of knowledge."

"But Freud himself attempted to reduce everything to one explicative factor, one simple way of understanding all phenomena."

"Early on that was true. But later he discovered that things couldn't be explained by the pleasure principle alone, so he had to come up with another factor, a more complex understanding of human nature than he'd originally conceived. This is a good lesson to learn, Mr. Eisen, that there are no singular explanations. Everything is multifaceted and can be viewed differently from different perspectives. The whole is simply much greater than the sum of its parts. I suggest you think about this. If you want to focus on the philosophical piece, that's okay, but demonstrate its interdependence with science and psychology, not its distinctiveness." He paused, stared into space for a moment, and took another puff before continuing, "And while you're at it, ask yourself why you seem to feel this need to find a singular explanation for things that are really rather complicated. Introspection is always healthy for the true philosophy scholar."

Oh yes, I guess I haven't done enough of that lately. Rebecca's going to love this one. Talk to the philosophy professor about Freud, and he becomes a psychoanalyst.

I arrived at my parents' house a few minutes after my father had already left for the synagogue. As I opened the front door, out of breath from running the three blocks from the subway station, my mother called out from the kitchen, "Yankeleh, you're late! Your father's already gone off to *shul,* and I'm just about to light candles."

"It's okay, Mama. You can light now. I don't need to shower. I took one before I left the city," I yelled back as I hung my coat in the front closet.

"Come in here and let me look at you! I haven't seen you in so many weeks."

"It's only been three," I commented as I walked through the hall toward the kitchen.

I came into the kitchen and there she stood, her back turned to me, her head covered with a pot holder, as she finished the blessing over the candles. Everything smelled as it always did just before *Shabbos.*

She turned around, looked me over as if she hadn't seen me in several millennia, and then enveloped me in her usual embrace. She planted a warm wet kiss on my cheek and suggested that I hurry off to the synagogue so that my father would see that I had arrived home in time. I consented.

When I got to the synagogue, the service was just beginning. My father looked at me in the pews and gave a nod of welcome, and then took an obvious glance at his wristwatch.

After the service, on the walk home, we were accompanied by guests, a family that had recently moved into the community and joined the synagogue. My father always made it a point to invite newcomers for a *Shabbos* dinner. Coincidentally, they happened to have a nineteen-year-old daughter.

Her name was Rina. She was shy, reasonably attractive, and

seemed intelligent from the few words we exchanged. Like all proper girls her age in Borough Park, she attended the Shulamit Teacher's Seminary, a place where women went instead of college while waiting to find husbands. I was a bit annoyed at my parents for having arranged this, but behaved politely nonetheless. The atmosphere at the table was awkward.

"So, Yankel, what have you been learning in yeshiva these days?" my father asked to get the conversation flowing. Another curveball from him, I thought, taking me back to my childhood. It had been a long time since he asked that particular question, and the first time ever that he referred to Yeshiva University as a *yeshiva*.

"Well . . ." I began as I cleared my throat, "just yesterday we studied the laws concerning how long one must wait between eating meat and milk." No harm in playing this game, I thought.

"Ah yes, there are some interesting opinions on this subject if I remember correctly." Feigned modesty—of course my father remembered. These, after all, were matters in which he was quite expert. "So what are the different opinions?" he asked, looking to the others around the table to contribute, Rina in particular.

She knew she was on the spot. There was a brief moment of silence, and then she spoke up. "We wait six hours," she said softly as she looked to her father for approval, "and there is another custom among German Jews to wait only three hours." Nervousness.

My father turned toward me, twirling his goatee, waiting for me to add something. Not wanting to embarrass him and his efforts, I went along. "That's correct," I said, "but the laws are really more complicated than that."

My response made him uneasy. He wasn't sure where I was going with this. "And in what way are they complicated?" he asked hesitantly.

He wasn't looking at me when he said that, but I assumed I was supposed to answer. "Well, to begin with, the prevalent customs, as Rina said, are either six or three hours. But the truth is that there is no actual source for the custom of three hours."

Rina looked bewildered. "But the German Jews do wait only three hours," she asserted. "I have many friends in the seminary whose families came from Germany and they only wait three hours."

"I know that is the custom," I stated, "and it is our custom here in this house as well, but there is no textual or legal source for it."

At this point, my father was definitely uncomfortable. "Ah, yes, Yankel is correct," he interjected as he looked at Rina's father. "He is referring to the fact that the custom for German Jews according to strict interpretation of the law should really be one hour, not three." Rina's father tried to appear as if he had heard this before, but probably hadn't. People tended to act that way with my father.

"Yes, that's true," I said, "but there's more. You see, there's also another opinion on the law that very few are aware of."

My father looked at me nervously. He now knew where this was heading and was sorry he'd started it. Too late, I thought to myself, taking pleasure in his chagrin. The others waited for me to continue, and I was about to before he preempted me a second time.

"Yes, again Yankel is right," he continued while looking at Rina's father. "You see, according to *Rabbeinue Tam,* a famous medieval rabbinical authority, one really doesn't have to wait at all. He believes that dairy after meat should be regarded the same as meat after dairy, where the only requirement is to cleanse one's mouth thoroughly."

Very clever, I thought to myself. Had I been the one to say it, Rina's father would probably have been discomfited, but such words from the mouth of the great Rabbi David Eisen engendered only acceptance. My father immediately started humming a tune, a tactful way of telling me to say no more on the subject. But I wasn't finished.

"It's interesting," I began as his humming grew louder.

"Isn't it? The way we pick and choose the laws we follow. We always accuse the Reform and Conservatives of doing that, but we do it as well. This dairy and meat thing is a perfect example of that . . ."

"Our Yankel likes to analyze things a bit too much some times," my father interrupted, still looking at Rina's father.

"Yes, I can see that," the man responded with an arrogant smile.

"But this is no deep analysis," I replied with equal arrogance. "In fact, it's fairly obvious. Most of the Orthodox world does what they do because they see everybody else doing it that way. Just listen to what Rina said about her friends in the seminary." Now I wasn't being polite; my mother wore a disapproving look. But I didn't care. It was an opportunity to speak and have my father listen; that was all I cared about. "We've become so accustomed to living by the community's standards that most of us have become completely ignorant of what the Torah really says. We don't know the law or its nuances, we know only what's acceptable to others around us!" This came out more animated than I'd intended.

"It seems you have figured many things out from the laws of Kashruth," my father said humorously. "Only a true Talmudic mind can infer so much from discussions of dairy and meat." The others all laughed. Had they not been present, his response would have been quite different. Then again, had they not been present, the conversation probably wouldn't have occurred to begin with.

He resumed his melody, and the others joined in. Another slow, soft tune from years gone by. He closed his eyes and tried to forget what had transpired. His gentle singing grew much louder than usual, but not nearly loud enough to drown out the echoes.

He closed the front door after the guests left, stood at the foot of the stairs, one hand on the banister, and looked at me in the dining room as I cleared the table. I met his eyes with mine, anticipating a disparaging remark, but none came. Instead, he stared at me impassively as if he were waiting for me to say something.

"It was a nice try," I declared with half a smile, referring to Rina.

He didn't respond with words. He just gave me one of his knowing looks, then turned away and ascended the stairs.

I finished clearing the table and joined my mother in the kitchen. As I stood next to her at the sink, handing her dishes to be washed with liquid soap and cold water—hot water being prohibited on the Sabbath—I began to speak of the yet unspoken business that had brought me home in the first place.

"Mama, I know what happened," I declared softly.

"What happened with what?"

"Mama, you know very well what I'm talking about. The thing about Rebecca's mother and . . ."

She stopped what she was doing, looked me in the eye, and voiced, "Ah, yes, Yankeleh! But do you know *exactly* what it is you're talking about?"

It came out like the warning it was intended to be. "I think I do," was my meek response.

"And you want to talk about this? Do you really expect your father and me to discuss something so personal with you? It is *pas nicht,* not proper, for us to discuss such a thing with you. We knew you would find out, but we thought you would have the good sense not to bring it up with us, at least *I* thought so. Your father, he must know you better than I, for he was certain that this was the reason for your visit."

Her tone was indignant, her eyes laden with tears. I stood there, staggered by the energy of her words. What had I done? Had I alienated her as well?

"I didn't intend for this to happen. I mean, I'd no idea at all," I offered apologetically.

"I know," she responded softly as she regained her composure and took my hand.

"Mama, I really love her and I know that is going to cause a great deal of pain for you and *Totta.*"

"I guess we'll have to deal with it." She looked up to heaven. "Like we deal with everything else. At least, thank God, you didn't turn out like your cousin Chaim. That boy causes his parents so much *tsuris,* so much hardship. You're really a wonderful son, Yankeleh, and I'm very proud of you."

"What's going on with Chaim?" As I asked this question it dawned on me how far removed I had become from my family. It had been months, maybe even longer, since I'd seen or spoken to Chaim.

"Nothing is going on with Chaim," she retorted hastily, realizing she had said something she shouldn't have. "It's just the things you already know, that he's always been a problem and will never amount to anything," she continued. A weak attempt to cover her tracks.

I let it lay, but it stayed in the back of my mind. There were more important things—or so I thought—to discuss. Things that might rapidly change her mind about the "world of difference" between me and my forlorn cousin.

"Mama, there's more about my relationship than you and *Totta* know, maybe even some things you don't want to know. But, they are things I need to tell you."

"What are you saying, Yankeleh?" she asked innocently, her tone indicating that she had no doubt that the issue concerned neither sex nor pregnancy, things most other parents would immediately assume.

"I'm saying that the situation is much more complicated than you already think it is."

"What could possibly be more complicated than what's already going on, Yankeleh?"

"That Rebecca is very different from other women."

"Different? In what way different?"

I could no longer evade the truth. I would tell her plainly, and let the cards fall where they may.

"Mama," I took both her hands in mine, "we haven't even

talked at all about what Rebecca does." I could feel the tremble in my voice. "I mean, she's a student like I am. *Very much like I am.*"

The look in her eyes was completely bewildered. "Yankeleh, I don't really understand what you're saying."

"I know, I'm having a hard time with this." A deep breath. "What I'm saying is that Rebecca is studying to be a rabbi."

My mother's face turned pure crimson. She covered her mouth with both hands. Her eyes looked like they were about to bulge right out of her skull.

Her silence was worse than any words could possibly have been. It lasted for what seemed an eternity, until I broke it, saying, "Mama, please, say something."

"What can I say?" she offered. "You, Yankeleh, you are very much full of surprises," she went on softly, staring into space as if she were in a daze.

I knew at that point that I had reached the limits of our relationship. There was nothing in the universe that I needed more at that moment than her reassurance that everything would be okay. I realized it would not be forthcoming.

"I'll tell *Totta* tomorrow," were the only words that came to my mind.

"Don't tell your father tomorrow, please, don't," she pleaded. "He has had so much on his mind and, I . . ." she lifted her hands to her eyes to cover the tears, "I don't think he can take this." She tried to cry quietly, took a napkin to wipe away the tears. "I don't think he can take this," she repeated.

She asked to be left alone and told me she would be all right. I reluctantly left her there, and went up the stairs. When I came to the closed door of my father's study, I stopped and stood for a few moments in silence. I could hear his faint humming and wondered over what book he was pondering, what words of wisdom he was filling his mind with. A fleeting temptation to knock came upon me, but I quickly mastered it. I had never knocked on that door before, and probably never would.

I went to my room, got into bed, and lay there, staring at the ceiling. At some point I heard my father come out of his study and close the door behind him. As it closed, the sound reverberated in my mind, and I felt I was destined forever to be locked out. I thought about Harry's words, his belief that God would eventually help me find a place for myself. I wondered if that would really ever happen.

The next day my mother acted as if nothing unusual had occurred. My father hummed through lunch. I obeyed the silence.

After *Havdalah* I went upstairs to pack my things to return to the city. I came down with my bags, removed my coat from the closet, and went to the kitchen to say goodbye. Each action felt, somehow, as if it were the last time I was to do it. My father was sitting at the kitchen table reading the newspaper. My mother was tending to the dishes from lunch. I stood in the entranceway for a moment and watched them both, trying to take a picture with my mind, one that I knew would have to last for a very long time.

I entered the kitchen and approached my mother. She turned around and we looked into each other's eyes. I leaned forward to kiss her goodbye, a tender kiss on her lightly wrinkled cheeks. She embraced me only slightly, both of us struggling to maintain a facade of normalcy. I could feel her quivering and she could feel mine. I shook hands with my father. No words, just a nod and that same impassive look he gave me the night before. I left them both in the kitchen as I walked out the front door with my bags. The door closed behind me, and with it a part of my life that I knew I would never recapture.

CHAPTER 21

SEVERAL WEEKS had gone by, and still there were no calls from my mother. Rebecca's parents, on the other hand, had taken a renewed interest in her life since I had reentered the picture. They saw me as the path to her salvation, as she put it. Life certainly had its paradoxes.

In truth, however, it was Rebecca who was influencing me, stirring up cravings and passions I'd never imagined I had. Our bond strengthened as we grew to understand each other, though there still remained some barriers that we hadn't crossed.

On a Saturday night, three weekends prior to Thanksgiving, we were coming out of the Tribeca Cinema, a small theater in lower Manhattan specializing in revivals. Rebecca's appreciation of films had been refined significantly since our days at The Pineview, and she'd become an avid fan of nostalgia. I must also have come some distance, for I was able to see the value in this.

The feature was *To Have and Have Not,* a title bearing much similarity to the current state of our affair. It was an old Bogie and Bacall wartime romance that often plays the late-night TV circuit, where it loses the attributes afforded by the big screen. Rebecca sat through the film completely engrossed, mesmerized by the larger-than-life black-and-white figures. Though she admitted to having seen the movie several times, she had wanted to see it again, with *me.* She seemed to want to share everything.

As we walked out onto the sidewalk, she took my arm and drew me closer to her despite her awareness of my discomfort with any type of physical contact in public. I was paranoid, as she frequently teased, fearful of being seen by the Rav Trachtenbergs of the world. She was also proud of reminding me how she used to feel similarly, back in the days when she was ashamed of her own aspirations. "I really worried about what others would think of me if I followed my heart," she once told me, "but as soon as I began following my heart, I stopped worrying."

This time, I made no effort to disengage from her. It felt good. And it felt right.

Noticing this, she stopped, turned, and kissed me gently on the cheek. Innocent enough, my mind told me, though other parts of me said something else. When I looked at her with a smile, she remarked, "I'm glad you're happy."

"I am happy," I responded. And for the first time, I was.

"By the way, Rabbi Samuels is having a dinner party on Thanksgiving and he's asked me to invite you along as my date.

"Just like him to make a big deal out of a Gentile holiday." I thought I was being humorous.

"Oh, yeah!" she responded, preparing herself for battle, "what makes you think it's not a Jewish holiday?"

"Come on, be serious!"

"I am being very serious!"

"You mean to tell me that Thanksgiving is in the Torah!"

"No, but neither are *Chanukah, Purim,* and *Tisha B'av,* are they?"

"But they're different."

"How so?"

"Well, to begin with they center around the Jewish people and the land of Israel."

"Not so with *Purim.* That was about Jewish survival in Persia, wasn't it?"

"Okay, but Thanksgiving was a holiday instituted by Gentiles and for Gentiles."

"But that doesn't mean it can't also be meaningful to Jews. It's not Christmas or Easter—it has no Christian connotation per se. There's no special mass or particular rituals associated with it. It's just a day of giving thanks to God for being good to us and bringing us to a place of freedom. Do you honestly mean to tell me that this isn't something that Jews should be celebrating?"

"We do celebrate those things, but we have our own way of doing it."

"I understand that, but what's wrong with celebrating this in the same way that everybody else celebrates it? Do you think it will threaten our distinctiveness if we join other people in celebrating something that we all value, and do it all in the same way? I mean, it's not about going to church; it's about families and friends getting together for a festive meal and enjoyment. What's not Jewish about that?"

"It seems you have a much broader definition of what's Jewish than I do."

"You're kidding," she jested.

"You know, you *would* have made a great lawyer," I responded in kind.

"I've heard that somewhere before. I think it's getting stale. Anyway, don't you think I'd make a great rabbi?" A crafty smile.

I didn't respond.

She stopped walking for a second and turned toward me once again. She leaned forward and kissed me on the lips. No innocence, not this time.

I took her hand, stepped into the street, and hailed a cab. When we got in, I told the driver her address. We held hands for the entire ride uptown. As the cab turned off Broadway onto her block she asked if I wanted to come up for a while. I knew that if I did, this could mean the end of the last boundary still standing between us. I was certain that she knew it too.

What was there to hold me back? I had already broken my mother's heart, and who knew what I had done to my father? Why not take the final step, perform my final act of defiance? Stop the pretense! Follow your heart! No more paranoia!

An image of Chaim appeared in my mind. Why couldn't I be like him, able to do what I wanted? Why did I worry and think so much? Why was everything so damn complicated? Who cared about ancient, oppressive rules? To hell with the books and laws. To hell with Waldman and his complexities. Praised be the pleasure principle! The singular explanation. The pursuit of personal indulgence.

The cab pulled up in front of her building. As she reached to grab the doorknob, she turned to me with a lascivious grin and said, "Well?" I looked at her and past her, out the window. There stood Sandy the doorman who, having seen the cab pull up, readied himself by the door. He was watching and waiting. The cabdriver was watching and waiting. The meter was ticking away. I lost my nerve and told her I couldn't. She seemed to understand, reached over and kissed me on the cheek, said good night, and closed the car door behind her.

I watched her run in as Sandy held the door for her. They chatted as she walked toward the elevator. I wondered what gossipy urge he was fulfilling—at least someone would be satisfied tonight.

The driver was taking me home, but after about four minutes I asked him to stop. I wanted to get out and walk the rest of the way. It was a pleasantly nippy night and I needed some air. I gave him the fare and a generous tip for his patience.

I continued up Broadway. It was just after eleven-thirty and the bars and eateries were still crowded. On the sidewalks some people were strolling leisurely through the evening, others were pacing briskly as if they were anxious to get where they were going. I must have been moving exceptionally slowly, for it seemed all of them were passing me by.

In front of me was a young couple, playfully hugging and kissing as they walked. The girl laughed loudly. The boy reached out, grabbed her, pulled her toward him, leaned her up against his body, and then glued his face to hers. I couldn't help watching. They didn't seem to care about where they were. It was much better than Bogie and Bacall's "you just put your lips together and blow" scene in *To Have and Have Not.*

They turned a corner and went up a side street in the same manner. I had to stop at the corner to let the cars go by, so I watched them continue up the darkened block until the pedestrian light said WALK. They gradually faded from view, but their laughter could still be heard.

As I approached the corner of my block, I saw Tina, the prostitute, standing off the far curb, leaning her head into the window of a red Porsche. I turned the corner to go up the block, but stopped for a moment to watch. The car pulled off without Tina—he probably wasn't able to make a deal—and as she straightened up, she caught me looking. She offered her familiar smile, waved to me, and called out, "Hey, Rabbi, ya lookin' damn cute tonight."

Embarrassed, I turned away and continued walking up the block toward my building. A moment later, she caught up to me, slid her hand around my arm, and said, "Well Rabbi, seems we got a little situation here, what d'ya think?"

"Pardon me?" I responded tensely. I was sweating and knew she saw. We stopped walking, and I looked around. The entire block was empty except for us.

"It's my business to know when people are interested, and I think you're interested," she said, her eyes peering into mine.

"Interested?" Very defensive.

"Yes, *interested.*"

"In what?"

"In me."

I took a step back and released myself from her hold. She moved closer to fill the gap. My knees began to shudder.

"I think you like me, Rabbi."

I didn't respond.

She took her hand and stroked the front of my jacket. I looked around, still no one in sight. I didn't stop her just yet. She began to stroke a little harder. I felt an erection coming on. She knew exactly what was happening. I grabbed her hand, removed it from my chest, and slowly placed it down by her side.

"A bit shy, are we?" she reacted.

I said nothing, but continued looking at her and sweating. She stood there silently, reached into her jacket pocket and took out a cigarette without removing her eyes from me.

"Want one?" she asked.

"I don't smoke," I answered, though it probably wasn't a bad time to start.

She placed it in her mouth. The way she caressed it with her tongue was enticing. The bulge in my pants was getting quite uncomfortable. She struck a match and lit up.

"I think I'd better go," I said.

"Where to?"

"Home." I pointed toward my building.

"I bet you could use some company," she pressed.

"I bet I could," I agreed. A rare moment of honesty. "But I can't do *this,*" I added, as if I were talking to myself and letting her listen.

I started walking away. She didn't follow, but I had only gone a few steps when I heard her say, "You know what you need, Rabbi?"

I turned, my eyebrows raised in curiosity.

"I'll tell you what you need," she continued. "You need to get laid."

I stopped for a moment, struck by the simplicity of her diagnosis. She smiled, turned toward the avenue, and walked away. I watched her go.

She moved proudly, not as if she'd been insulted or scorned. She even turned around to get one last look at me. She smiled again, waved goodbye, and disappeared into the night.

I remained still for a few seconds. I was no longer sweating; my erection had subsided. But I couldn't go home, not just yet. I needed to walk, to think.

My mind swelled with images: a child, watching his father being taken off in an ambulance, and turning on a light on the Sabbath; a teenager, washing his hands to cleanse his soul from a wet dream, and cheating on a chemistry test; an adult, kissing Rebecca in the street, and conversing with a whore.

Other images appeared: Ezra, lecturing me on how everything is part of God's ultimate plan; Ezra again, sitting with my father, swallowing the man's wisdom like a starved bird; Trachtenberg, on one of his tirades against modernity; Waldman, lashing into me for being too literal; Harry, pointing at his pictures of dead faces hanging on the walls; Rebecca, touching me and making me tremble.

I asked myself, does God exist? How can He allow so much suffering? Can science and philosophy solve the riddles of existence? What about the greatest riddle of all: me? Am I to be a rabbi, a philosopher, a lover, or a whore-chaser?

Suddenly, the answer dawned upon me. Perhaps there *is* a singular truth, perhaps complexity is the real illusion. At last, all conflicts *can* be reduced to a common denominator. The solution has finally been revealed. Praised be singularity! *I need to get laid!*

I stepped out into the street and hailed a cab. It was close to one in the morning by the time he dropped me in front of Rebecca's building. Sandy was dozing in his chair. He awakened as I came into the lobby, but only opened the corner of one eye, nodded slightly, and gestured me toward the elevator without bothering to pick up the intercom to announce me.

I walked off the elevator; the door closed behind me. I felt calm, confident in what I was doing. My heart was at one with my mind. I knocked on the door so as not to startle Rebecca with the bell. From the other side of the door I heard her ask softly, "Who is there?" I identified myself and the door immediately opened. We did not speak.

The sun glared through the window, caught my eye, and transformed a sound sleep into a sudden jolt of wakefulness. The first thing I saw was the white ceiling overhead. As I regained my orientation, I realized that I'd awakened in unfamiliar surroundings.

I reached out with my left arm to feel for Rebecca, but the other half of the bed was empty. I turned to let my eyes confirm what my hand had discovered. She was not there. Then I sat up, and it occurred to me that I was naked. I pulled the sheet around me as I frantically searched the room for my clothing. My underpants and slacks had managed to make their way under the bed. It seemed everything had a life of its own.

Gradually I became more alert. There were noises coming from the kitchen. I walked out of the bedroom, through the living room, and into the kitchen where Rebecca stood, barefooted in a long light-blue terry cloth robe, preparing breakfast. She looked at me with that familiar smile, and said good morning. My eyes wandered for a second to the clock on the wall behind her. It was already eleven-fifteen. She made a cute comment about what a good night's sleep I must have had.

She then poured me a glass of freshly squeezed orange juice, followed by an affectionate kiss on the lips. She suggested I take a seat at the table, for breakfast would be ready in a jiffy.

"Not very talkative this morning, are we?" she called from the kitchen.

"Sorry," I responded.

"Feeling guilty about last night?"

"Not sure what I feel."

"That's fair enough, and typical I might add."

"Can we talk about something else?"

"Just like that?"

"Well, I don't mean to sweep anything under the rug. I just don't know what to say right now."

"You can tell me how it was, for openers," she said as she

came out of the kitchen and placed a plate of scrambled eggs and fried potatoes in front of me.

"What do you mean, 'how it was'?" I reacted as she sat down next to me.

"You know what I mean: how it felt . . . emotionally, physically."

I blushed and didn't answer.

"Come on, Yakov, you have to tell me something. You can't just make believe nothing happened."

"I don't intend to."

"Then how was it?" she pressed.

"It was very nice."

"That's it—'very nice'?"

"I'm not sure what you want me to say."

"You're really not sure of anything, are you?" she intoned angrily.

"I'm sure that I want this to work out," I asserted in the hope of assuaging her.

"Just 'very nice'?" she reiterated.

"It was the best thing that ever happened to me!"

"*Happened* to you?"

"That I ever did, I mean."

She took my hand in hers, leaned over, and kissed me again on the lips. She used her left hand to fix my hair and commented, "You look very cute in the morning."

"So do you," I responded.

CHAPTER 22

RAV TRACHTENBERG was in full form. The topic: contemporary *bar mitzvah* celebrations. The precipitant: an article in the *New York Times* describing the *bar mitzvah* celebration of a famous banker's son that had cost in excess of a hundred thousand dollars.

"What an incredible waste!" he harangued. "It is unbelievable how these people throw away money!"

The students sat around the desk in awe of his infinite wisdom. You could hear a pin drop.

"Did you see that piece, eh, in this morning's, what's it called, *Times,* Eisen?"

Was he talking to me? I heard my name called, but it wasn't my day to recite. He had caught my attention, which he knew had escaped him until that moment.

"No, *rebbe*, I haven't had time today to read the paper," I explained, trying to give the impression that my hours were spent, instead, reviewing the text for class.

"Ah, yes," he reacted in a measured tone as he stroked his beard, "I don't really read the paper either, I just look at it for a moment to see if maybe there is anything important there, just for a few seconds, you know, Eisen," he continued with feigned embarrassment.

Why was he picking on me? Had he found out about my weekend activities? Oh my God, he knew! I was finished! No, you paranoid jerk, he didn't know anything! He just figured you're the only one in the class who might have read a paper, and he figured wrong. Yes, that was it.

I nodded my head in approval.

"Well, it is obscene, that money they spend on these things, boys, it is obscene!"

The entire class nodded in agreement.

"What is it anyway, this thing, a *bar mitzvah?* Why do they make such a big *tsimmes* out of it? The truth is that if a boy does nothing at all on his thirteenth birthday, he is still a *bar mitzvah,* even if there is no caterer for hundreds of miles!"

The class chuckled. My mind was elsewhere, in Rebecca's living room on a Friday night. She was recounting her impressions of a *bar mitzvah* that was held in her temple that same evening. She was indignant, and her tone, was terribly similar to Trachtenberg's. She described a life-size photograph statue of the *bar mitzvah* boy at the entrance to the temple; the buttons inscribed *Michael's Bar Mitzvah* handed to each guest as they left the sanctuary to enter the catering hall; the live parakeets in cages on each of the tables for guests to take home as mementos. I was sitting on the couch in disbelief, listening to her lamentations about this and similar affairs she had seen. She was criticizing Rabbi Samuels, her preceptor, for not joining forces with some of his Reform colleagues, rabbis who enforced strict limitations on such extravaganzas in their temples. She was going on about how this type of materialism was a modern-day form of idol worship, directly antithetical to the teachings of Judaism. She argued that maybe the Reform Movement had a good idea years ago when it proposed to do away with *bar mitzvahs* altogether and replace them with confirmations, unpretentious ceremonies to take place several years after *bar mitzvah* age, thereby encouraging the continuation of religious studies beyond one's thirteenth birthday.

If Trachtenberg knew that some of his sentiments were shared by members of the Reform rabbinate, he might change his mind and champion the institution of *bar mitzvahs* instead.

I'm sure he would conjure up some rationalization to distance himself from any conceivable association with his liberal enemies.

Again, my mind drifted. This time I found myself reading from the Torah at my own *bar mitzvah. Relatives and friends are watching, but I do not see them for my eyes are in the scroll and my body is facing the ark. Between portions, the only person I see is my father, sitting on his throne beside the ark, facing the congregation. He looks full of joy, but frail from the heart attack he had suffered a month earlier, his second during my lifetime. He had returned from the hospital a week before the event, and my mother felt it best to cancel what was to be a modest celebration at our home the following afternoon.*

I am reading the Torah and the words come out of my mouth with ease and familiarity. I had spent months in preparation, first learning the entire Torah reading, then the Haftorah, *and then the* Musaf, *the concluding service which I would lead for the entire congregation. I can hear myself, the unseasoned voice of a thirteen-year-old, singing out resoundingly the text of more than two thousand years' vintage. It is said that Rabbi Akiva, the preeminent Talmudic sage, used to interpret the crowns that sat upon the words in the Torah scroll. He continued studying and teaching despite the Roman prohibition against doing so. When he was caught, they slaughtered him by flaying his skin. He died for the sake of Torah, and here I am, tens of centuries later, celebrating, chanting the traditional melody that gives life to those words and crowns. And unlike the characters in Rebecca's and Trachtenberg's scenarios, I understand the meaning of it all. Yet, like them, I feel very little, very little except the affliction of my father as he sits there, trying to catch his breath, trying to stay alive so that he can finish the work that Rabbi Akiva left behind. So much work.*

I caught myself almost dozing off, my head dropping and losing support from my neck. I looked around for a second, shook my head slightly to restore my consciousness, and there I was, back in Trachtenberg's classroom.

"And what a *tsimmes,* what an ordeal they make! First they have a, eh, how do you say, when they have all the different foods on the tables?"

"Smorgasbord!" some students shouted out in unison.

"Ah, yes boys, smorgasbord. And after that they all go in to begin eating. And then they have that candle lighting *nahrishkeit,* that nonsense when all the relatives light the candles and march up and down the aisle, dripping wax all over the floor. And finally, after everyone is all filled up, what do they do? They bring in the Vietnamese table."

The class, believing he was unaware of his faux pas, struggled to suppress its laughter. One brave student politely corrected him stating, "I think you mean Viennese, *rebbe*." Everyone else was silent.

"Vietnamese, Viennese, who cares?" he roared.

He looked over in my direction and caught me smiling. I thought he was going to ask me what was so funny. Instead, he simply smiled back and said, "You agree, Eisen?"

"Yes, *rebbe*."

CHAPTER 23

My eyes opened suddenly from the piercing noise. Habitually, I reached over to shut off the alarm clock, but realized midstream that the sound was emanating from somewhere else. I lay in bed for a moment, still sweating from the dream I must have been having, until it was apparent that what I was hearing was the downstairs door buzzer. I looked at the clock; it was two-thirty in the morning. I dragged myself out of bed to the intercom, pressed the talk button, and asked who it was. The voice through the static reception belonged to my cousin Chaim.

I went to the bathroom to urinate, then to the kitchen to put on some coffee. A few minutes later, there was a knock at the door. I turned the latches to the locks, opened the door, and saw him standing there in the hallway. He looked sick, sweating profusely, and peaked. His face had been unshaven for days; his black trench coat was torn at the pockets and missing two lower buttons; the collar of his white shirt was yellowed; his black pants were filthy and frayed.

"My God, you look like death," I pronounced.

"I feel like death," he responded as he raised his hand to rub his nose while sniffling.

"Come in, please!" I stepped aside so he could enter. He moved past me quickly, looked around for a brief moment, and walked toward the window. The kettle was whistling. I slipped into the kitchen to turn off the flame, but didn't bother taking the time to pour any coffee. I came back out and he stood there looking at me.

"I heard weeks ago that you were sick, but I didn't imagine . . ."

"I'm not sick!" he yelled. "I'm sorry, I didn't mean to get angry at you. I haven't seen you for a long time, I have no reason to be angry with you."

He was pacing around as he spoke and he seemed not fully rational.

"What's wrong? Why are you here at close to three in the morning?"

"I had nowhere else to go. Haven't you heard? I haven't been home for days, I've even stopped counting how many. Nobody knows where I am. Hell, I don't even know where I am half the time."

"I haven't heard anything." I paused. "I'm not exactly in touch with my parents right now."

"Listen, Yankel, I'd like to sit and listen to your problems, but I got *real* problems to deal with right now." He continued to pace nervously in circles.

"What is it, Chaim?" I stepped forward, placed my hands on his shoulders to stop the pacing, and looked him in the eye. "What is it?"

"Look, I just need some money to hold me over for a while." He broke free of my hold.

"Money?"

"Yeah, money! You do know what that is, don't you?" he exclaimed.

"Chaim, what are you so upset about? Talk to me!"

"Talk to you? Good little Yankel, the *gutskeit* of the family, little prince and rabbinical student!" He laughed out loud.

I was silent. I couldn't believe what I was seeing.

"Well, Yankel, what's it gonna be—the money or nothing? I can't stay here discussing this all night, you know."

"No, I don't know. Where could you possibly have to go this time of night?"

"Boy, you are really one ignorant fool. I mean, you can't even see what's in front of you."

I ignored his insults, for he clearly had no control over what came out of his mouth.

"Chaim." I walked toward him again and grabbed his shoulders the same way as before. "I know what's in front of me! I know you're sick and need help."

The smell was repulsive. He broke away again, this time almost violently.

"You know what I need, I need money, that's it, the long and short of it. I need money," he yelled in my face. "Are you gonna help me, or am I wasting my time?"

"You need the money to buy drugs, don't you? You're on drugs, aren't you?" I shouted back in his face.

"Well, good morning, cousin Yankel! A brilliant deduction!" He backed off.

"What is it, Chaim—cocaine? Is that it?"

"That's some of it." Pause. "Cocaine, crack, and even heroin when I'm lucky."

We both stood silently and looked at each other for a moment, he with shame, me with pity.

"Chaim," I said gently as I approached him again, "I can't help you by giving you money. I just can't."

"There you go, judging me again, I can see it in your eyes. All your life you stand in judgment of me, and you know nothing about my life. Better, you don't want to know anything about my life! You say you heard I was sick a few weeks ago? Okay, righteous Yankel, why didn't you call to see how I was? No, I'm not good enough for you to care about, heh?"

"I thought it was just a cold or something," I answered meekly.

"Oh, come on, Yankel, you haven't spoken to me in over a year. And last time we did bump into each other, it was 'hi and bye,' no time for my troubled older cousin. Come on, admit it, and then I'll leave you alone forever. Just admit it, you're too damn good for me!"

This time he had both his hands on my shoulders and he was shaking me as he bellowed in my face.

"Why don't you sit down?" I offered in an effort to calm him. But he remained distraught and insistent that the only thing I could do for him was to give him money.

"Will that prove to you that I care, if I give you money to go out and buy more drugs?"

"Forget it!" he said as he moved toward the door. "I should have known better than to turn to you for anything."

I lunged at the door and held it closed, my back against it.

"Listen, Chaim, I can't let you leave here like this!"

"Then give me the money, and let your conscience be eased."

"You know I can't give you the money. But I can give you food, and a bed, and a shower, a place to stay for as long as you need to sort things out."

"I have places to stay, and places to go, if you don't mind." He motioned for me to get out of his way. I didn't budge.

"Yankel, please don't make me force you to move."

"That's just what you're gonna have to do to get past me."

He backed off, seemed to soften a bit, and suddenly burst into a crying fit, kicking and punching the wall. "Please, Yankel, let me go. I need to go!"

"Chaim, just stay for the rest of the night. You'll get some sleep and food, and we can talk about things in the morning. I'll get you help for this problem, I will."

"The only problem I got is you're standing in my way."

He resumed pacing. I followed him, continuing my appeal. "Chaim, just hear me out. I know I haven't been close to you over the past few years, but I haven't been close to anyone. I've been in my own world. Now's not the time for me to share my problems with you. I'm just asking you to believe that I do care and that you're important to me. I want to help you! Please!"

"Are you gonna let me go now?" he responded as if he had heard nothing of what I said.

"I can't stop you anymore, can I?" I asked sadly.

"No you can't. And I can't stop myself either," he added in a similar tone. He then pushed past me and ran out the door.

When the door closed behind him, I just stood there for a while, staring into space. Go after him! You gave up too soon. Pull him back in and convince him to get help! Call the police, call Uncle Zelig, call your father! But I continued to stand there.

After a few moments, I took hold of myself and went to the window. I looked down below and there he was coming out of the building. I stayed there watching him, my hands, nose, and forehead pressed against the glass, as he walked toward Broadway.

An image entered my mind from when we were children. *We are holding hands, running and jumping on the way to* shul. *He is stockier and taller than I. He is the leader and I follow with glee. He holds my hand tightly, not letting go for a second. I feel safe and loved.*

I returned to the present, still leaning against the window. He was out of sight, vanished into the darkness.

Several hours later I hung up the phone after having spoken to my aunt Sheindy. I breathed a sigh of relief. She had made no effort to kill the messenger; on the contrary, she was full of appreciation and explained that she and Zelig had been aware of Chaim's drug problem for over a year. They tried to get him help but he refused adamantly. There had even been a physical encounter between him and Zelig, which led to this latest disappearance. That Chaim came to call upon me seemed to bring her a sense of comfort. At least Chaim still realized he had a family, as she tearfully put it.

Her pain was evident in every word she spoke. She loved her child and wanted to protect him at all costs. I offered whatever help I could provide, anything at all. She asked only that I not tell my parents about this. She and Zelig had thus far managed to keep it a secret and wanted it to stay that way. She had no idea that not telling my parents wouldn't be a problem at all.

PART III

CHAPTER 24

Rav Trachtenberg waited until the end of the class to announce that he had finished grading the first exam of the year. The grades were in his office, where he would be found the following morning to meet personally with each student and review each test. This was the procedure he followed for all five exams throughout the year.

The next day, I figured I could avoid the rush by waiting until just before lunch to retrieve my exam. I came off the elevator onto the fourth floor of Furst Hall and went through a door to my left that had a sign stating, "Faculty Offices." I entered into a hall—the same yellowish color as all the other halls in this building—with a series of doors on both sides. The second door to my right was room 423, Trachtenberg's office. I knocked gently and a voice from within invited me to enter.

The simple cubicle had no windows. The walls were barren and the institutional gray erector-set-type bookcases that covered the wall directly across from the door were virtually empty as well. Rav Trachtenberg sat in a swivel chair behind a gunmetal aluminum desk—identical to the one in his and every other classroom—pushed up against the wall to my left. On the desk were some books, his worn brown leather briefcase, and a large manila envelope containing the test booklets. Behind him, against the wall, stood a coat rack where his wool coat and hat hung, and to his right, in a space between the side of the desk and the bookcase, was the chair in which I was to sit and face him. It appeared that he spent little time in this room aside from these brief meetings with students.

"Come, Eisen," he motioned, directing me to the seat.

I held my jacket and books in my left arm and placed them on my lap after I sat down. He reached inside the envelope. There were only three test booklets remaining, the one on top was mine.

"Ah yes, here it is," he said as he placed it in front of me.

It was a light-blue essay booklet with an honesty attestation in the middle of the front cover, just above the place where I had printed my name. On the top right-hand corner, written in red ink and circled, was the number ninety-seven. I looked at this and smiled.

"It is, eh, a very good grade, the second best in all of the class," he remarked without expression.

It didn't bother me that I was bettered by another student. At the moment, my only ambition was to defeat Trachtenberg. I was certain he sensed what I was thinking, yet that didn't matter either. It was clear to both of us that I would get through his exams and there was nothing he could do about it.

"You know, eh, Eisen, there's more to being a rabbi than just passing these tests," he commented.

"Much more, *rebbe*," I offered in agreement.

He looked at me with piercing eyes. I felt uncomfortable and needed to look away: at the walls, the floor, the ceiling. He continued to gaze. He definitely had more on his mind.

"Is there anything else the *rebbe* would like to discuss with me?" I inquired, using the respectful third person to hide my disdain.

"I would like you to come to my class dressed more like a yeshiva *buchur*. Those, how do you say, jeans and sneakers are not, eh, the proper clothes to study Torah in." A stroke of the beard.

"I'm sorry if I offended the *rebbe*; I will try to dress more appropriately in the future," I responded, squelching my anger.

"But how do we change what is on the inside?" he contemplated out loud.

"Pardon me?" I responded, pretending not to understand what he was getting at.

"It's not just your, eh, outward appearance that I'm concerned about, Eisen," he clarified.

I sat and waited for what was coming next.

"I have great respect for your father—he is a tremendous scholar! Does he know, eh, that you wear jeans and sneakers in my class?"

"No," I faltered, "I don't think so."

"I didn't think so either," he added.

"But what do you think is wrong with my insides?" I asked innocently.

"I think you are troubled and live in, how do you say, confusion." Direct.

I wanted to ask him how he knew this, but instead said nothing.

"I know that you study, eh, *goyishe* philosophy, but I don't understand why you need to. Isn't everything in the Torah? Why do you think you need other things?"

I wasn't surprised that he knew about my second life at NYU, for it was pretty much common knowledge by this time. Keeping secrets in this place wasn't as easy as I'd thought. I presumed, in fact, that the extra attention he gave me in class was related to this. But now he wanted to discuss it openly, and *that* I wasn't prepared for. I sat silently, hoping that one of the owners of the other two test booklets would knock on the door. Fate wasn't so kind.

I thought about confronting him about his own secular education, but deemed that an unwise strategy. I could, however, focus on the theoretical arguments without any personal references, but to what avail. He continued looking directly at me, stroked his beard, scratched his nose, and waited for a reply. It was, at once, a momentous and unnerving occasion, an opportunity to sock it to him with the truth and dig my own grave in the process. I opted for the passive approach and played dumb.

"I never thought of it that way," I began. "It's not something that competes with Torah, it's just something I enjoy studying in addition to Torah, something that I might like to teach one day, for a living." I hoped this gibberish might mollify him.

I could tell he saw right through it. He appeared pensive as he observed my discomfort. Once again, he played with his beard. The tension grew.

"There are many ways to earn a living. One does not have to become a, how do you say, heretic in order to put food on his table."

"I do not intend to become a heretic," I responded defensively.

"I'm sure you do not. After all, eh, you are the son of Rav Duvid Eisen, and it would be a tragedy for you to become anything other than a great Torah scholar. But how can one study *goyishe* philosophy and not become a heretic?"

"One must have deep faith, like Rav Liebowitz," I answered a bit too smartly.

"Ah yes, Rav Liebowitz," he mused, stroking his beard. "He is a man of deep faith, and he is also a man of, eh, incredible understanding. But, above all, he is a man of great strength. Are you all those things, Eisen?"

I supposed he had figured that I wasn't. He was right. I'd dug a hole for myself by invoking Liebowitz's name. I'd given him just the ammunition he needed.

He waited for an answer. I hesitated slightly, then heard myself say, "I hope to be."

"Than you have much work to do," he replied. "And you should start by dressing properly when you study Torah."

"Yes, *rebbe*, I will." At that point I would have agreed to anything to get out of there.

"Good, you may go now."

CHAPTER 25

REBECCA TOOK ME SHOPPING. She picked out a black and maroon argyle sweater, charcoal corduroy pants, and cordovan penny loafers. She also found a pair of socks and a belt for the finishing touches. The sweater was her gift, a way of motivating me into purchasing the other articles. She wanted me to wear this outfit for Rabbi Samuels's Thanksgiving bash. I complied.

She was quite gentle when it came to my wardrobe. It amused her that I had only two categories of clothing—dark suits or jeans and sneakers—reflecting, as she put it, the two extremes of my personality. Introducing me to new clothes was another of her ways of trying on new ideas, and helping me find a niche somewhere in the middle.

When we arrived at the rabbi's home, a housemaid answered the door and took our coats. I could hear voices from another room as we stood in the foyer waiting for her to hang the coats and direct us to the gathering. Before she finished, however, Rabbi Samuels emerged from a hallway straight ahead.

"Rabbi Kleinman and Rabbi Eisen," he called out heartily as he walked toward us, "good evening and welcome."

He held out his hand, first to shake Rebecca's, next to shake mine. When he took my right hand, he used both of his hands, and then he warmly put his arm around me to escort us in. We proceeded down the hall which was marked by its unusually expansive width, tall ceiling, lustrous white marble floor, and lavish artwork hanging on the black silk–papered walls. As we walked, I noticed a staircase on my left leading up to another level. I had never been in a duplex apartment before, nor any place this magnificent.

At the end of the hall, he led us into a room filled with seven other people. "Don't despair," he looked at me with a bright smile, "we're expecting three or four more, so you'll be able to remain at least somewhat anonymous."

I was beginning to see what Rebecca liked in him, despite my predisposition against what he stood for. Rebecca sensed this, and looked at me with a smile. I smiled back. I started to feel comfortable now.

Samuels introduced me to the other guests, who were already well acquainted with Rebecca. There was his brother the cardiologist and his wife, another couple from the congregation whose family lived out of town, and a black minister from a nearby church with his wife and young daughter. Mrs. Samuels was still in the kitchen working on last-minute preparations.

The doorbell sounded. The last guests had arrived, a rabbinical colleague of Samuels's with her husband and two small children. Rebecca scrutinized my expression upon each introduction.

I was the only person with a yarmulke, though Rebecca assured me that the rabbi kept a strictly kosher home. Not necessarily for himself, she pointed out, but for the many prestigious guests he regularly had at his table. He was very politically involved and had entertained personalities the likes of Israeli cabinet members and chief rabbis from all over the world.

We all sat in the room chatting for a while. Rebecca left me to go into the kitchen to help Mrs. Samuels—Karen, as she referred to her. I sat, listened, and smiled a lot, but offered little to the conversation, which centered around the latest Nazi war criminal to have been discovered in the United States. It was an unusual case because he was a Bishop in the Episcopal Church and a board member of the National Council of Churches. The talk was interesting enough, but I found myself overwhelmed by the physical surroundings.

It was a den, not a living room. The walls were all mahogany and the floor was polished oak parquet. The room was small and cluttered, seemingly out of character with the rest of the apartment. All the furniture and ornaments were antique, right down to the fountain pen that sat in a holder upon a magnificently preserved pine rolltop desk. The walls were adorned with plaques and awards, just like the walls of Samuels's office, but some of these were different, more personal in nature. There was, for example, an honorable discharge from the army dated 1947, and a basketball award he had received as an undergraduate at Yeshiva University. Soldier, athlete, and rabbi, I thought to myself. Seems I'm not the only complex sort around here. As I continued perusing the walls, the rabbi came up behind me and asked if I'd found anything interesting. The others were still involved in their conversation.

"Yes, in fact I have," I responded, pointing to the discharge.

"Your father didn't fight in the war?" he asked.

"No. He had heart problems from a very young age," I explained, assuming that to have been the reason.

"I'm sorry to hear that. Is he well?"

"He holds his own."

Rabbi Samuels seemed truly genial and sensitive. He was in the business of consoling others, but it appeared he enjoyed his work. He placed his hand on my shoulder again and began telling me about how he was among the troops that liberated the Bergen-Belsen concentration camp.

"That was when I decided to become a lawyer," he stated as I looked at him in astonishment. "I saw what Hitler did to those people, to our people, and decided that I would become a champion of justice."

"Did you become a lawyer?" I asked.

"Oh yes," he answered as he pointed to the Columbia law degree that I hadn't gotten to yet.

"So what happened?"

"Well, to make a long story short, I ended up in the Manhattan DA's office as an assistant and found myself entangled in politics and deals. After a while I felt like I wasn't doing much for anybody. So I decided to switch careers and went to Cincinnati to become a rabbi. The rest, as they say, is history."

His grin revealed the satisfaction he felt from my interest in his tale. I was embarrassed for ever having slandered him. He ignored his other guests and had just begun telling me of his love for basketball when we were interrupted by his wife's entrance into the room. She greeted all the guests and extended her hand to me saying, "And you must be Yakov." Rebecca stood behind her watching lovingly.

She was tall and slender, meticulously put together, and held herself most gracefully. Her facial features were rather ordinary, but dignified by the contrast with her short black hair and stark eyebrows. Adding to her mystique was an English accent, which I later learned was really South African. She was more reserved than her husband, but in every other respect they were quite similar.

We were invited into the dining room, a spacious area with the same white marble floor as in the foyer and hallway. There was a long rectangular black lacquered table with matching chairs, and a large square crystal chandelier. Aside from the table and chairs, there was no other furniture. The walls, on the other hand, were amply decorated with paintings. It struck me as odd that this room would be found in the same house as the room we had just come from.

Most of the paintings bore the signature of our hostess who, I was told, had achieved some notability in the art world. This meant nothing to me—a proud ignoramus in such matters—until my untutored eyes beheld her work. She used dark colors, and the themes of her paintings seemed to reflect man's inhumanity to man. I found this most striking, considering the lively decor of the surroundings and the artist's far from morbid personality.

There were six oil paintings, four of hers and two that might just as well have been. One was of an elderly Jew trying to pray in a concentration camp barracks; another of a black prisoner receiving his morsels of food from a South African prison guard; the third of a Jewish woman trying to tear herself away from an SS guard pulling at her dress; and the last of a black woman in identical circumstances with a white Klansman. The other two pieces, by an Israeli artist whose name even I recognized, were of scenes involving Jews and Arabs. The first depicted the hanging of a Jewish civilian by an Arab mob, and the second showed an Israeli soldier holding his gun to the head of a Palestinian who was on his hands and knees.

The neat balance and even-handedness reflected keenly the liberal proclivities of the rabbi and his wife. And as this thought came to mind, I saw commonalities, rather than dissimilarities, between them and my parents. For they all saw the world in particular ways, based on the backgrounds from which each emerged. That they happened to find themselves on opposite sides was only the product of their experiences, not the result of some interpretation of truth. In a kinder moment, I might even have given such benefit of the doubt to Rav Trachtenberg as well.

But with Rebecca and me, the matter seemed very different. She was certainly no prisoner of her past, and I had made much headway toward breaking away from mine as well. Had I hit upon something here in recognizing the varying levels in which people are entrenched in their ideological heredities? Is the root of divisiveness more psychological than philosophical? Perhaps Freud, Nietzsche, and Spinoza rejected the faith of their fathers simply because they were motivated by a psychological need to distinguish themselves from those who came before. An interesting hypothesis, though Professor Waldman would probably accuse me of being too singular, once again.

In a flash I was brought back to the party by the touch of Rebecca's hand on my thigh under the table. She seemed to have a keen sense of whenever I was lost.

The conversation had just shifted to a new topic: the issue of patrilineality. Rabbi Samuels, an ardent proponent of fathers having equal say in the religion of their children, was arguing that if men and women were to be considered truly equal in all aspects, then the man's religion should be as strong a determinant as the woman's in deciding the religion of the child.

Rebecca and I smiled at each other. We both recalled when I told her about Rabbi Roth's speech lambasting the Conservative rabbinate for deciding to ordain women, and how Roth had made the same exact point that Samuels just articulated, but used it as a warning against egalitarianism.

The female rabbi, the reverend, the cardiologist, and their respective spouses all nodded in agreement. Rebecca was the only dissenter, and it seemed she was trying to get me in on the action.

"But don't you think that all you will accomplish is to create a situation of incredible division in the community with the Conservatives and the Orthodox against us? I mean, their children will be unable to marry our children because they won't be Jewish by *their* definition," she contended, her hand still on my thigh, squeezing to hold my attention.

"There already is such a division," Rabbi Samuels responded, looking in my direction for a rejoinder.

I was still silent, but now attentive.

"I think whenever a religious movement does something this controversial, it risks dissociation from more fundamentalist groups," the reverend contributed.

The rabbi nodded his head in agreement and looked back at me again for a reply. But I was trying hard to remain a mere spectator, so he pushed the issue, though in his skilled, amiable style.

"I'm wondering what you think of this, Yakov."

The heat was on. There was no place to hide now.

"Well, I think Rebecca has a point, but I don't believe she agrees with herself," I began as the others chuckled.

"Don't be too surprised," she responded with a full smile. Everyone seemed amused by our emerging repartee.

"Really?" I said placing my hand over hers, which was now on the table.

"Well," she began, "it's a very touchy issue, and I wouldn't necessarily be so quick to apply the principles of egalitarianism in this case."

"Why not?" the female rabbi asked aggressively.

"Because there are differences between men and women, and this particular issue, in fact, points to one of the most obvious of all," she answered dauntlessly.

"And what is that?" the female rabbi continued, a slightly vexed look coming upon her.

"That we always know exactly who the mother is," I interjected before Rebecca could.

We looked at each other, surprised that we could be taking the same side, and more astounded at being so much in sync. The rest of the conversation didn't seem to matter that much.

"And you think that this is really a problem today?" Rabbi Samuels asked.

"I think it could be," I responded, "although I do admit that the state of affairs today is significantly different from what it was in other times of history when Jewish women were being raped on a fairly regular basis."

"So you feel that since there is more certainty as to the mother's identity, she should exclusively determine the religion of the child," Karen Samuels threw in for clarification.

"I think it's a good argument," I explained tentatively.

"I think its a weak argument, frankly," the female rabbi contended, "because it's the usual Orthodox stuff of resolving present inequities by referring to historical conditions that no longer exist."

"If I might add something," the reverend's wife offered with a Southern accent, "it seems a much more dangerous problem to be creating an irreparable division in your community than this business about knowing who the mother is. These days, we always know who the father is also, although we may not be able to find him."

Her words and forthright delivery brought a refreshing reality to the esoteric tenor of the discussion.

"Well I don't see why we have to worry about that," the female rabbi responded with equal command while looking to Rabbi Samuels for approval. "They don't regard us as Jews anyway," she continued, this time with eyes on me. "Even if we do things their way, they don't regard it as legitimate just because it's *we* who did it and not they."

"Like what?" I asked defensively.

"Like conversion for openers." She waited for my response; I waited for her to continue. "If a Reform rabbi performs a conversion, even if it's done according to Orthodox standards, it's still not accepted."

Notwithstanding my desire to remain impartial, to them I was The Orthodox Jew. It didn't matter that I was Rebecca's boyfriend, or that I was sharing Thanksgiving with them. They saw me as they needed to. So there I was, the representative of everything from which I had always strove to separate myself.

"I don't think it's really possible for a Reform rabbi to perform a conversion according to strict Orthodox standards. After all, the most important of those standards is that the *Beis Din,* the three judges or rabbis that preside, be completely observant of Orthodox law. In addition to that, the convert also has to accept the authority of Orthodox law," I countered.

Rabbi Samuels broke the silence that followed my reply. "You're sadly correct, Yakov. What we have here are two very distinctive definitions of Judaism that can't seem to achieve any compromise."

"I will go even further," I asserted, feeling valiant because of the rabbi's affirmation. "Even the term *Judaism,* in this context, becomes meaningless. If you have a word, for argument's sake, and so many people disagree so ardently as to its meaning, then, in essence, it has no objective meaning. There's no way to measure what it is, no criteria at all. It is, therefore, meaningless."

"So what are you saying?" Rebecca asked with a confused expression.

"What I'm saying is that, practically speaking, these groups are practicing different religions, and they're engaged in a semantic argument over which group has the right to label their practice "Judaism." It's a ridiculous argument—let's just call a spade a spade and get on with it, like Christianity did."

"So which group can call itself Jewish?" the female rabbi asked.

"Frankly, I don't think it much matters. Each group should use a name that adequately reflects the different practices."

"But what about the things that we believe and do that are similar?" asked the cardiologist's wife.

"But what of the things that we believe and do that are similar to Christianity or Islam?" I countered.

"So, according to your analysis," Rabbi Samuels figured, "you're involved with a woman who practices a different religion than you." His words were followed by a cutely devilish smile on his face.

"That's only if you assume that I am Orthodox as you define it, and she is Reform as you define it. In either case, you would probably be wrong," I responded.

A good counter, no doubt, but not good enough to allay the powerful effect of his words. Rebecca and I stopped looking at each other for the moment and seemed, rather, to be simultaneously turning inward. Could we find some mutual ground upon which to build a life together? I could hear each of us asking just that in our hearts.

It was time for dessert.

CHAPTER 26

REBECCA'S PARENTS had been pushing to see us together ever since the day they first learned of our reunion. Rebecca could hold them off only so long, but after close to five months she herself was becoming uncomfortable by my reticence. I wasn't ready for such a meeting—considering the significance that would be attached to it—but she simply regarded this as another manifestation of my problem with making commitments, a problem I would have to overcome if I wanted to hold onto her.

It was a Sunday afternoon, coincidentally the third day of Chanukah, an appropriate time for family gatherings. Rebecca was as nervous as I. She had not seen her parents since that *Shabbos* when she had told them of our involvement, although she had spoken to them on the phone more frequently and the tenor of their relationship had improved.

It was an unusually mild day for the middle of December. The sun was bright and the temperature was in the low fifties. The plan was for brunch at Rebecca's apartment.

I arrived at about eleven-thirty to help her prepare, a good half hour before Benny and Devorah were expected. I had brought two boxes of assorted cookies and cakes that I had picked up at Gruenbaum's Kosher Bakery on my way. Rebecca was pleased with the selection and added that her parents would probably bring dessert also. A real party.

Upon entering her apartment, I could smell a distinct aroma, reminiscent of my mother's house at this time of year. It was homemade potato *latkes,* a traditional Chanukah staple. As a child I believed that this was what Judah Maccabee himself actually ate in order to gain strength to defeat his enemies. Now, I jested that the significance was really in the oil, each *latke* containing enough to burn for eight days.

Rebecca led me into the kitchen to show off the feast she'd prepared. Aside from the *latkes* and the applesauce that goes with them, there were bagels, lox, cream cheese, and assorted salads. "Enough food for the entire Maccabean army," I commented. I was always struck by how much of a Jewish mother Rebecca really was.

"I know I overdid it," she responded with a slightly embarrassed look. I assured her that nothing would go to waste. My refrigerator was completely empty and I would gladly accept any donations.

She was amused and moved closer to embrace me. As we held each other I could feel the scant vibrations of her anxiety. I put both my hands on her head, which was resting on my shoulder, and moved it back till our eyes met.

"Everything is going to be okay," I assured her.

"I hope so," she responded.

We proceeded to set the table and before we knew it the intercom was buzzing. Sandy announced the guests and Rebecca told him to send them up. The crescendo was building.

"Maybe you should answer the door, I'll wait in the living room, and you'll bring them in," I suggested nervously.

"Of course not. Don't be silly. I want you to answer the door with me. I want them to see us together from the very start," she responded as she took my hand.

I would have preferred to give her a chance to greet her parents after not having seen them for so long, and then bring me into the picture. She apparently had a different plan.

Instead of just standing around waiting, we continued busying ourselves with the table. We still hadn't finished by the time the doorbell rang. Noticing my hesitancy, Rebecca took me by the hand and led me to the door. She unlocked the two latches and, before turning the knob, took a noticeably deep breath.

Her mother embraced her and kissed her immediately; her father was a bit more reserved. Benny looked me over for a moment, and offered a respectful smile. Devorah's expression was more enthusiastic, but I knew they were both very pleased by my presence.

Rebecca turned toward me and said, "You both remember Yakov, of course." She seemed more awkward than the rest of us.

I jumped in, shaking hands first with Devorah and then with Benny, and offered the greeting *chag sameach,* happy holiday. They responded in kind. Rebecca directed us into the living room while she hung their coats in the closet and took the bakery box they had brought. We weren't in there a minute when Benny opened by asking me about my *smichah* exams. He appeared genuinely interested in the details. It was easy for me to talk about this. He laughed when I described Rav Trachtenberg, and he made an observation about how Yeshiva University must have changed since his days. He offered a few humorous stories of his own, but none as outlandish as mine.

I was feeling comfortable with this line of conversation. Devorah sat politely as Benny and I went back and forth. After a few minutes, Rebecca entered the room and quietly sat on the couch next to her mother. It seemed the women enjoyed watching us share anecdotes. When I noticed what was happening, I interrupted myself and apologized for my obliviousness to their presence. "Oh, I'm sorry," I said, turning to Rebecca and Devorah. "I always get carried away when I talk about Rav Trachtenberg."

"And Benny also gets a thrill reminiscing about the old days," Devorah added with a charming smile.

Rebecca just looked on, seemingly relieved at the smoothly flowing interchange between her parents and me. There was a brief moment of silence, and then she said she was famished. We all agreed and proceeded to the table.

"You know, I think Rebecca has impeccable taste," remarked Devorah as she examined the surroundings.

"Impeccable is a well-chosen word," I said.

"I mean, I've been here a few times before—she hasn't invited us too often you understand—but I can never get over the way she puts things together," she added.

"I think that's enough, Mother," Rebecca leaped in cutely.

I wasn't sure if she was reacting to the compliment, or to the criticism of not having them over more often. Benny was silent, and seemed amused.

We all sat around the table and began eating. I was much more relaxed than I'd imagined I would be. Some small talk ensued, mostly catching up on Kleinman family matters such as the latest about Moshe and his musical career. The pain on Rebecca's face at the mention of his name was revealing. I had known from what she had told me that he had all but disowned her when she had decided to become a rabbi. It was quite lamentable, I thought, remembering the first time I'd met her with Chaim and Moshe in The Pineview lobby.

It was interesting to watch them interact after all these years. She seemed a bit uneasy, as did they. There was much water under the bridge. But they had come back together, probably never to be severed so drastically again. I wondered if I would ever be as fortunate.

Barely five minutes went by before Benny turned to me again, but this time with a more personal bent. "You know, Yakov, I remember when I told you that you looked just like your father, but you're actually a cross between him and your mother. You have her eyes," he observed. The proverbial cat was out of the bag.

I wondered if he wasn't also alluding to my slightly thinning hair, an inheritance from my maternal grandfather. "So I've been told," I responded uncomfortably.

I looked over at Devorah, trying to be inconspicuous, and imagined her as my father's youthful love. She shared most of Rebecca's features, the same mint-green eyes, unflawed facial structure, and a thin yet ample figure. It seemed natural that, in addition to inheriting our parents' characteristics, we also inherited their preferences.

"How is he doing?" Benny asked with an air of sincerity.

"He's okay." Awkward.

"His health is good?" added Devorah with a slight nervous tremor in her voice.

"He hasn't slowed down any, that's for sure," I said with greater enthusiasm. I wondered how far we were going to take this line of inquiry.

"He always was a tenacious fellow," observed Benny.

"Still is, as much as ever," I replied.

"And your mother, how is she?" Devorah inquired.

"She's well, too," I answered, trying to hold back any clue of the recent rift between us. Rebecca had assured me that she hadn't shared what went on between me and my mother with her parents, that they had no idea whether I had told my parents about her or not. It was none of their business, she declared. But I was sure they were damn curious. And wondered, at this moment, if I wouldn't have preferred her telling them. This way they would have been satisfied and wouldn't feel the need to broach the topic with me. That was my greatest fear. How could I possibly tell these people that the pain they had caused almost thirty years ago was still very much alive, and as destructive as it ever was. I now understood what Benny had been so concerned about that summer at The Pineview.

"Well, Rivki," interjected Benny, "what ever do you intend to do with all this food?" I was relieved at the change of subject.

"Oh, Yakov has a pretty good appetite, and if you and Mom want to take something . . ."

"Now don't be ridiculous," interrupted Devorah, "your father and I don't eat this kind of food at home anymore anyway."

Benny shrugged his shoulders.

"Wait till you see what's in the cake box we brought you," he added.

"Let me guess," offered Rebecca, "chocolate black-out cake!"

A giant smile came to his face.

"Still your favorite?" he posed.

"Still my favorite," she replied.

"That's my Rivki, Ms. Chocolate Black-out Cake," he boasted with his eyes on me. "You just know her as Ms. Serious Philosopher, or something," he added sardonically, "but to me she'll always love black-out cake more than anything in the world." I noticed he couldn't bring himself to use the term *rabbinical student.* I also noticed that he took much enjoyment in turning Rebecca back into his little daughter, assuming the role of gracious daddy, providing his child with her most desired treat. A momentary excursion into elusive fantasy. It was obvious that he needed to do this.

Rebecca fell into the trap and blushed at the caricature. Devorah's expression matched Benny's. I smiled along, but felt slightly envious of their reconciliation.

The conversation remained fairly superficial. There was no further discussion about my parents. They were either being tactful, or afraid to learn the truth. There were also no questions about my relationship with their daughter, about our intentions or future together, about how I would fit into her life or she into mine. At least not from them.

It was safe to assume that they regarded me as a "white knight," as Rebecca had put it, sent by God Himself to rescue their daughter from the clutches of iniquity. They'd hoped I would bring her to her senses, that through my influence she would find her way back to where she'd come from. How ironic.

CHAPTER 27

As the next few months passed, Rebecca's desire for a commitment grew. She never actually spoke about it, nor did she pressure me, but I could tell that she was waiting. I also knew she wouldn't wait forever.

An unspoken tension had developed between us. She seemed unhappy, and was gradually losing some of her enthusiasm. Yet again, she wouldn't talk about it, and I certainly wasn't going to press the issue. Until one day, the last Sunday in February to be exact, when her silence finally broke.

It was unusually warm for the time of year, a very premature glimpse of spring. So we decided, after breakfast, to take a walk through Central Park. Suddenly, just as we were about to step out the door, her phone rang. We looked at each other as Rebecca decided whether to answer. By the fourth ring her curiosity had gotten the better of her.

"Hello . . . Oh, hi, what's up?" she said into the receiver as she mouthed to me, "It's Stephanie." Since that *Shabbos* lunch when I was first introduced to Stephanie and Bob, they had joined us on a few occasions for double dates. I'd gotten to know them better and had developed quite a liking for them—her, for her charm; him, for his innocence.

Rebecca listened for a moment and then became happily excited. "Oh my God, you're kidding," she yelled ecstatically. She continued to listen, smiling gleefully, and mouthing to me something that looked like, "They found a hall and set a date for the wedding." I pretended not to understand what she was trying to say.

"They're tying the knot in just three months!" she blurted out.

"Mazel tov," I responded, pretending to be happy. I knew what was coming next.

The conversation between them was brief. After hanging up, Rebecca recounted to me, with fervor, where it was to be held, her excitement over buying a bridesmaid's dress, and other little details. She was acutely unaware of how girlish she sounded.

The simplicity of it all—two people finding each other, falling in love, marrying—must have made her envious, though she managed to hide it. I felt similarly and managed to hide it as well. As we left her building, she took my hand and said, "I know I'm not supposed to do this, especially in broad daylight, but today I'm going to hold your hand the entire day whether you approve or not."

For her, this was an obviously empowering act, to ignore the constraints of our relationship and make things as she wanted them to be. I was happy to comply, seeing that some of the luster had been revived. My fear of being seen this way took a back-seat to the pleasure of the moment once again.

We talked about nothing: school, the weather, the surroundings, what movie we would see next. We had gotten halfway through the park walking toward the East Side when she broached the inevitable.

"There's something I've wanted to discuss for a long time but I've been too scared to bring it up," she opened.

I was fully attentive. The unusual sound of birds chirping in winter had been hushed.

"I don't even know if *scared* is the right word. I just always promised myself that I wouldn't be the one to bring up this issue," she continued. Her lips began to quiver and her eyes looked as if she were holding back tears.

"I think I know where this is going," I added.

"I'm sure you do," she reacted, almost angrily. "It's not fair for you to put me in this position!"

"What position am I putting you in?" I asked, feigning innocence.

"You really want me to say it, don't you. You want *me* to ask *you,* or maybe you want me to beg you." Anger.

"Stop!" I demanded as I softly sealed her lips with my forefinger. "I know what you want and it's the same thing I want. I just don't know about the logistics. I mean, how can we possibly get married or even think about getting married under our present circumstances? It's absurd."

"If you really want to spend the rest of your life with me than you'll have to change the circumstances, won't you?" she added emphatically.

"And what about you, what changes are you prepared to make?"

"I don't know—we've never discussed them. You've never asked me to change or give up anything. You've never said 'Don't be a rabbi,' or 'Try returning to Orthodoxy,' or anything of the sort. And that's part of the problem—you've never been committed enough to me to give me any ultimatums, and you've never been committed enough to your Judaism to force you to make any. You've been able to have it both ways only because you don't know what it is you really want. Well, I know what *I* really want, so I know what I'm willing to give up and what I'm not."

"That's just great that you have all the answers."

"Well, it sucks that you don't have any."

"I have some, at least more than I used to. And I've made choices and given things up also. Remember, I'm the one whose parents don't speak to him anymore."

"Oh, come on, Yakov, don't lay that one on me. *You're* the one who doesn't speak to them, not the other way around. Okay, so your mother doesn't call since you told her about me, but what have you done to change that? Have you called her and told her how you feel? Have you gone to your father and confronted him with the truth? No! You just sit passively, hoping that she hasn't uttered a word, and letting things go on as they always have. It's just another sign of your lack of commitment. It's all over the place!"

I stood in silence. She wanted me to make my choices and sacrifices as she had done; she wanted me to struggle and fight, and to emerge.

"Yakov," she said as she took my hand and tried to calm herself, "I love you and I love my Judaism, and I know exactly what I'm prepared to give up and what I can't because of that. And one of the things I know is that I can't stay around forever waiting for you to figure these things out. I'm a woman and I want to be married and have children and all the things that go along with that. I'm going to be a rabbi and I need to have a family to help me be completely fulfilled so that I can give of myself to others." She paused. She could no longer keep back the tears. "You need to decide what you want and what you love, what you're truly willing to sacrifice and what you aren't. Even if you chose to give me up because of your orthodoxy, at least that I could respect. But this total indecisiveness, I detest it, and sometimes I detest you for it."

"I do know that I love you," I responded softly, snuggling her hand. "I knew it from the very first time I saw you, and I know that I was dead all those years without you. I also know that I can't imagine spending any more years like that."

"I believe you. But I need you to love me more than the first time you saw me, because that was in a fantasy world and this is reality. And I need you to imagine your life *with* me rather than imagining it *without* me."

She took her hand from mine and wiped her tears as she spoke. I watched and listened. I had no more responses to offer. I reached out with both my hands to hold her and bring her closer. She complied tentatively. I knew that I did not have many of these conversations left.

Sometimes you must make choices. Sometimes you must sacrifice.

The next day, I surprised her when I suggested that we go somewhere out of the city for a weekend. Find a place where no one would know either of us, where we could just be, where we could spend a simple weekend focusing on what we shared rather than worrying about what stood between us. "I think it could give us some perspective," I suggested. She agreed.

We had settled on a small inn up in the Berkshires outside the town of Great Barrington, far away from anything that would be familiar to either of us. The place, which was recommended by one of her classmates as the perfect getaway, didn't have a vacancy for two weeks because it was still skiing season. Our reservation was for the second weekend in March.

We split the entire cost which included the room, renting a car, and buying kosher food to bring with us. We even divided up the drive which took a little under four hours, all the way up the Taconic Parkway, and then eastward on Route 23 toward Massachusetts. When we saw the sign for The Meadow View Inn, I made a left into the entrance. Straight ahead of us was a quaint white colonial building not more than a quarter of a mile back from the road. We drove toward the building on a pebbled approach that cut through a flat landscape of grass covered slightly with the season's last residue of snow. I removed my yarmulke and placed it in my pocket. Now I was, for the first time, completely anonymous. And with that anonymity came a surge of liberation that I knew I could easily get used to. Rebecca made no comment.

I pulled the car up to the front entrance and an elderly man immediately came out to help us with our bags. I felt bad letting him carry the suitcases but he insisted, stating, "You're the one who's here for a rest, young man."

We entered through the front door into what appeared to be a large living room full of comfortable-looking couches and chairs, an oversized television, and a baby grand piano. The lighting was subdued to accentuate the countrified feeling of the oak floors, walls, and ceilings. A few scattered area rugs added to the homeyness.

Behind a small registration desk was the same fellow who took our bags. I gave him my name and we both chuckled as he referred to us as Mr. and Mrs. Eisen. He gathered the paperwork, took an imprint of my credit card, and then offered to show us to our room. As he led the way up a semicircular staircase, another couple, dressed in ski clothing, was descending. The old man then asked if we had planned to do any skiing this weekend. When he saw the curious look on my face, he jumped in, boasting that the season could sometimes run as late as the end of March. We hadn't really considered it, I explained, but asked if he knew of any other activities we might be interested in. He led us to the room, put the key in the door, and opened it as he proceeded to enumerate a list of attractions ranging from historical sightseeing to dining. He spoke as he brought the bags into the room, opened the curtains, and turned up the thermostat. When he was finished, he asked if we would be eating at the inn or elsewhere that evening. "Reservations for the dining room need to made by three each day," he declared. We replied that we would not be having dinner in the dining room, and I reached into my pocket to take out a few dollars for him. He stopped me by placing his hand on my arm and informed me that the owner doesn't take tips. Embarrassed, Rebecca and I both laughed and thanked him for his help.

When he closed the door behind him, it remained shut until the following morning. Sometime during the evening we managed to unpack and eat some of the chicken and *kasha varnishkes* we had brought with us. Rebecca lit *Shabbos* candles, I made *Kiddush,* she recited the *Motzi*—a politically acceptable division of labor. Although we had come to a new place with the plan of leaving everything behind, there were some things we just couldn't forget.

We awakened early in the morning to the sounds of footsteps in the hall. The diehard skiers were hurrying to catch the slopes. When I opened my eyes, I looked around the room for a moment. The wallpaper was an old-fashioned flowery design—greens, yellows, and crimsons—that matched the curtains and the bedquilt. Bright sunshine blazed through the windows and landed against the wall in front of me.

The room was warm; the pillows were fluffy; the bed was hard; the quilt was soft. I felt I could stay there forever, and when Rebecca reached over to embrace me, I wanted to. It was as if I had never awakened before in my life.

The day was ours to spend together. No synagogues, no families, no school, no other commitments, just the two of us and this place. And so it wasn't surprising that we spent the entire day without any of our usual debates. There was nothing to impel us into philosophical contention. There were Ping-Pong and pool tables, and much beautiful scenery to hike through. And there was just sitting around enjoying the solitude. We did it all.

We held hands and talked about nothing. We read newspapers and didn't talk at all. And before we knew it, the day had passed.

We had seen in the local newspaper that the theater in town was playing a revival of the movie *Laura,* the classic detective story in which the hero, a hard-nosed cop played by Dana Andrews, falls madly in love with a portrait of a murder victim, played by Gene Tierney, who he later discovers had never been killed. Rebecca was ecstatic. She related every detail she could remember from the many times she had already seen the film. A romance like this was the perfect icing on the cake for this weekend, she insisted. So off to town we went.

We were just about leaving the room when I remembered that we'd forgotten to perform the *Havdalah* service to end the Sabbath. I reminded her and she quickly took out the special three-wick candle she had brought with her. I lit it and she held it in her hand while I filled a cup with the leftover wine from the night before. Folklore has it that a woman's husband will be as tall as the height at which she holds the *Havdalah* candle, and Rebecca smiled as she positioned it perfectly parallel to the top of my head. I then began to recite the prayer, mumbling speedily through the words so that we could get it over and done with, so that we could get back to the other world and make the movie on time. But my efforts were slowed by a looming irony stirred by the very essence of the words I was saying: *Blessed are You, Lord our God, King of the universe, Who has separated the holy from the profane, light from darkness . . .*

Holy and profane, like light and darkness, seemed to be neatly divided categories, but our lives had managed to blend them into obscurity. A weekend away, in the same bedroom, in the same bed. Yet dare we neglect the Sabbath, dare we allow our profanity to abrogate all last traces of sanctity?

It was right out of one of Rabbi Roth's speeches about Jewish law and premarital sex. He had addressed such issues on numerous occasions, always concluding that while he didn't endorse premarital sex, having it didn't exempt one from putting on *t'fillin* the next morning. The metaphor of not throwing the baby out with the bathwater was one he commonly used.

He undoubtedly seemed courageous when making such assertions, unlike so many other Orthodox rabbis I'd known. His eyes were open and he recognized the needs and demands of the community he served. And here I was, living proof that there was somebody out there in the pews listening. At last, I was listening to The Rabbi.

I had intermingled the holy and the profane, probably even confused the two. Nevertheless, I remembered to thank God for separating them, for bringing clarity to what would otherwise have been blurred. Then I went to the movies, held Rebecca's hand, ate popcorn, and enjoyed watching two people who yearned for each other light up the screen. To me, the world was still blurred.

We arrived back in the city at around seven-thirty the next evening. The ride home was marked by an obvious strain between us. We didn't do much talking; the time was passed driving and sleeping. It occurred to me—and probably to Rebecca as well—that the weekend, which was perfect by every conceivable definition, would likely worsen the problems we'd left behind. Our intention had been to grow closer to each other and to a decision about our future. And though I felt enmeshed with her very essence, it only served to intensify my conflict.

I let her off in front of her building. The plan was for me to go on to my place, drop off my luggage, return the rental car, and come back to her apartment to spend yet another evening together—to prolong the weekend as much as much as possible. We were both wiped out from the drive and probably in need of some solitude, so when I suggested that we call it a night, she offered no objection. Sandy came out into the street, gave his usual salutations, and helped her with her bags. We exchanged a restrained kiss on the lips and a flimsy hug goodbye.

I called when I got home after returning the car. It was a short conversation—how it went with the car, how tired we both were, talk to you tomorrow, and the rest. I needed to reconnect, to recapture what we'd left in the Berkshires. It was not there for the taking, not unless I was prepared to accept all the consequences that such a relationship in the real world would impose. There was no need for any further discussion between us on the matter, it had all been said and was understood. All that remained was to choose.

CHAPTER 28

OVER THE FOLLOWING WEEKS I was forced to focus my energies on an upcoming *smichah* exam and plow through some serious dissertation writing. Waldman had insisted that giving me deadlines for the completion of different chapters would help me elude the trap of procrastination and avoidance that so often plagues graduate students. It also helped me deflect my attention from the other matters that I was indeed avoiding.

My apartment had turned into a disaster area. Papers and manuscripts had piled up from wall to wall. Even the bed, which I was using more often these days, was covered with clutter. Except for classes and phone calls or dates with Rebecca, I became reclusive. And the dates—which had already begun waning in intensity—were also beginning to occur less frequently. The "dissertation/*smichah* exam" excuse was wearing thinner with time.

Rebecca talked frequently of Stephanie's wedding, of her excitement over being a bridesmaid. I would be invited of course, she insisted, cloistering any reservations about my actually still being part of her life when the time came. It was clear that she wasn't going to raise the issue of commitment again, until she was completely out of patience and ready to be rid of me. I hoped she would at least grant me the leeway of finishing my *smichah* exams, maybe even my doctorate. Perhaps the doctorate was pushing it.

We saw each other a bit more frequently over the Passover holiday. She had me over for several meals and we spent a few spring afternoons walking through the park. I knew that she noticed I had been particularly saddened at not having had any contact with my parents despite the holiday, but she, wisely, kept her observations to herself.

I often wondered what my father was thinking. Had my mother lied to him? Had she maintained the illusion that she spoke with me regularly and that I just couldn't make it home because of exams and the like? Or had he finally learned the truth?

After the first seder, which Rebecca hosted for me and some other friends including Stephanie and Bob, I found myself walking home along Broadway at about two in the morning. It had been a late evening with much commentary and song. Somewhere along the way I stopped, looked in the window of a shop, and saw my own reflection staring back at me. I was disheveled, probably because of the hour and a slight case of intoxication. I also appeared lost.

I looked at myself and wondered how I'd come to this moment. Images of the past entered my mind, of myself around fourteen or fifteen, sitting at the large table in my parents' dining room on the first night of Passover. *Chaim, his sisters, and his parents are with us. Zelig and my father are wearing* kittles, *the white robes traditionally worn for marriage, special holidays, and burial. They are busily discussing the meaning of a passage in the* Haggadah *while Chaim and I are playing around and laughing.*

The scene continues. My father is eating a large chunk of horseradish. His eyes are tearing from the bitterness, but he is smiling with rapture over performing this mitzvah. *He then turns to me, sitting next to him, and offers me some as well. "Here, Yankel, take it!" he says. "It's not easy to fulfill the* mitzvah *of eating the bitter herbs," he tells me, "but it is important to taste the suffering of the Jewish people." With his strong hands, he holds the root with his left and cuts out a sizable piece with his right. I make a face and Chaim laughs. I cannot decline; Chaim's turn will come next. My face turns red as a beet and I feel like I'm going to faint. Now it is my father who is laughing and my mother along with him—another rarity.*

Another image appears. We are all sitting at the same table, but I am even younger, a child of five or six with a funny-looking mustache from the grape juice I've been drinking. The men are singing. I can hear my father's mellifluous voice, my uncle trying to stay on key. The women hum modestly along. I only know some of the words, so I try to fake it. I appear content, even happy, sitting there in song with my parents.

Suddenly, I returned to the present, recalling a conversation I'd had with my aunt Sheindy a few days earlier. She reported that Chaim had been doing much better. A few weeks ago he'd been caught stealing from a charity box in a local yeshiva, and the yeshiva decided not to press charges under the condition that he return home and enter a drug treatment program. Apparently, he had kept his part of the bargain and was now attending a specialized program for Orthodox Jewish addicts run by the Jewish Board for Mental Health Services. I was surprised that such a thing even existed.

She sounded enthusiastic in describing the parent group that she and Zelig had become involved with. The number of people in the community touched by this problem, they had learned, was astounding. There were alcohol, heroine, cocaine, and even crack addicts. There was talk about AIDS, which had infiltrated the community through the use of intravenous drugs and the practice of homosexuality. She thanked God that her son had been spared the worst of these things.

She sounded both optimistic and sad. The lines of communication had been opened between Chaim and his parents, and for that she was grateful. I felt a touch of jealousy upon hearing this, a similar feeling to the one I'd had when Rebecca had reconciled with her parents. Would fate be as kind to me?

It was a painful education Sheindy and Zelig had received. They'd learned, firsthand, of how the scourge of society had visited itself upon a community that, because of its insular character, was unprepared to meet the challenge. And yet, despite strange currents to conceal these problems, they'd become part of a movement that had emerged among those whose lives had been touched.

I asked Sheindy if my parents had known of any of this, and she said no. Strangely, she didn't elicit any further commitment of confidentiality from me. Perhaps she had gained confidence in my discretion, or maybe she was just more aware of my estrangement from my parents than she'd previously been. She did sense, in fact, that one of the reasons for my call was to find out how my parents were faring. She told me they were well and that they spoke of me often, as if nothing unusual was going on. "Don't worry," she said, "I'm good at playing dumb. I make believe I don't know anything. That's how you get along in this family. That's how we used to deal with your grandfather, of blessed memory."

What a family, I thought to myself. So many secrets, lies, and pretenses. Could life's truths really be so threatening?

I was relieved to hear that my father was healthy, which only meant that he had still not learned of my last conversation with my mother. My aunt was glad that I had called and encouraged me to do so more often. She also suggested that I break the ice with Chaim. "He's much too embarrassed to make the first move," she said. I told her I would do just that, but knew in my heart I probably wouldn't. More pretense.

"This will be a real Passover of redemption," she said, "May the messiah come speedily in our time." And then with a sullen tone she added, "And maybe next year you will come home and join us."

My reverie was over and my sobriety was returning. I turned away from the window and looked around, realizing that it wasn't the safest time to be wandering the streets. I continued walking up Broadway. I was now an adult and very much alone.

CHAPTER 29

Professor Waldman's midterm exam for the spring semester was scheduled for what was also the second day of Passover. He agreed to allow me to write a paper to make up for missing the exam. The topic of the paper dealt with Nietzsche's attitude toward sex. Apparently, the great philosopher had a powerful aversion to the activity and also had troubled relationships with women. As I was doing with Freud in my dissertation, I explored whether Nietzsche's views had been influenced by his psychological needs or purely by his philosophical convictions. I concluded, à la Waldman, that it had probably been a bit of both. I was certain he would love the argument. When I got back the paper with a B on it, I was dismayed that he hadn't.

I approached him after class and requested a meeting with him during his office hours. Such was the usual procedure for setting up an appointment with The Professor. "No need," he replied as if he knew that this was not about my dissertation, "I'm on my way there now, just have to take a quick pit stop at the john. What do you say we meet there in about five minutes, okay?"

When Waldman arrived, I was waiting by his door. He invited me in and we both sat down. He swiveled around toward me, leaned back in his chair, and waited for me to open the conversation. I didn't.

"So, Mr. Eisen, what can I do for you today?" he asked congenially.

"It's about the grade I got on the paper, the one about Nietzsche."

"Ah yes, that's what I thought you wanted to discuss. You know it was an excellent paper, just about the best I've seen on that topic." He took a fresh cigar from the box atop his desk, unwrapped it, punched a whole in the back, and lit up as he spoke.

"Then I'm even more confused—"

"You mean about the grade," he interrupted. "That's not a reflection of the quality of the paper in any way," he affirmed. Puff, puff.

"I don't understand," I reacted with bewilderment. He sat there and looked right at me as if there was something obvious that I just wasn't getting. "Then, what is the grade about?"

He took a deep breath and continued staring at me. I could tell he wasn't completely comfortable by the way in which he nervously seesawed the cigar between his fingers. "I thought it would be clear," he began, "but I guess few things really are in this world," he added sarcastically as he paused once again.

I waited for him to continue.

"The reason I gave you a B was because I felt it necessary to penalize you for not having taken the exam. The paper *was* very good," he offered defensively as he saw the burning look in my eyes, "but it's far easier to write a paper than to take an exam. And that gave you an unfair advantage over the others."

He must be kidding, I thought. I sat there for a moment, trying to digest this, trying to conjure up an appropriate response without brandishing my anger. I was afraid of losing control. And that damn smoke wasn't helping either.

"I'm sorry, Dr. Waldman, but I don't agree with your analysis of this situation," I presented with detached philosophical demeanor.

"What do you disagree with?" he probed innocently.

"Well, to begin with, I see significant differences between opting to write a paper, which I agree is easier than taking an exam, and not being able to take the exam because it was given on a religious holiday on which I neither travel nor write. In one case there is an option, in the other there is no choice."

"But still you have the advantage," he answered smugly.

"But that's because . . ."

"Yes, I know, you had no choice," he preempted. "But consider this, Mr. Eisen. It is not so clear that you didn't, as you insist, have any choice. After all, the decision to miss the exam because of your religious convictions is a choice, is it not?"

"But Dr. Waldman, you yourself are Jewish, surely you understand these restrictions."

"My religion, Mr. Eisen, is, frankly, irrelevant here. You are making the argument that you had no choice. I could be Jewish, Buddhist, or Episcopalian, and it wouldn't change the fact that you *did* have a choice. And that means that you also had an advantage over the others for which I must somehow penalize you."

I knew at that point it was senseless to continue. He was convinced that his motives were purely rational, though I suspected a more unconscious reason at play—good old ethnic self-hatred. It wasn't often that I personally encountered anti-Semitism, and here it was coming from a Jew no less, a Jew I'd admired and emulated.

I picked up my book bag from the floor and stood up. Not knowing if my expression in any way betrayed my inner rage, I said nothing as I moved toward the door.

"I'm sorry if you still don't understand, but I hope you will think about it some more. The important thing is that the paper was excellent, even publishable I might add, and I still regard you as one of my most brilliant protégés." Puff, puff.

I shuddered at the thought, yet still nodded in acquiescence. And as I was just about out the door, I turned to him and asked, "Tell me one thing." He peered up with curiosity.

"Have you ever scheduled an exam on Martin Luther King's birthday or even the day before Christmas?"

He offered no reply. I gestured goodbye and continued out the door.

CHAPTER 30

I HAD SPENT the evening at the library and hadn't arrived home until well after eleven. The light on my answering machine was blinking. I wondered who it could be. Rebecca was the only one I'd been speaking to these days and we'd talked just a few hours earlier. I dropped my books on the chair and before even removing my coat I rushed toward the machine. I pressed the playback button; it was the voice of my mother.

She was calling from a pay phone in the emergency room at Maimonides Hospital. My father had been rushed there by ambulance. She said only that he had collapsed after dinner and that he was being worked on by the doctors. This was all she knew.

I ran out in the street and hailed a cab. It was late and the driver didn't exactly relish the idea of going all the way into Brooklyn. I anxiously explained the circumstances and he agreed.

The drive should have been about ten minutes shorter, but we were held up by a traffic jam getting onto the Brooklyn Bridge. No other city in the world has traffic at midnight. It was the longest forty minutes I ever experienced.

When we pulled up to the emergency room the meter read thirty-seven dollars and some odd cents. I gave the man fifty and hurried out of the cab before he could give me any change. "Good luck," he yelled from the window as I rushed through the hospital's electric doors.

I entered a waiting room filled with people. I stopped and looked around for a moment. My mother was nowhere to be found. I approached what looked like a nurses' station at the other end of the room. There was only one nurse and she was already talking to someone else. I tried waiting for a few seconds before I found myself interrupting.

"Eisen. Rabbi David Eisen," I said excitedly.

The nurse looked up at me, and the woman she was talking to gave me an angry stare.

"Could you please tell me where Rabbi Eisen is? He was brought in earlier by ambulance. I think he had a heart attack. He's my father."

The lady's look disappeared and the nurse typed the name into the computer.

"He's not in the computer," she said, "so he probably only arrived in the past few hours. Let me check inside and see what his status is," she added politely.

"And if my mother's in with him, could you please tell her that I'm out here," I said as she walked through a double swinging door.

She was gone for less than a minute before reappearing, expressionless. She told me that my father was inside, still being worked on by the doctors, and that my mother was with him. The utter professionalism of her manner frightened me.

She buzzed me in through a visitors' entrance which was off to my left. As soon as I was inside I saw my mother, with my aunt and uncle standing at the other end of the hall, speaking to a man in a white coat. They saw me coming, and my mother turned toward me and started running in my direction with her arms open and tears in her eyes. Zelig and Sheindy stayed back with the doctor. She grabbed me, held me, and continued crying. I wiped her tears away, but more kept coming. I put my arm around her and walked back to the others, who were standing beside the entrance to a room that was closed by a white hospital curtain.

"Yankel, this is Dr. Benjamin," my aunt said.

I looked at him and introduced myself. He was the resident on duty that night, a good-looking young man, about thirty years old, tall, thin, with dark curly hair. His manner seemed pleasant and straightforward.

"I'm afraid the situation is quite serious," he said, responding to my question about my father's condition.

"Where's Dr. Rubin?" I asked, referring to my father's regular cardiologist.

"He's inside working on him now," he answered.

I looked at the white curtain for a moment, then turned to the doctor and asked when I could go in.

"Right now, no one can go in. It's touch-and-go and we're doing all we can, but we need room to work."

He was barely finished speaking when the curtain opened. It was Dr. Rubin, with a defeated look on his face that I shall never forget. He was not only my father's personal physician, but one of his avid followers as well. He moved toward my mother, took both her hands in his, and said he was sorry, but there was nothing more they could do.

"What does that mean?" she asked as if not getting his point.

"He's gone, Esther," he said, while struggling to maintain his composure.

My aunt Sheindy fainted and was caught by Zelig. A nurse came right over to assist him. My mother stood there, gasping for breath, gushing tears and bellowing, with Dr. Rubin trying to comfort her. I slipped inside the curtain to see for myself.

The last nurse was just finished disconnecting the apparatus and covering the body that lay there on the table. She picked up a plastic bag filled with soiled sheets and rags, gave me a sad glance, and left me alone. The room was filled with the stench of human waste.

The commotion outside faded into the background as stillness descended upon my surroundings. For the first time ever there was just the two of us. And he was dead. I stood there looking at him. He seemed to be asleep, all but his head covered by a sheet. His features were rigid, his mouth slightly contorted from the respirator. His hair was wet from perspiration.

I moved toward the table and grasped the sheet. I stood there, holding it in my hand, trying to imagine what lay underneath. Suddenly, my hand had a life of its own. It lifted the sheet, and my eyes beheld his nakedness. I stared at him, the body of a great Torah scholar, as if expecting to have discovered some wondrous secret or anomaly. There was nothing but his corpse, and the lingering smell of feces, his last mark upon the world.

When it occurred to me that what I had been doing was expressly forbidden by Jewish law, I replaced the sheet. The sanctity of the dead had to be preserved. I then moved to the end of the table, and stood directly above his head. I began stroking his damp hair, straightening it out so he looked proper when he met his maker. Our encounter remained undisturbed; perhaps God was giving me this moment. And then came the tears.

I had contained my tears so often, fought them back so many times, for so many years, but could no longer do so. I held his head with both my hands. I hated him for having deprived me of his touch, and myself for having accepted those boundaries. I bent over and placed my cheek against his. I could feel the wetness of my tears running down his face. I moved slightly upward and pressed my lips on his forehead.

I was kissing my father, holding him, and crying. He was dead, and I was alive in a way I'd never known. The moment was fleeting, suddenly broken by the presence of others.

My mother ran to his body and smothered his face with hers. My aunt was beside her as I stepped away and watched with my uncle. I wiped the tears from my cheeks but more kept coming.

I am sorry I am crying, *Totti.* I am sorry I am not strong like Jewish men should be. I am weak. Please forgive me. I am sorry.

I quietly opened the curtain and stepped out into the hallway. I looked for a pay phone and found one at the end of the corridor. I walked toward the phone, oblivious to the goings-on around me.

I took the receiver off the hook and a quarter from my pocket. I hesitated. I knew I had to tell Rebecca what had happened, but I didn't know what to say beyond that. She would want to come and be with me, but I had to think of my mother.

I dialed Rebecca's number. She answered, half awake, after two rings. She probably looked at the digital clock on her night table. She probably knew something wasn't right.

"I'm calling from the hospital, it's my father—"

"Yakov, is everything okay?" she interrupted.

"No. It's very bad," I responded, trembling. I couldn't bring myself to say it, to accept the reality and speak the words.

"Yakov, tell me what happened," she urged.

"He's gone," I responded, using one of those euphemisms that don't quite capture the essence of death but make the point nonetheless.

"Oh my God, Yakov, I'm so sorry, I'm so sorry." She began to cry. "Where are you, what hospital?"

Just what I had feared. She wanted a latitude and longitude so she could come to me. I couldn't deal with this now. I shouldn't have called.

"It's Maimonides in Brooklyn, but you really don't have to come. I'm okay, and I don't think I will be here much longer anyway. I have to get back to my mother. She'll go home with my aunt and uncle and I'll stay with his body until the funeral parlor comes for it." The meaning of my own words overcame me and I erupted, weeping again. "I think I should be at my mother's house in an hour or so. I'll call you when I get there."

She sensed my resistance to her coming and acceded. "Okay, but please, call me as soon as you get there," she pressed.

"I will."

"I love you very much."

"I love you too," I said, biting my lip to keep it from trembling.

I hung up and proceeded back down the hall. When I got there, Dr. Rubin was escorting my family out. "They'll take the body downstairs until it is picked up by the funeral home," he was saying to my mother.

"I have to stay with the body!" I interrupted. "Someone has to stand guard over it until the burial," I explained a bit more calmly.

Dr. Rubin, being familiar with Jewish law, understood what I was saying. He told me he would explain to the nurses and make appropriate preparations for me to remain with the body. He walked over to the nurses' station and the three of us remained by my father's side. I was surprised at my own zealousness in insisting to stay with the body. It was almost instinctual. My mother gave me a proud look.

I suggested that Zelig take them home and I would wait and accompany the body to the chapel. My uncle agreed and told me that he had already called the leader of the *Chevra Kadishah,* the burial society that consists of members of the community who take it upon themselves to perform all the necessary preparations for burial. I would be met at the chapel and they would take over the guarding and ritual cleansing of the body. From there, I could walk to my mother's house.

The laws and requirements kept me occupied with thoughts concerning the sanctity and protection of my father's body, almost as if he were still alive and I had to take care of him. This helped impose structure and purpose on a moment of sheer desperation. And in a sense, I believed that a part of him was still alive and watching to make sure that I attended to everything correctly. I was believing in something.

The funeral was to be held at noon that same day. Although there were but a few hours to notify people, a mammoth crowd appeared likely. I knew I couldn't keep Rebecca away—nor did I want to—but I hoped she would be inconspicuous.

We were picked up by a limousine in front of the house at around ten-thirty in the morning. My mother and I got into the backseat with Zelig and Sheindy. Rachel and Leah rode behind in their car. Chaim was not there. I asked Sheindy where he was, and she responded with a dispirited expression. I figured out the rest.

When we arrived at the chapel, we were met at the door by the funeral director. He expressed what appeared to be genuine condolences. He had known my father throughout the years—one might say they were business associates of sorts. He directed us to a reception area where we were to sit while everyone would greet us and offer their sympathies. We sat and waited.

I had been in a complete daze from the moment I entered my mother's house about nine hours earlier. I had tried to sleep but couldn't, so I went downstairs into the living room and just sat there staring at the walls. I cried off and on. It was a strange thing, crying, and every time I started I was afraid I would be unable to stop. It wasn't about memories—my mind was unable to focus on the past—but about his missing presence. He was gone, and this time for good. There were no more conversations to be had, no more battles to be fought. There was no more unfinished business to be finished, at least not with him. Anything that remained between us was mine to contend with, and mine alone.

I wanted him to come back, even for only a second, to have a last opportunity to look at him and say that, despite the arguments and estrangement between us, I loved him, and all I ever really needed was to know that he loved me. Nothing else mattered. All the other issues, conflicts, and quarrels were mere diversions from that one utterance that would never be spoken.

My mother had also been up the entire night, aimlessly wandering through the house as if searching for something she couldn't find. She sat with me in the living room for a while, even took my hand and told me that she wouldn't know what to do without me. I thought about Rebecca and wondered. I wanted to ask if he had been told about her, but restrained myself. She was in enough pain already.

We had been in the reception room for about ten minutes when the first guests arrived—Ezra and his wife. As soon as he saw my mother he burst into tears.

Ezra was to conduct the service and deliver one of the eulogies. I knew it would be most difficult for him to do so. A few hours earlier, over the phone, he had told me he had asked three other rabbis, all close friends of my father, to deliver eulogies and that he felt I should speak as well. I declined.

I had thought about the request, even mentioned it to my mother, who deemed it a fitting idea. But I knew that the things that I would talk about might not go over too well with this audience. These were people who saw my father as some sort of godly being, totally self-sacrificing and faultless. This was what they believed and this was what they would want to hear. Not that I would dare say anything negative or inappropriate, but my reflections might be just a bit too human for their tastes.

Other people soon began arriving. There were neighbors, congregants, rabbis by the dozen, and even some dignitaries like the local assemblyman and city councilwoman. They paraded before us, took our hands, and commiserated with us.

Among them was Rav Trachtenberg, who had been given a ride by a group of my classmates. Despite my alienation from my fellow rabbinical students, it was a *mitzvah* to attend a funeral, and these guys took that seriously. It was also an opportunity for them to do the *rebbe* a favor by driving him, and sucking up to the *rebbe* was another thing they took seriously.

It was very close to twelve when Rebecca finally appeared. She entered the room and my heart pounded in much the same way as it had the very first time I saw her. She was so absolutely gorgeous, so exquisite in the way she held herself. She looked around for a moment, and then walked toward where we were sitting. I watched her intently as she approached, the elegance of each and every move. And then she stood in front of me and took hold of both my hands. We both knew that a kiss or embrace wouldn't exactly go over. Tears came to her eyes. My eyes were dry—*old habits die hard.*

She leaned over and whispered in my ear that she loved me very deeply and always would. "I know," I said as I tightened my grasp on her hands. She then moved along with the rest of the line and offered condolences to my aunt and mother. There were so many people in succession, I was fairly certain she would go unnoticed. I was mistaken.

After the guests had been escorted into the chapel, we stood up to make our entrance. My mother held my arm as we proceeded and leaned up to my ear with her lips. I thought a kiss was coming. "She looks so much like her mother, very lovely," were the words I heard. I looked into my mother's eyes and nodded. The expression on my face said, "I love you very much, Mama."

We entered a sanctuary that must have been filled with more than three hundred people, standing room only. Everybody rose for the traditional greeting of the mourners as we were escorted to our seats in the first row. A modest pine box, plain and unfinished, sat directly in front of us. Its simplicity was in keeping with the traditional requirements.

I looked at the box and imagined my father lying inside, peacefully, draped in shrouds and wrapped in his *tallis.* I wanted to see him, to behold his face after the mortician's touch. But a viewing is strongly frowned upon by the Orthodox, so the image I would be left with would have to be as he appeared in the hospital, the contorted face and disheveled hair, the smell of human waste, the reality of death unadorned.

The service began with a few memorial prayers, and then came the eulogies. They were much as I'd expected. Ezra was very emotional and broke into tears at several points. He spoke of my father as a teacher of unswerving dedication, as a community leader with wisdom and integrity. He compared him to his namesake, King David, who devoted his life to the pursuit of spiritual perfection. And as he spoke I pondered on the superb irony of this analogy. For King David, more than any other figure in Jewish history, stands out as the perfect example of one who is exalted through distortion of the truth. It was, after all, this great king who intentionally sent a soldier out into the front lines of battle to die just so he could marry the poor man's wife.

Toward the end of his speech, Ezra talked about our family, how my father deeply loved my mother and me. How did he know that? How could he possibly speak with such certainty of things of which he was so ignorant? But that is the rabbi's trait, to make others believe he knows. And as I listened to Ezra, I knew he had been the perfect protégé for my father; at least *he* had learned his lessons well.

It wasn't that I felt my father didn't love me, for I knew he did. The sad truth, however, was that no one else would have known it. For his love, like his pain, was borne in silence.

So I sat there and listened as one after another offered their perceptions of purity and saintliness. And I knew that the man I had known, like his namesake, was much more than the portraits they were painting. Yes, he was dedicated to the community, but to the point of neglecting his family. Yes, he was zealous in his beliefs, but to the perversity of alienating his only son. Yes, he may have been a superb teacher, but he was a wanting example.

Amidst the praise and tribute, his humanness had been keenly flouted. For notwithstanding his social savvy, he was a man who had contempt for most of the people he encountered. He was angry and pained, scarred by a crippling childhood illness and the harshness of his own father, unconsciously determined to pass that on to another generation. Yet once, he had been a lover, starry-eyed and helplessly besotted. But this, like his sweet *Shabbos* melodies, was elusive, obscured by tragedy and anguish.

Soon the speeches and prayers were over. The room was filled with tears, but my eyes were still dry. Zelig, Ezra, some other rabbis, and myself carried the coffin out to the hearse. We placed it inside and closed the large door. I walked to the limousine behind it and took my place in the backseat next to my mother. She was hysterical and grabbed my hand with one of hers while her other hand held a soaked handkerchief.

The motorcade began as we commenced our journey to the cemetery, the last journey that Rabbi David Eisen would ever take. It was a sizable procession, a fitting send-off.

The New Montefiore Cemetery was far out on Long Island, but the time passed quickly. From the Belt Parkway, we turned onto the Southern State Parkway, and along the way I stared out at the trees, flowers, grass, and houses bordering the highway. It was a warm, sunny day, the middle of spring, and I opened the window to catch the breeze. Yet the sights and scents of nature did little to erase that last image of my father in the hospital. I could only hope that in time, other memories would replace the unsightly scene that had now seemed permanently fixed in my psyche.

We arrived at the cemetery, the limousine following the hearse as it pulled through the entrance gate. We drove up a narrow two-lane road with monuments and greenery on either side, until we came to a stop. Straight ahead of the hearse, in the middle of a circle in the road, sat a large gray stone building with a sign over the front door that read ADMINISTRATION BUILDING. The funeral director got out of the front seat of the hearse and walked to the building. The rest of us remained in place.

I turned around to see who was behind us. There were cars lined up, one after another, all the way back to the entrance about a quarter of a mile down the road, and then even more that were still on the main road. The loud horns of angry drivers trying to get past the procession could be heard in the distance. My mother sat silently beside me and my aunt next to her. We were all holding hands, waiting.

A few minutes passed before the funeral director came out of the building. He walked past the hearse to the limousine and spoke to our driver, giving directions to the burial site.

He returned to the hearse, which began to move shortly after he got in. We followed slowly, toward our right, and then straight down another narrow road until we arrived near what appeared to be the edge of the cemetery. We pulled up a few feet past a large pile of earth from a freshly dug plot—my father's eternal resting place. The cars stopped, the driver of the limousine got out and opened the back door on my aunt's side. My uncle was in the car behind us with my cousins, Sarah and Leah.

My mother was having difficulty getting out of the limo, she stumbled and stalled. I got out on my side and hurried around to assist her. She lost her balance and almost fell, but I held her firmly. My aunt stood next to her. They were both wailing.

Zelig and I left them in the care of Sarah and Leah and walked over to the back of the hearse to carry the box. We opened the door and there it sat. I was still for a moment. Soon I would be carrying my father to his burial. Nothing seemed real. I was disconnected from myself, from everything around me, feeling as if in the midst of a horrible nightmare, waiting to be awakened.

There was a hand on my shoulder; it belonged to Ezra. I hadn't felt that touch since I was seven. He squeezed my shoulder to let me know he was there, he was there to lean on and to help. I felt his sincerity. He and the others assisted with the coffin. Clumsily, we removed it from the hearse and carried it over to the grave. The crowd formed two lines through which we passed while Ezra recited the *Tziduk Hadin,* a prayer declaring the perfection of God and the imperfection of man. His voice became louder and more trembling as we approached the grave. When we reached it, he was howling. We placed the box upon large canvas straps attached to a metal apparatus that held it above the hole. The people gathered around; it was a crowd of about a hundred.

I looked into the hole and saw the earthen walls and base. A few feet away was a tall monument with the name Eisen in large capital letters. Off to the left of the monument, rising about eight inches above the ground, was a footstone with my grandfather's name and the dates of his life. Next to it was a similar stone belonging to my grandmother.

This had been a familiar place to my father. Every year as far back as I could remember, he had come here before the high holidays and on *yahrzeits,* death anniversaries. Sometimes my mother had accompanied him, But never I. He felt that since I hadn't had any relationship with my grandparents, it wasn't necessary. "You will one day have plenty of time to spend in the cemetery," he used to remark.

The box sat atop the hole, and Ezra signaled for one of the workers to press a lever. Suddenly the box was slowly descending. My mother's bawl could be heard for miles. I was holding her in my arms. It was still not real. The box moved further down into the hole and when it was just a few inches from the bottom, the workers performed some trickery to remove the canvas straps from underneath. The coffin then rested in its final position.

Ezra belted out a few more prayers, some final words of solace, and then the burial began. It is customary among the Orthodox to bury their own dead and not allow cemetery employees to do the work for them. Only pious, observant Jews should come in contact with the body of the deceased. It was considered an honor to be among those who were chosen to carry the coffin and participate in the burial. It was a special honor for the son to bury his father.

And so I took the shovel in my hands and—in keeping with the tradition of demonstrating hesitancy in the act of burial—I began by using it backwards to push only a small amount of earth into the grave. I could see the dirt flying through the air, almost in slow motion. And when it landed, the sound of it falling upon the pine box rang hollow, an echo that could never be forgotten.

I turned the shovel upright and continued. The sound became harsher, more poignant with the heavier clumps of dirt. Each one, after the other, until the box was completely covered. Then the echo faded into the trifling sound of earth being piled on more earth.

There was sobbing all around me, but I was lost in the task of filling the grave. I was doing my duty, fulfilling my obligation as a Jewish man. No tears. Sweat dripped from my forehead, down my temples. I removed my jacket and gave it to one of my cousins to hold. The second shovel was being shared by several of the men, but the one I held belonged to me alone. I should have stopped and rested, placed the shovel down so someone else could help, but I was determined to continue until the ground was level. My heart raced, I grew short of breath, my arms ached—a welcome outlet for whatever was building up inside of me.

Time passed in a flash. The work was finished. I was drained of all my strength as I placed the shovel on the ground. The sobbing around me continued. Unrelenting. I could hear my mother's voice as she cried, but could see nothing but the square patch of dirt before me. To its right was an empty plot that would one day belong to my mother.

Ezra's hand appeared beside me, offering a prayer book. It was time for me to recite the age-old *Kaddish,* the prayer of affirmation, of glorifying and sanctifying the name of God in the face of death.

It was fitting that this moment of ultimate despair and doubt be marked by an assertion of God's dominion. Fitting and paradoxical. I took the book, already opened to the appropriate page, and looked at the words. I looked at the dirt in front of me. I began to pledge my faith.

"Yisgadal veyis-ḳadash she-me rab-bah." As the words departed from my mouth I could hear my voice, but it felt like I was not the speaker. The words had a life of their own. I was not present. I was somewhere else, lost between despondency and denial.

My voice continued with the exaltation. The phrases flowed smoothly, unencumbered by emotion. The others responded *amen* when required, everyone obediently performing his duty. We were imposing order on chaos, giving purpose and meaning to a random, capricious universe, assuaging our greatest anxieties.

I concluded the *Kaddish* and the crowd split, once again, into two lines for us to walk through. My mother barely moved. I placed my arms around her and we stumbled together back to the limousine. As we passed through the line, each person offered the traditional prescription for mourners, *Hamakom Yinachem,* may God comfort you among the mourners of Zion and Jerusalem. The forever faithful, always to the letter of the law.

We took our seats in the limousine, my mother still weeping. In the background I could hear the sounds of car doors opening and closing. The driver started the engine, waited a few minutes, and then slowly pulled away. I turned and looked behind me. I could see the patch of dirt fading in the distance.

Rebecca was among those who came back to the house after the cemetery. She tried to be helpful with serving the food, but my cousins discouraged her assistance and made her feel like the outsider she was. My mother was too lost in her grief to notice anything.

The living room and dining room were filled, wall to wall, with people and would probably remain that way for the duration of *shiva,* the seven days of mourning. They came from around the world: Israel, South Africa, and even New Zealand. Some were unable to attend the funeral because of the short notice, but would be there for the *shiva* to pay their respects. And we would have to sit on our little boxes and endure the barrage of well-wishers, many of whom would be total strangers, intruders on our time of anguish.

There was a part of me that understood only too well the rationale for this ritual. It was a way of postponing the inevitable sense of desolation by surrounding the mourner with friends and family. But at this point, the only thoughts I had were those of resentment. Why were all those people here? Why were they robbing me of the opportunity to be alone, to feel the sense of misery I was supposed to be feeling? It was easier to blame the presence of the multitudes than to admit to the real reasons for my numbness.

The evening brought a new shift of people, no smaller nor quieter than the first. Rebecca was still around, managing cleverly to keep her distance, yet letting her presence be known to me. She moved in and out of the crowd, at one moment sitting alone on a couch on the other side of the room, at another moment chatting with a group of women over in a corner. I was proud of her display of self-sufficiency but expected no less.

At about nine-thirty the house was still crowded. I got up and made my way to the staircase. I caught Rebecca's attention and signaled her to meet me upstairs, away from the gathering.

I walked up the stairs and went into the hallway bathroom. I stood over the sink and sprinkled some cold water on my face. Then I tried to look at myself in the mirror, which had been deliberately clouded beneath a sheath of glass cleaner. It is a requirement to cloud up or cover all the mirrors in a house of mourning. Among the many reasons I'd heard for this law, the most sensible was so that the mourners not concern themselves with matters of vanity.

But vanity was not my motive, clarity was. I wanted to see myself so that maybe I could get a clue about how I felt. I stood there for a few seconds trying to decipher my face through the white film. Whoever had worked on this mirror had done too good a job.

I went and opened the door and there she was, outside in the hall, waiting for me. I put my index finger over my mouth, indicating "quiet." I was still afraid some people might hear or see us. I then pointed to my right, to my bedroom. She went first and I followed her and closed the door behind us.

I was met with an immediate embrace. She started crying as soon as she held me. We stood there for a few moments in silence, engulfing each other. I ran my fingers through her hair.

The embrace came to a natural conclusion. She stood in front of me, put her hand on my face, and whispered, "I'm so sorry."

"I know," I said softly. I paused, and then turned to show her the room. "So, *this* is where I grew up."

She rotated to take in the surroundings, examining the pictures and posters on each wall, every piece of furniture, even the bedspread. "Interesting," she observed.

"How so?"

"Well, most boys have posters of sports and music figures on their bedroom walls, and you have pictures of rabbis."

"I was a bookish sort."

"No kidding." She smiled.

I started staring into space.

"Are you okay?" She caught herself. "Of course not." She reached out to touch me again.

I caught her hand with mine and held it. "I'm fine," I said without conviction. "We should be getting back downstairs."

She looked disappointed but understanding.

"You know you don't have to stay around here all night," I said.

"Would you like me to go?" Two rejections in a row. She was beginning to take it personally.

"Of course I don't want you to go. I was just thinking how uncomfortable it must be for you to be here like this."

"No Yakov, it's not uncomfortable at all. Never. It's never uncomfortable to be anywhere that you are."

I was wordless.

"But if you feel I should go, I will," she offered sullenly.

"Rebecca, you've got me all wrong. I'm just concerned about your traveling all the way back to Manhattan this time of night."

"I'll be taking a car service. It's safe. But if you feel I should . . ."

"Now stop that, please."

"Okay, I'll stop. But I think you should realize that it's *you* who are uncomfortable, not me."

I looked at her, thought for a moment, and then nodded in agreement.

"I'd like to stay for another hour if it's okay with you."

"Of course," I answered, her hand in mine.

I opened the door of the room to make sure the hall was clear. We came out and went toward the stairs. I stopped her on the way and said, "By the way, your cover was blown the minute you entered the chapel."

"I know. I could tell by the way your mother looked at me."

"She knew you the second she saw you. Said you were beautiful, just like your mother."

"Did she say anything else?"

"No, and I was surprised she said even that. You're the only thing outside of herself that she's noticed all day."

We glanced at each other in mutual bewilderment and then went back down to the mob.

The house didn't empty until after twelve. I was exhausted, said good night to my mother and aunt, and went upstairs to bed.

I passed the study door, stopped, and beheld the lavish mahogany that had so effectively stood between my father and me over the years. It no longer seemed towering and ominous as it had when I was younger. Now, it was just a fancy slab of wood.

I put my hand on the knob and turned it. The door opened easily. The room was dark, the lingering scent of my father's presence was overpowering. I stepped over the threshold and, for the first time in my life, entered this sanctum without the trembling sensation that I was somehow intruding.

I moved slowly and then stood for a moment without turning on the light. Some illumination came from the hallway. I moved to the other end of the room, behind the desk, to try and imagine the world from his perspective. A slight tinge of guilt ran through me as if I was doing something I shouldn't. I went even further and sat in his chair. The light from the hall was scant, but my eyes adjusted to the darkness. Everything in the room was clear, yet seemed very different from what I'd remembered.

I sat there, exploring my surroundings. The chair was soft and comfortable, the leather creased and worn from years of use. On the desk in front of me sat a few volumes with torn pieces of paper used to mark specific places—my father's last toils before his departure.

I reached out to pick up a book that looked familiar. As I brought it closer I recognized it as one of my grandfather's published commentaries. I started flipping through the pages, just to feel their texture as they waved by my fingers. I had never bothered to read my grandfather's work and was surely not going to start now. But I needed to hold the book, to touch it, to be close to it. Suddenly I began to feel something welling up inside, a sudden surge of despondency. And then, tears.

The book remained open before me as I began to weep like a child, droplets falling upon the frail pages of Hebrew lettering. My grandfather's wisdom, my father's nourishment, my tears. I tried to control myself but couldn't. I began to wail. Louder. And louder.

I was hoping that my mother and aunt couldn't hear me. But I needed to let go, to cry out for my dead father. Yet as the tears flowed, I knew that I was lamenting his life more than his death. I was weeping for what I never had, rather than for what I'd lost.

I also realized, at that moment, why I had been unable to cry during the funeral. Yes, it had to do with old habits and the fact that the entire event had seemed surreal. But beyond that, it had to do with him. His rules and ordinances. His demands. It was *he* who had always deemed it improper for me to cry. And in the privacy of the hospital room, as he lay dead on the table, I could defy him. But at his funeral, in the public view of all his amen-sayers, he had his way. I was finally the true Jewish man he wanted me to be.

I stood up, moved to the door, closed it, and locked myself inside. Now, nobody would be able to hear me. Before I could make it back to the desk, my knees gave way, my legs collapsing beneath me. I crashed to the floor and found myself lying on the stale red carpet. The crying was unrelenting; I could barely pick myself up. I got as far as resting on my knees and stayed crouched in that position as I began bellowing at God. Cursing, yelling, screaming.

The room was much darker now than before. The profanities kept coming. One after another. And then I began to yell out one word repeatedly, *why. Why,* with nothing following but more sniveling and more *whys.* I banged my fists on the floor and started tugging at my hair. The yelling became louder, the crying more profuse, until I heard the knocking on the door.

The person in the hall turned the knob to no avail. It was my mother, banging frantically, calling for me to open the door at once. It took a few seconds for my fit to subside.

"I'm all right," I called out, "I'm all right," I responded, trying to regain my bearings.

"Okay, Yankeleh, I know, but just open the door, please." She kept banging, though a bit softer.

I stood up, repeating that I was okay, and took some deep breaths. I opened the door and saw her standing there. She approached me and put both her arms around me. I began to weep again, and could feel tears rolling down her cheeks as well. She held me tightly, close, the way she used to when I was a child.

Rebecca visited each day of *shiva,* always in the middle of the afternoon when the crowd was smallest. For the first two days my mother was appropriately polite and affable. By the third day a rapport started building between the two of them. I even caught my mother begin smiling during one of their conversations. On the fourth day they sat together and talked for over an hour. I busied myself with some of the other guests and purposely kept away from them, all the while observing out of the corner of my eye. What was developing was the last thing I'd ever expected.

That same evening, before retiring, my mother told me that she understood what I saw in Rebecca. No condemnation, no anger, only understanding. "A very fine girl, good sense of humor, and much intelligence," she said. There was no additional mention of her beauty—my mother never repeated herself.

I chose not to ask about the things that had previously been a problem, and was content in assuming that they had died with my father. My mother was alone now and wanted to be close to me. She would somehow deal with the past and welcome the future, so long as we would never again be estranged.

I held her hand, smiled, and responded, "Yes, Mama, she is."

CHAPTER 31

I DECIDED TO STAY with my mother for a little while longer after the *shiva* had ended. There was less than a month left of school and I could handle the commute for that short amount of time. Rebecca understood and was supportive. But we both knew that this would make it more difficult for us to see each other.

One morning, two weeks after the funeral, the alarm woke me at exactly six o'clock. The daily morning prayer service at the synagogue was at six-forty-five and I had been attending regularly in order to say *Kaddish,* which requires the presence of a *minyan.* I would follow this routine for the next eleven months, the prescribed length of time one is supposed to mourn for a parent.

In most respects, this was to be a morning like any other. I would arrive at the synagogue just in the nick of time, there would be the same group of regulars in attendance, the service would be held in the same sanctuary, we would recite the same prayers, and I would experience the same harried feeling about finishing up in time to catch the train. But as soon as I got to the bathroom and saw myself in the mirror, I knew something was different.

In keeping with the laws of mourning, I hadn't shaved for the past two weeks. But this was the first time I'd taken any notice. I stood there in amazement, examining myself closely, how the stubble blended with my features; how it altered every contour and crevice of my face. The resemblance was uncanny. I was looking in the mirror and seeing a ghost.

I stared for a while, trying to shake my head back to reality but to no avail. I got on with brushing my teeth, washing up, and combing my hair, attempting to avoid the mirror as much as possible. But each time my eyes caught the mirror, I saw *him.*

It was an eerie feeling that stayed with me until I came downstairs and realized from the clock on the kitchen wall that I was late for the synagogue. I quickly grabbed my briefcase and jacket and hurried out the door. I ran all the way to the synagogue and arrived there just in time for the start of the service.

I removed my jacket, placed my briefcase on the seat beside me, and donned my *tallis* and *t'fillin,* all with great alacrity. As usual, I was ready precisely at the start of the first *Kaddish.*

One of the older men, a regular worshiper and devoted congregant of my father's for many years, was sitting in his usual place just a few seats away from me in the same pew. He looked over to me, as he had at this time each morning, with a warm, receptive smile. I responded similarly.

I began *davening,* uttering under my breath the perfunctory phrases of the morning service, words that had never packed much inspiration in the past. When the preliminary prayers were over, the men waited for me to approach the *bima* to lead the rest of the service as I had done every other morning that week. It is customary that the leader for weekday prayers be one who is in mourning.

I stepped up to the *bima,* but this time, as I ascended the two steps, I was again struck by that eeriness. I stumbled for a second, caught myself, and took my place at the podium. I placed my right hand on the open page of the oversized prayer book that lay upon the red velvet cloth covering the *bima.* The page was worn and discolored, the words faded from the years. I looked in the book and began chanting. The others joined in. My thumbs rested on both sides of the book, holding down the pages, preventing them from turning on their own. My body began to *shuckle,* to sway back and forth in an almost sexual motion, like I was making love to God with my body as I prayed with my mind.

This was not me. I had never *shuckled* before, at least not since I was a young child trying to imitate my father. In fact, I had always made it a point not to sway while I *davened,* not to manifest too much enthusiasm, not to get too involved in the act. Always going through the motions with minimal commitment. As with life itself, I stayed on the edges, the sidelines, neither an actual player nor a mere spectator. And here I was, engrossed in the game, getting lost in the words, and unable to restrain myself from doing so.

As I said the phrases, my mind focused on their meaning. And all the things that I was always supposed to feel, wrapped in my grandfather's *tallis,* all the things that I never felt . . . were the very things that I was feeling. I was unable to escape, to think about getting through with my dutiful act so that I could get onto more important "things." At this moment, this was the single most important thing; it was the only thing.

Before my eyes stood the ark in which the Torah scroll was stored. To its right, my father's chair. It was empty now, but not for long. After an appropriate amount of time, it would again be inhabited, most probably by Ezra.

I thought about the ark, the scroll, and the chair, all inextricably intertwined in the divine scheme of my father's life. The ark protected the Torah, and so did he. "You must be extra strict in your interpretations," he used to say, "for even the slightest leniency only leads to the path of deterioration."

His existence was bound up in that singular intention, fighting off the enemies of the Torah. And for years I mocked and scorned, and raved my jealousy at being second. But not today, not at this moment. For now I was beginning to focus, to see not the things which I was denied, but those to which I had been blinded and had denied myself—a sense of purpose, of connection.

With each utterance, I moved further and further beyond

what I had ever imagined my spiritual capacities to be. Like Franz Rosenzweig, the great philosopher who wandered into a synagogue one Yom Kippur only to awaken his dormant religious instincts, I was calling out to God, beseeching guidance, and, for the first time, believing that it would be revealed to me. I was saying *Kaddish* with its full spirit in mind, affirming God's eminence and ultimate design for my existence. It was, at once, wonderful and frightening.

CHAPTER 32

THE DOOR OPENED SLOWLY and in came Rav Trachtenberg. He carried his books under his arm and placed them on his desk before sitting down in his chair. He faced the class and looked in my direction. He stroked his beard.

"Eisen, it is your turn to recite today, but if you're not up to it . . ."

"No, *rebbe,* I'm fine," Conviction.

He paused for a moment, stared into space, and looked over to me again. "In that case, boys, let's begin."

The text for the day dealt with the issue of how long it is appropriate to wait between eating meat and dairy.

This, coincidentally, was the exact same topic I had discussed with my father at our very last Shabbos meal together, just a few months ago. Again, I felt eerie.

There were several opinions to be considered and, of course, various rationales behind each. There was the strictest approach of waiting six hours; the most lenient of merely washing out one's mouth without waiting at all; and a few approaches between the two.

I read out loud, and carefully translated and explained each argument and interpretation, all of which stemmed from the simple biblical commandment not to boil the calf in its mother's milk. As I recited, it occurred to me that I was not experiencing my usual sentiments of mockery. To the contrary, I found myself enthusiastic and interested.

The words on the pages in front of me came to life, and Rebecca came to mind. She had always pointed to the diversity of opinion in Jewish law as the basis for her break with Orthodoxy, which she felt had become monolithic in its present-day form. Even the fundamentals, like how to separate meat and dairy, had differing opinions, and here lay those opinions, right before my eyes. She was indeed correct, and I always knew it. But I had been less concerned with that than with the more vexing questions about God's very existence, and whether the whole enterprise of Judaism was a hoax to begin with. For some reason, those questions weren't haunting me today.

So it was here and now, in front of these future Orthodox rabbis and their devout master, that I realized that amidst all the various opinions and positions, a choice had to be made. Trachtenberg, Waldman, Harry—they had all made their choices, in one form or another. Benny and Devorah Kleinman, and David and Esther Eisen had also made choices. Tough, hard choices. And Rebecca, too. Choices and sacrifices.

I looked down at the open book of laws that sat on my desk and pictured the weathered pages of my grandfather's book. I pictured the prayer book in the synagogue, the ark, the chair, the image of my father in the mirror. I was receiving a message from somewhere beyond myself. I could no longer retreat in indecision. I could no longer opt out, sit on the sidelines as the observer, the detached philosopher. I was no longer detached. I *was* connected. True, the pages before me bore much diversity, but one can get lost in diversity if there is no commitment. I knew then that a verdict was soon to come.

After class, I left the building and was about to turn left toward the subway station, but found myself compelled to make a stop before returning to Brooklyn. I turned right instead, walked to Amsterdam Avenue, and then left toward 187th Street. It was a bright sunny day, warm and slightly breezy. I walked up past the library and further, past the main building across the street from the dairy restaurant—sights that in a few short weeks would be relegated to mere memories. When I came to 187th Street, I crossed Amsterdam and continued another fifty feet until I stood in front of Harry's building. I entered the front door, pressed the buzzer, and announced myself.

He was waiting at the threshold of his door by the time I got off the elevator. He looked brittle, even more worn than before. The isolation had taken its toll. His face was almost barren of life, poorly shaven with bloodshot eyes and tousled hair. His shirt was full of wrinkles and his trousers were barely held up by a frayed leather belt fastened at its last hole.

"Vell, vell, the soon-to-be rabbi has come to visit," were his words of greeting as he gestured for me to come in. I walked in but said nothing.

We entered the living room together. It looked drearier than the last time. The curtains were drawn to block out the sunlight, newspapers and unwashed dishes covered most of the available surfaces, and a musty odor of oldness filled the air.

He sat down on his chair and I took my place on the couch across from him. I tried to ignore the surroundings. He apologized and said that he would have cleaned up if he had been expecting anyone. I could tell that nobody visited.

I nodded, indicating that I understood, but still had no words. I wasn't sure what had driven me or what I should say. There was a long silence between us; he obviously wasn't one for conversation these days.

Then the words came out of my mouth. "My father's dead." It was the first time I had actually said it out loud. Harry looked at me, dismay in his eyes. "He died two weeks ago, it was a heart attack." I felt a lump in my throat, my body quivering.

His immediate response was *"Baruch Dayan Emes,"* blessed is the Judge of truth, the traditional formula one recites upon hearing of the death of another. His words were barely audible. It was laborious for him to speak. "I am very sorry for you, very sorry this happened." His tone gained a bit of strength.

I sat there and nodded my head in thanks.

"Your father, he vas a special man." He paused to take a breath. "I never met him, I vas vone of the few people who had never even heard of him until I met you . . ." Again, a pause. "But I know that he vas a special man because he had a son like you." Another deep breath. "Only a special man can have a son like you."

"Thank you," I uttered under my breath. I, too, was finding it burdensome to talk.

"So now, vhat vill you do?"

"What do you mean?"

He looked at me and hesitated for a moment, and then he spoke. "You have come here to tell *me,* a decrepit old man, that your father has died?" Another pause. "But you have also come for something else. There is something you are looking for from me, yes?"

"I don't know exactly why I have come." I stared out into space and whispered the words as if I was speaking to myself.

"You have always been looking for something, from the day I met you. And now your father has died. Have you found vhat you've been looking for?" His speaking was becoming less strenuous.

"I'm not sure. Something is happening to me, but I don't know what it is."

"But vhatever it is, it brought you here to see me."

"Yes."

"You have come to *me* for answers." Irony was in his tone, almost laughter. "Vhy me?" He reveled with unexpected energy.

I held my hands up and gestured, "I don't know." He sat and waited for a better answer. I began to speak again. "Something has been happening to me today. Since I woke up this morning, I've been feeling things, strange things that I've never felt."

"Vhat kind of things?"

"Spiritual things, I guess. I'm not really sure. But it feels as if

I have a purpose, as if I belong in places that I've never imagined belonging, as if I should be doing things I never felt I should be doing. I don't know, maybe I'd be better off telling this to a good psychiatrist instead of you."

"So, vhy me?" Pressing.

"I don't know," I paused, "maybe because you've suffered so, yet you still believe; because I see you as someone with a true sense of purpose in his life."

"And that is how you must see yourself!" he exclaimed. "It is time for you to find your purpose, to stop fighting vith your father! He is gone, you don't have to fight anymore." He stopped for a moment to calm himself and added, "Maybe now God vill help you find a place vhere you belong."

I sat, silently, thinking about his words.

"Your name is Yakov, yes?" he asked.

I nodded.

"Do you know that this is a special name, Yakov? That it has much meaning?"

"I know what the Torah says about it," I responded.

"And vhat is that?"

"It is written that Yakov was born immediately after Esau and came out of the womb holding onto Esau's heel. The Hebrew word for heel, *aikev,* is the root of the name Yakov. Its funny," I added in a sad tone, "I've often thought what a 'heel' I was."

He ignored my last line and said, "That is *gut,* but it is no great accomplishment for a soon-to-be rabbi to know only vhat the Torah says. Simple explanations like this are taught in *cheider,* in elementary school. There is much more to your name that you should understand."

He went on to offer some elaborate interpretation of why the biblical Yakov had his name changed to Israel after wrestling with the angel and how that shed light on the meaning of my name. I was barely listening, thinking instead about the strange things I'd been feeling all day.

"Do you understand vhat I mean, Yakov from Brooklyn?" was the next thing I heard clearly.

I nodded in assent.

"I'm not certain you do," he continued, "but vone day you vill." He stopped for a second, stared into space, and then repeated, "Vone day you *vill* understand."

I was quiet and could see that he was growing tired. The therapy session was over. I stood up to leave and he followed. We walked toward the door. "Is there anything I can do for you?" I asked.

"No, don't vorry about me. I'm not alvays this bad." He looked himself over as he said that. "It is just this veek, it is an anniversary for me." He pointed to one of the faces on the wall. "So many anniversaries, that's vhat happens vhen you become my age, anniversaries. But I accept it," he added with certainty. "I accept it as part of God's plan for me. Vhen I see Him I vill tell Him that he could have had a better plan." He smiled.

I smiled back. We were standing by the door.

"Your father vas a very lucky man to have had a son like you."

"I'm glad at least *you* think so."

"Ah, but *he* thinks so, too. He's not gone, you know. He lives on through you, like all my anniversaries live on through me. Everything is connected and has a purpose; it is all part of God's plan. You vill see. You vill understand."

With those words we shook hands and parted. I knew now what I had to do.

Interlude

VHAT EXACTLY do you think happened in the Torah to our patriarch Yakov vhen he drifted off to sleep? The next thing ve know is that he is wrestling with someone. Then he is victorious, and his name is changed to Israel. But vith whom vas he wrestling? Many think it vas an angel, but the Torah doesn't really tell us who the opponent vas.

But I vill tell you. And it is an important lesson you must never forget. It vill help you to understand your name, and who you are.

You see, it all began vhen Yakov was born. His twin, Esau, came out first. And then, as you said, Yakov came out grasping onto the heel of his older brother. So he is named Yakov, meaning, "vone who takes by the heel." Now I know you just told me this, but vhat I vant to add is that Yakov vas not secure, not sure of himself, and that vas vhy he needed to hold onto his brother in order to come into the vorld.

And years later ve see Yakov bargaining vith Esau for the birthright vhich he believes should rightfully be his. Here, instead of asserting himself, he tricks Esau and takes advantage of him in a veak moment vhen Esau is starving and needs food. Yakov gets the birthright by striking a deal, exchanging it for the food he has cooked, not by being a man and standing up for vhat he believes.

After that, ve see Yakov again involved in deceit, this time vith his father. He pretends to be Esau by dressing up like him, and goes into his father and steals the blessing that vas intended for Esau. And vhat does he do next? He runs avay, like a coward, because he is afraid of Esau's revenge.

All this trickery; all this underhanded behavior. Vhy?

It really is very simple to explain. You see, Yakov vas afraid to be who he vas, afraid to assert himself as an individual. So he alvays tricked, and pretended, and held onto the heel of his brother. And then he runs avay.

And it is not until Yakov is returning, tventy years later, that something very strange happens to him. He vas afraid of meeting up vith Esau after all these years, and tries to appease him by sending messengers with generous gifts. But still he learns that Esau is coming out to meet him vith an army of four hundred men.

He is scared. Petrified! And it vas that night, vhile he slept, that the Torah tells us, "And Yakov vas left alone; and there wrestled a man vith him until the breaking day." And the Torah continues, "And vhen he saw that he did not prevail against him, he touched the hollow of his thigh; and the hollow of Yakov's thigh vas disjointed as he wrestled vith him."

And who vas this man? Who exactly did Yakov wrestle vith? The Torah does not tell us. In fact, it confuses us, for until it says that it vas Yakov's thigh that vas vounded, ve don't really know who is doing vhat to whom. He did this to him, and he did that to him, but who is he *and who is* him?

And vhen it is all over, this other man blesses Yakov, and changes his name to Israel, "for you have fought vith God and men, and have prevailed."

But Yakov is vounded, seriously vounded. He walks avay victorious, but limping.

Now, I vill explain this all to you. You see, Yakov vas really wrestling vith himself, his inner self, that is vhy the Torah gives the man no identity. He has *no identity! He is part of Yakov. He is the strong, determined, assertive part that has been buried for all these years. But now, as Yakov fears having to do battle vith Esau, he must awaken and face this part of himself. He must fight vith himself and be victorious. He must no longer hold onto someone else's heel, or pretend to be who he is not. He must become an individual who is not afraid to stand up for vhat he vants and believes.*

This is the lesson, and it is a hard lesson. Remember, Yakov emerged from this struggle limping. For no one does true battle vith himself and emerges vithout vounds.

That is the lesson!

Do you understand vhat I mean, Yakov from Brooklyn?

I'm not certain you do, but vone day you vill.

Vone day you vill understand.

PART IV

CHAPTER 33

THE BRIGHT JERUSALEM SUNLIGHT dazzles through the bedroom window and lands upon my slumbering eyes. Within a few seconds, I am awakened by the glimmer. My lids open wide to the world I left behind some eight hours earlier. It is six, time to begin yet another day.

But today is different. Today I will not be going to work or following my usual routine. For today, I am taking a special trip.

Like clockwork I hear my son David, his pattering bare feet running down the cold stone hallway toward my bedroom. He appears anxiously in the doorway, stops for a brief millisecond just to see if I am awake. Upon finding that I am, he lunges toward the bed.

He jumps up onto my side of the mattress with the force of an earthquake. Beside me, I hear the familiar, ritualistic groaning from his mother. Each morning it's the same. She turns face-down to the bed, puts her pillow over her head, and tries to grab just a few more moments of sleep.

He crawls up over the covers under which I lie, half awake. The look of the devil sparkles in his large brown eyes. He is getting so big, I think to myself, so tall for a seven-year-old.

Our eyes meet. *"Boker tov, Abba,"* he says to me with a playful grin. Good morning, Daddy.

"Boker tov, Duvidel. Good morning, my little David," I respond.

He is sitting on my chest, his knees digging into my sides. "Do you want to fight, *Abba?*" he asks as he pins my hands behind my head.

"Do I want to fight?" I react energetically as I lift myself up and him with me. "Do I want to fight?" I grab his torso in a bearhug.

"Abba, Abba!" Yelling and laughing at the same time.

By now his mother is fully awake, her eyes on us with a gleeful smile. She should be tired of this typical morning rite, but she is not. Her son is struggling with his father so that he can grow up and become a man. It is a playful and loving struggle, but imbued with much seriousness nonetheless.

I release my hold. David gasps for breath. *"Boker tov, Imma,"* he says with the last of his strength.

"Good morning, Duvidel," she responds as she caresses his face with her fingertips.

He leans over and kisses her.

"I think you forgot something!" I interject with feigned jealousy.

"Boker tov, Abba," he repeats as he approaches and kisses my cheek. I take his small head between my hands, move toward him, and rest my lips on his forehead. "Good morning, my little David."

In the doorway, with blanket in hand, watching us, is the other little one. She is only three, and much more docile in temperament than her older brother. She stands there until she is noticed, until she is invited to join us. And she doesn't mind, for she seems to be contented. I wonder when that will cease.

As her name, Shoshanna, suggests, she is a delicate flower, a lily. She shares her blue eyes with me and her light skin with her mother. She shares her blanket with no one.

"Shoshi," her mother beckons with open arms, "come to *Imma.*"

She proceeds slowly, sauntering across the floor, the blanket dangling behind. She approaches her mother's side of the bed, tries to climb up, and makes it with a little motherly assistance. David is lying quietly in my arms.

Shoshanna's mother kisses her on the lips. "Good morning Shoshi, my precious flower," she says in Hebrew.

"Boker tov, Imma," Shoshi responds in her soft, placid three-year-old voice.

I turn toward my left, where David is lying against me, and Shoshanna is next to him against her mother. She looks at me with her captivating eyes. *"Abba,"* she says as her hand extends out to me. I grab it and lean toward her to hoist her over her brother and into my arms. She lands upon my stomach. I reach up and almost hug the life out of her.

This is my family, my children Duvidel and Shoshi, and my wife Yehudit, or Judith as she is known among her American friends. And this is the way we all wake up just about every morning.

But this morning David and Shoshanna are unusually clingy because they know that it is the last morning that they are going to see their *Abba* for a week. They have never gone this long without him.

"Okay, lets all get going. *Abba* has to be at the airport by eight," Yehudit instructs.

The children hesitantly vacate the bed. David goes first. Perhaps a part of him is looking forward to playing the man for a while. Shoshanna moves ever so slowly. Again, her mother assists her.

I watch Yehudit with Shoshanna. She is an exceptional woman. I knew that the very first time I met her. It was in the pediatric oncology ward at Hadassah Medical Center. She was a nurse and I was in the first week of my new job as chaplain. That was ten years ago.

I was fresh off the plane from America. And there I found myself, in this large Israeli hospital providing religious guidance to the sick in my choppy Ashkenazic Hebrew. And there she was, that day, administering an IV to a ten-year-old girl suffering from leukemia.

I was walking through the ward, trying to get my bearings, to adjust to my new position, when I saw this scene. I stopped and watched. She seemed oblivious to my presence, totally engrossed in the task at hand.

I was mesmerized by the delicate way she interacted with her patient. The same fingertips that now stroke David and Shoshanna were then brushing through the few strands of hair on the sick girl's head. And a smile came upon the girl as she reached up to hold Yehudit's hand.

And then Yehudit turned toward me and looked at me with wonderment. She stood upright. "Can I help you, sir?" she asked in almost-perfect Hebrew, only a minuscule trace of an American accent.

"Oh no," I responded defensively, as if I was intruding on something. "I'm just the new chaplain," I explained.

"Ah, you're Rabbi Eisen." Somewhat surprised. At my youthful appearance, I supposed.

She was definitely a beauty, by every definition of the word. Taller than most women I'd been attracted to—about five foot nine inches—with short, straight, dark blond hair, soft features, brown eyes, and a large-boned figure that fit perfectly with her height. I knew at that moment that I was going to marry her.

She was twenty-three and had moved to Israel with her family ten years earlier when her father, a Chicago rabbi, had accepted a prestigious position as the American Jewish Committee representative to the Israeli government. Spending her adolescent and young adult years in Israel gave her a sense of values that were uncommon among most American woman I'd known.

Although she was from an Orthodox family, she chose nevertheless to serve her time in the army. Afterward, she pursued a career in nursing with deep commitment, yet she also wanted to establish a traditional Jewish family. We were married within six months.

She helped me with my work, especially with my Hebrew.

She introduced me to all the doctors and nurses. Her friends became my friends. It was precisely the new life I had hoped for.

In addition to the chaplaincy, I had another job (most people living in Israel have at least two jobs). It was as an assistant professor of philosophy at Hebrew University. This had been Waldman's graduation gift to me. When he heard I had accepted the position at Hadassah, he told me he thought it would be a terrible waste for me to abandon philosophy. He had friends at Hebrew University and prevailed upon me to consider teaching there if he could arrange it. He did, and I did.

Over the years my work has focused on medical ethics, analyzing moral and religious issues connected with the problems of euthanasia, abortion, gene manipulation, et cetera. It was a perfect way to combine what I did in the hospital with what I did at the university. I published several papers about the Jewish perspective on several themes, and had become a special consultant to the Chief Rabbinate on questions concerning medical ethics. I climbed the ranks from assistant to associate professor, and had become internationally recognized as a scholar in this field.

But nothing meant as much to me as the time I spent administering to the frail and needy. Here, all the philosophical questions became practical questions, intellect made way for compassion, theory was replaced by action. Here I was able to achieve what I believed God had always intended for me, the inevitable conclusion of what had preceded.

It is difficult talking to dying children about faith and hope. It is next to impossible responding to the anguish and desperation of the sick. It is a thankless and basically unprofitable endeavor that leaves one drained and depleted most of the time. But there is that rare occasion when you do get through to someone, when you do make a tangible difference in the way they regard their suffering. Those are the moments that seem to make it all worthwhile. Those are the moments when my faith is strengthened.

The car is loaded and the children are waiting in the backseat. I wanted to take a cab, but Yehudit insisted that since she is already off from work for the week to spend extra time with the children while I'm away, they would all take me to the airport.

Yehudit always prefers to do the driving. She claims my mind often wanders too much and my driving makes her nervous, especially with the children in the car. I don't care; in fact, I like it this way. There are few things more pleasurable to me than looking out the window at the hills and landscape along the road from Jerusalem to Tel Aviv and getting lost in thought. And there is nothing as unpleasurable as having to drive that road.

She starts the car and backs out of the little parking alcove in front of our building. I look up at our third-floor terrace as we pull away and I see some of David's toys: his soccer ball, and the blow-up Samson punching figure that he plays with in the living room, much to his mother's consternation.

The four-story walk-up is fairly typical of Jerusalem. It is squared off with sizable terraces and faced with golden-tan stones. The building has eight large apartments, two on each floor. Ours has three bedrooms, two baths, a living room, dining room, and an eat-in kitchen. It is comfortable and roomy, especially by Israeli standards.

We head down our block, Rehov Abarbanel, a quaint, serene street in Rehavia, a suburb immediately adjacent to the center of the city. In Jerusalem, all neighborhoods outside the center of the city are considered suburbs.

Yehudit turns the car west to Rehov Hillel, and then heads toward the outskirts of the city to the Tel Aviv–Jerusalem highway. There is much traffic. Israelis begin their days early.

Within fifteen minutes, we are outside the city and on the highway. Soldiers hitchhike along the road. No matter how long I am here, I cannot get over the sight of Jews in army uniforms, some even with yarmulkes and beards. The true army of God.

We descend out of the hills of Jerusalem toward the flatland of Tel Aviv. There are large newly built villages atop some of the hills, and on the sides of the road lie the remnants of wars past, rusted half-tracks and jeeps, left as memorials of the struggle to capture Jerusalem.

I am always struck by the view of these memorials against the backdrop of burgeoning towns. The past and the present; the triumphs of the past, the struggles of the present.

I often wonder, and worry, about the challenges of this society. Not the external challenges—we have an army and hordes of experts to ponder those—but the internal ones: the equally dangerous and destructive conflicts between the secular and religious Jews.

As a chaplain in the hospital, I deal with all types of Jews. It doesn't matter to me what they are, nor to them what I am. It only matters that I'm there. They are sick and my purpose is to help however I can.

In the streets, however, it is a different matter altogether. For this is a very polarized society. The resentments and enmities between groups are immense. And the tactics used in these conflicts are nothing short of embarrassing to the outside world.

There is no strong presence of organized Reform or Conservative Judaism here. Maybe a smattering from place to place at best. The Orthodox rabbinate has too strong a hold on the government to allow more than that. So instead there are, for the most part, the Orthodox and the non-Orthodox. And very few try to bridge the wide gaps or create alternatives.

I am outspoken about these things at the university where most of my students are from exclusively secular backgrounds. They are amazed sometimes when they hear that I am an Orthodox rabbi, that I keep the Sabbath, that I attend an Orthodox synagogue, and that I send my son to an Orthodox yeshiva in the city. They are amazed that I am often consulted by Orthodox authorities to assist them in their rulings on questions of Jewish law and medical ethics. They are surprised that I am accepted in that world. I am surprised that I am accepted in either world, and occasionally wonder how long it will be until I get into trouble. But I have been in trouble before.

The green-and-white sign says that we are only three kilometers from Ben Gurion Airport. I turn around to David and Shoshanna in the backseat. Soon I will be on an El Al flight to New York, a place that I haven't been to in the six years since my mother's funeral.

Shoshanna's middle name is Esther. Shoshanna is named after Yehudit's mother, who is also deceased, four years ago from cancer.

I pleaded with my mother to join me in Israel, especially when she came for our wedding. "You can stay here and live with us," I said the evening before she returned home.

"My place is in Borough Park, where I lived my life with your father of blessed memory. I cannot leave that house. His spirit is in that house and I cannot leave him," she responded.

I told her she was being irrational and ridiculous. Yehudit told me I was being unfair and unsympathetic only because of my guilt over having left her alone in America in the first place. Yehudit was, as usual, correct.

But the guilt never left me. Not for a second. It haunted me when she suffered her fatal stroke; it plagues me still to this day.

And here I am, about to embark for that place of many memories. My purpose: to deliver a paper, "Jewish Law and Heroic Life-Saving Measures in Terminal Illness," at the International Conference on Jewish Medical Ethics. My intention: to find some peace with my past.

My baggage is checked and it is time for me to take the escalator to the gate on the second floor of the Departures Building.

The sign in front of the escalator says, "Only Passengers Beyond This Point."

David and Shoshanna are standing beneath their mother's wings. Yehudit has one hand on each of their shoulders. Shoshanna clings to her mother; David stands upright.

I lean down to say goodbye. Shoshanna reaches her hands around my shoulders and hugs me. She is fine, secure with her mother by her side.

David has tears in his eyes. I reach out to him and draw him to me. The hug is intense. He is silent but his tears say much. I take out my handkerchief and help him dry his eyes. Then I hand it to him. "It is okay to cry," I tell him, "it is okay."

CHAPTER 34

THROUGH THE WINDOW I can see the shores of the Rockaways on our approach to Kennedy Airport. The plane dips lower as the roofs of buildings appear, then there is more water—Jamaica Bay, the Marine Parkway bridge—as we come in closer for the landing. We pass briefly over some swamps, the runway appears, and the wheels hit the ground smoothly.

The passengers applaud the landing. The pilot's voice comes on the loudspeaker, instructing us to remain seat-belted until the plane stops taxiing. Outside it appears to be a pleasant autumn morning with a mild overcast.

The plane soon comes to a stop. The seat-belt light goes out, a bell sounds, and everyone gets up at once. It is a restless group, hurrying to leave the plane after the fifteen-hour ordeal, pushing and shoving in the aisles. I remain seated, waiting for the plane to clear a bit. The flight itself was only eleven hours, but the departure from Ben Gurion had been detained four hours due to security concerns. I can stand to wait just a little while longer.

A few minutes pass and I gather my things. I spent much of the trip reviewing and amending the notes for my lecture. I place the papers into my briefcase, stand up, stretch, and reach into the overhead compartment for my coat.

I exit the plane and follow the signs to the baggage claim area. The enormity of the airport is intimidating. Despite being a native New Yorker, the years in Israel have altered my perspective on many things.

The baggage claim area is in the International Arrivals Building next to Customs. At least five flights have arrived in the last thirty minutes. I know from previous experience that I will be here for hours.

As I wait for my luggage, I examine the faces of my fellow travelers. They look worn, tired from the tedious trek. It is now twenty minutes past six in the morning, New York time. I slept for a few hours on the plane. By the time I get out of here and make it to my destination, there will not be much opportunity to nap. I hate these trips, and now I understand why, despite the numerous invitations from places all over the globe, I seldom accept.

But this is a special conference, held every third year, and attended widely by rabbis and scholars of all denominations. To be solicited as a guest lecturer at this conference is the greatest compliment and recognition of my work. And since I've always craved recognition, here I am. Yet I know I also have an ulterior motive.

I exit Customs through electric metal doors into a waiting area. There are hordes of people standing around on all sides, waiting to greet family members and friends from afar. Many are holding signs bearing family names. I push my cart a little further into the crowd. My height has always been an advantage in situations such as these. I do a three-hundred-and-sixty-degree turn, and when I get back to where I started Chaim is standing in front of me, face to face.

"Yankel," he says with a wide grin and an extended right hand.

"Chaim," I reply in the same manner.

We shake, look each other over warmly, and then we embrace.

"Let me help you with your luggage," he offers as he picks up the larger of the two suitcases. "Follow me, the car is just outside. I paid off the guy to let me keep it there for a few minutes. Who knew I would be waiting this long?" Chuckling.

I pick up the smaller piece, which is really a suit-bag folded over, and follow. We pass through electric glass doors to the outside world. The air is brisk.

"That's it, right over there," Chaim says as he points to a beige Cutlass.

He sees the porter with an angry look on his face. Chaim slips him another bill for his trouble and the man reacts with an empty expression, neither angry nor thankful, as he turns away.

We put the luggage in the trunk, get into the car, and pull out onto the road. For a while there is silence, Chaim is concentrating on how to exit the airport.

Finally, Chaim asks, "So how was the flight?"

"Terrible."

"Oh, poor Yankel. I know how much you hate to travel. Hell, that's why you never visit."

"I don't see you coming to Israel so often," I respond cutely.

"I'd like to, but it would cost us a fortune with the kids and all. But you always have some university or organization offering to pay your way and then some, just to get you to speak to them. My cousin the scholar. We always knew you'd amount to something. But I'll bet you had your doubts about me!" Laughter.

Indeed I did, until about five years ago. And then, somehow, miraculously, he finally turned it all around. He got clean and sober after several failed attempts, and even went back to school to study social work. He met a nice Orthodox woman named Rachel Schwartz, married her, and has two little girls. Now he works as the director of a drug rehabilitation program in Borough Park under the auspices of the Jewish Board for Mental Health Services.

I had planned to attend his wedding but David had gotten sick. Chaim understood, and Yehudit and I sent them a beautiful hand-carved steel menorah, signed by one of Jerusalem's most famous artists.

Now, we write regularly. And though Chaim has never actually met Yehudit, he remarks often in his letters that he feels as if he knows her intimately.

"Mom and Dad are at my house, waiting with Rachel and the kids for your arrival," he warns. "I told Sarah and Leah that you were coming. They'll probably stop over for about five minutes on *Shabbos* to say hello. They couldn't really care less. They both live in their own worlds, married to real *frummies* who sit and learn in yeshiva all day while their wives work themselves to the bone. And they each have eight or nine kids, who knows, I've even stopped counting."

The thought of seeing my aunt and uncle saddens me. It reminds me of my parents. Chaim must know this for he is silent for a moment. It is impressive how sensitive he has become. Suffering can do this.

"How are the children?" I break the silence.

"What can I say? They're doing terrific and they're the best things that have ever happened to me. Just hope they don't give us trouble like we gave our folks." I join him in his laughter.

"Yes, I can definitely relate to that. I often worry about David. He has such an independent mind," I muse out loud.

"Well, there's no use making yourself crazy about it. After all, as we both know, there's nothing we can really do about it, so we might as well love them no matter what they become. That's always the best thing. And anyway, who says *we* turned out so bad?"

I place my hand on his shoulder as he drives. "I guess you're right. I should visit more often."

CHAPTER 35

THE CONFERENCE was being held at the Hilton Hotel in midtown Manhattan. I could have stayed at the hotel, but felt compelled to accept Chaim's hospitality. I was glad I did, except for having to take the subway into Manhattan for three mornings in a row. I remedied this after the first day by taking cabs instead.

It was now the last day of the conference, the day I was scheduled to give my lecture. The past two days had been exciting and enlightening. There were some of my fellow Israeli colleagues from various institutions, old friends and acquaintances from Yeshiva University, and famous names I'd recognized from my readings that now could be associated with faces. There were synagogue rabbis, community leaders, doctors, scientists, and even some clergy from other faiths. I recognized Rabbi Roth from afar yesterday. And this morning I ran into, of all people, Ezra. He told me that he was unable to attend the first two days but had made it a point to be present for my lecture. I was flattered.

It was an uneasy feeling following the impressive line of scholars that had preceded me. This would be my most distinguished audience to date. And my most difficult, by the tenor of what had transpired in some of the previous lectures.

My presentation was not without controversy, something I was acutely aware of and should have been used to by now. But

I was nervous. I wondered if it was about the presentation or something else.

I sat with Ezra at lunch, which was scheduled right before my speech. There were a few awards for exemplary this and that, and then came the announcement for the next event. Ezra patted me on the back. "Good luck Yankel, break a leg, as they say in Hollywood," he jested. "Don't worry, these guys aren't as smart as you," he added when he saw me hesitate getting up from the table.

I came into the large convention hall. Judging from the other speeches, I suspected the place would be full. A few minutes after I sat down at the dais, I looked out into the audience and saw that every seat was occupied and rows of people were standing in the back.

The conference chairman rose to the microphone to make his introduction. He began by remarking how this was the largest turnout for any speech yet, and that he hoped that the final lecture that evening would attract a similar crowd. Then he went on to cite my credentials and talked about my work. I was astonished at how much he knew.

The introduction was over. The crowd applauded politely. I stood up, notes in hand, and walked over to the podium. I began my presentation.

At first, I faltered a bit. Then, gradually, as I got into the material, I became more comfortable and animated. Soon, I imagined myself back home with my students. I felt fine. I was in charge.

I began by defining my terms. Professor Waldman had always stressed that the most important part of any presentation was providing clear, unambiguous definitions of what one was talking about. He was correct, especially with this sort of material and this type of audience. Practically every Jew fancies himself or herself a philosopher, an interpreter of reality. Leave nothing to interpretation—avoid being misquoted or misunderstood! These were the rules I strove to observe, though the odds were significantly against success in this setting.

Euthanasia, heroic measures, terminal illness, life support, living will, health care proxy, and a host of Jewish legalistic terminology—I meticulously clarified each category with specific illustrations. Then I went on to the central portion of my presentation. I talked about the value of life and how Jewish tradition placed it above virtually all other considerations. I alluded to the recent controversy over physician-assisted suicide and contrasted that with other forms of euthanasia. All the while, I tried to remain objective and scientific, tried to avoid imposing my own moral persuasion—a nearly impossible task. The audience was filled with people of varying proclivities and points of view. I tried neither to preach nor to alienate, but to enlighten and inform as best I could.

I talked about my experiences in the hospital and the various attitudes that people of equal devotion often have about these issues. I contrasted a case of a three-year-old victim in the last stages of terminal brain cancer to a case of a seventy-three-year-old with advanced lung cancer. I talked about the very real differences among the nurses, doctors, and relatives of these patients regarding their respective fates. "Make no mistake about it, they look to us—rabbis, philosophers, theologians, and doctors—for guidance. And in responding to this call, we must be both judicious and compassionate. It is a difficult balance to strike."

I offered some anecdotes from the Talmud, but didn't really provide any concrete answers or specific solutions. "I know that I have only heightened the questions," I said as I came to the conclusion, "and have complicated matters even further. But these *are* complex issues, and whatever resolutions we may arrive at, we must not give in to our psychological need to simplify reality, to provide ourselves with easy answers to life's most difficult problems."

As I offered these conclusions, it occurred to me that I was speaking about a great deal more than just medical ethics, and that the man I was really addressing wasn't even present, at least not in the flesh. I wondered how much of my work and opinions were forged by my relationship with my father. He would always be there, and my need to reach him would never wane.

The audience rose with a thunderous applause. I was both relieved and shocked. I thought, for certain, that they would be disappointed, but I had been happily mistaken.

Hordes of people swarmed around me as I descended from the podium. There were questions and congratulations, comments and greetings. Ezra managed to sift through the crowd.

"Would you like a ride back to Brooklyn?" his voice rose above the others.

"I was planning to stay for tonight's speech. It's Rabbi Friedman of Australia discussing abortion. Why don't you stay? You might find it interesting."

"I can't. I have a Talmud lecture tonight at the *shul.* And after your speech, anything would be a disappointment."

"Thank you," I responded shyly. "I really think I ought to stay. I believe my absence would be noted. It would be disrespectful."

"Yes, I'm sure you're right. Well, take care of yourself, and I guess I'll see you in *shul* on *Shabbos* with your uncle and Chaim."

"Most definitely. My flight isn't till Sunday afternoon."

He bade me goodbye and slipped out with the rest of the crowd. There were still plenty of people left in the room. I looked around, but saw no one else whom I knew. It was disappointing. I wondered about that ulterior motive for my being here.

Eventually, after chatting with some strangers, I made my way into the lobby. I figured I would find a quiet place where I could sit down and relax, maybe even close my eyes for a while. I walked over to a small alcove around the back where there were some deserted chairs and couches. I looked at my watch.

It was five of three, a good three hours until dinner, after which would be the final lecture. I put my briefcase on the floor beside me as I sat myself down on one of the couches. Within seconds, I was drifting off.

After what seemed a very short time, I had a strange sense that I was not alone. My eyes opened to see who was invading my privacy. And there, standing about five feet away, watching me, was Rebecca.

"I hope I didn't wake you?" she remarked in that distinctive voice that had haunted my dreams for the past ten years.

"How long have you been standing there?" I queried, wondering if this was yet another of those dreams.

"Well, let's see. I followed you from the lecture, which according to my watch was about fifteen minutes ago," she said as she looked at her wristwatch. "So I guess I've been standing here, in this same position, watching you sleep for fifteen minutes."

"Has it been that long?" I said as I checked my own watch. "I must have been asleep."

"You were. But there's no need to be embarrassed. I always used to look at you when you slept."

The entire interchange seemed comfortable, neither of us displaying any overt excitement over having run into each other after all these years. It was as if the rendezvous had been planned, or as if we had just seen each other yesterday.

"So you *were* at the lecture?" I asked.

"Of course! You knew I would be, didn't you?"

"I hoped you would be." No pretense.

"I'm glad."

"Would you like to get a drink?" I suggested as I stood up.

"Love to."

We walked together toward the main lobby, where there was a large open bar.

"Aren't you concerned about being seen with me in public?" she asked, half serious, half joking, as we walked.

"Not in the least. On the contrary, it's a privilege," I remarked with a smile. *Some things do change.*

And some things don't. Like Rebecca's beauty, a feature that refused to fade with time. She looked not like the woman of ten years earlier, but like the young girl of almost twenty years ago. The same image I had retained so clearly in my memory. The same image I would always keep.

We sat down at a small table. She ordered a Diet Coke; I, a Dewar's on ice. Over the years I had graduated from Harry's specials to more sophisticated vices.

Soft music came from a nearby baby grand piano. The collective voices of hundreds of conventioneers filled the atmosphere. And we sat there, and talked, and talked, for hours.

She told me of her synagogue in Scarsdale. How she'd achieved much success in making it more traditional than it had been before she'd arrived. It was a large congregation, more than eight hundred families, and by this point she had two younger associate rabbis working under her.

We also talked about our families and shared pictures. Her eyes became watery when looking at David, and a few full tears spilled over her cheeks when I spoke about my mother's death. Shoshanna's face made her melt. Her parents were still relatively well, and came over weekly to visit with their grandson, Jacob. I became choked up when I heard his name.

She talked openly of the difficult pregnancy, and how the doctors advised her not to have any more children. But she and her husband, Mark, desperately wanted at least one more. So now, they were in the final stages of an adoption. "We're waiting for the phone to ring," she said as another tear fell.

Mark was a bankruptcy attorney, working with one of the prominent firms in Manhattan. "There's plenty of work for him these days," she remarked humorously. They had been introduced by Rabbi Samuels about a year or so after we split up. In less than four months, they were engaged. I could tell by the look in her eyes that her marriage was good.

I filled her in on Chaim and his family. She told me that her brother still refused to acknowledge her or her son, and I could see that she still wasn't used to that.

She said Yehudit was beautiful when I showed her a picture. I replied that that was the least of her qualities. I talked about how we met, and how we lived. She seemed genuinely happy for me.

And through it all, there was no mention of the things that had come between us, that had made our lives take the paths they had taken. There was no sign of remorse, regret, or anger. We had both, in our own ways, come to peace with that part of ourselves.

It had been an agonizing time, but it was very much in the past. Ten years ago, on that day I left Harry's apartment, I knew I could not be who I needed to be while living in America. There were just too many things pulling me in conflicting directions. I had to go somewhere else, to make a fresh start. I thought she would be overjoyed, that she would join me. I proposed marriage and tried to convince her that we could be together in a place like Israel. But she believed that was the last place she could fulfill *her* dreams.

"They don't recognize Reform or Conservative rabbis there," she argued. "The government makes us into outlaws. What am I supposed to do with my life and everything I've become?"

I knew she was right, but argued anyway. "No one knows us there. We have no histories there. We can start anew and become whatever it is that we want to become, together."

"But we can't, Yakov. You just can't run away from who you are by going someplace else. And it's foolish of you to think you can. It's ridiculous! You will take yourself—and your history—with you wherever you go!"

I understood her point and, as usual, it was a good one. But *I* still had to go. There was just something, something inexplicable, calling me. The very same thing that seized me that morning I woke up in my mother's house. I couldn't identify what it was or where it came from. It simply called, and I had to obey.

And it felt ironic, at the time, that what finally undid us was neither philosophical nor religious, but geographical. We each, for whatever reasons, needed to be in two different places. And as far as I was concerned, that was all of it. At least that's what I had thought then.

But now, the years had given us new perspective. We had both come to realize that what had stood between us was much greater than either of us could fathom or fight. It was the very same thing that had brought us together in the first place. It was, to put it simply, God's plan.

The hours passed quickly. We had missed dinner and it was time for the lecture. She wasn't planning to attend, and had to return to Scarsdale. We got up from the table and I walked her out to the garage. We looked at each other in silence as we waited for the attendant to bring the car around. An air of sadness fell upon us.

The car came up the ramp and stopped a few feet away from us. The attendant got out and held the door open for Rebecca. She handed him a dollar, and he walked away, leaving the door open. She stood by the door. I walked over and stood next to her.

"I hate these moments," she said softly.

"So do I."

"It was good seeing you."

"You too."

We stood there, like children, not knowing what to do next.

"I guess I gotta go," she offered tentatively, as if there had ever been another choice.

"Yeah, I guess so," I responded in a similar tone.

"Maybe we'll run into each other again in another ten years."

I offered a faint smile.

"Well, goodbye, Yankel," she said with a tremor.

"Goodbye, Rivki." Holding back the tears.

She reached over, put her hand on my shoulder, stood up on her toes, and kissed me gently on the lips. Then she turned and got into the car. I stood there as she opened her window. She wiped her eyes with her right hand and extended her left for me to take.

She grasped me tightly and said, “I’ll always love you.”

“I’ll always love you, too.”

CHAPTER 36

I SAID GOODBYE to Chaim, Rachel, the kids, Zelig, and Sheindy early Sunday morning. Although my flight wasn't until two that afternoon, there was still some unfinished business for me to tend to. I had rented a car for the day despite Chaim's insistence that I let him chauffeur me around. What I needed to do, I needed to do alone.

I drove to Eighteenth Avenue and made a left toward Ocean Parkway. I then headed south on Ocean Parkway toward the Belt. A few blocks up on my left, I passed the Mirrer Yeshiva. I looked out the window and noticed some students in the usual black-and-white garb, carrying their books. I was tempted to stop and get out of the car, to talk to them, maybe even take a tour of the building for old times' sake. Perhaps on my next trip, whenever that was to be.

On the Belt, I traveled east. To my right was Jamaica Bay, and in the far distance the Rockaways. Soon I would be looking down on the same sight. On my left was Brooklyn as I drove past Canarsie toward Long Island.

It was a little over an hour's drive till I arrived at the New Montefiore Cemetery. I passed the gate and continued up the main road, looking for Herzl Street. I made a right onto the narrow Herzl, and continued for two short blocks to Second Avenue. I chuckled about how these pathways for the dead bore names just like the streets of the living.

I made a left onto Second Avenue and pulled the car over to

the right side of the road. I turned off the engine, reached for the prayer book on the seat next to me, and got out of the car. Although it was a sunny day, a chill filled the air.

I crossed over the road, stepped onto the grass, and stood before the graves of my parents. I bent over and cleared away some shriveled leaves from around each of the footstones. Then I removed a handkerchief from my back pocket and wiped off the earthen residue that had gathered in the crevices of the lettering.

When finished, I ran my fingers gently over my mother's name. I turned to my right and, with some vacillation, did the same to my father's. I rose, stood before them, and opened the prayer book.

I turned to the memorial prayer for the deceased, but I found myself unable to articulate the words. *"El Moleh Rachamim . . . ,"* God who is full of mercy, was all I could get out before my mind welled up with thoughts of the past.

I could see my mother sitting in her living room with me the night before I was to depart for Israel. "You are giving up much in leaving," she observed calmly.

"Totta always said, 'sometimes you must sacrifice,' " I replied.

"Yes . . . I suppose so," she remarked to herself.

"I still wish you would reconsider and come with me. We can live together there just as we do here!"

"I cannot leave here." Again to herself. Resolute, but serene.

I had begged and pleaded, but to no avail. My best arguments fell on deaf ears.

"I think it is right that you are going," she insisted. "I believe you should follow your heart in this matter. You have searched and struggled for so many years—I, more than anyone, know that. And now you have found an answer. Or at least a path to an answer. I want you to go and do what you feel you must."

My guilt has never left me, not for a single moment since I left you, Mama. It plagues me day and night. I have tried to rationalize, to see that things have all turned out for the better.

And for me, they have. David and Shoshanna show such promise in their eyes. If only you could see.

I turned to my father. If only *you* could see, *Totta.* If only.

But the guilt has a life of its own. Even Yehudit notices it from time to time. I used to be better at hiding things.

I looked down at the prayer book again and tried thinking about the words.

Can you forgive me, Mama? Can you ever forgive me?

"El Moleh Rachamim."

Can I ever forgive myself? Can I ever forgive you, *Totta?*

"El Moleh Rachamim."

I had to leave, Mama. I had to find a place for myself, a purpose.

"El Moleh Rachamim."

And I have, *Totta,* I have. Can you hear my lectures? Can you read my writings?

"El Moleh Rachamim."

Do you see me kissing my children? Can you see me hugging my son when he cries?

"El Moleh Rachamim."

I must finish the prayer. It is an obligation; it is a duty. I *want* to finish it. I believe in its power.

"Shochein bamromim . . ." who dwells on high . . .

I closed the prayer book, looked up to the heavens, and then back at the stones once again. I bent down to pick up a few small rocks from the ground, and placed some on each footstone to mark my visit. I then got up, took a final look at where I had been, and slowly crossed the road, walking back to the car.

As I drove off, I thought about the things I had left behind. I thought about Harry, whose death I had learned of when I'd returned for my mother's funeral. I imagined him as one of those pictures on his wall. Another anniversary. And I remembered his final words to me: *Everything is connected and has a purpose; it is all part of God's plan. You vill see. You vill understand.*

I thought about Waldman and Trachtenberg, both of them probably still at it.

I thought about Chaim and his family—the big surprise.

I thought about Rebecca and her family. Her life, her dreams. Achievements forged in strife and struggle. We would always have that much in common.

And I thought about Yehudit, the true guiding light of my soul. In her I have been reborn, have found strength of faith. In the children she has given me, I have found my life.

I understood.